FOUR DEAD M
TOGETHER

What had these four been involved in that had led to such a grisly ending?

She glanced around; the only one looking in her direction was the sick-looking young cop. Marian broke the rules and ducked under the yellow ribbon. A quick search of the four bodies revealed no identification on any of them; she was back outside the ribbon in less than a minute. But that minute of touching the bodies had been enough to bring home their *peopleness*. These four weren't just lumps of trouble unloaded on the NYPD; they were individuals, four people who'd led autonomous lives but shared a common death. One of the bodies, the fat man, was still warm.

"My god," an appalled voice said from behind her. "'If thy right eye offend thee, pluck it out.'"

You have the right to remain silent

BARBARA PAUL

WORLDWIDE.

TORONTO • NEW YORK • LONDON
AMSTERDAM • PARIS • SYDNEY • HAMBURG
STOCKHOLM • ATHENS • TOKYO • MILAN
MADRID • WARSAW • BUDAPEST • AUCKLAND

YOU HAVE THE RIGHT TO REMAIN SILENT

A Worldwide Mystery/November 1993

This edition is reprinted by arrangement with Charles Scribner's Sons, an imprint of Macmillan Publishing Company.

ISBN 0-373-26132-2

You have the right to remain silent

ONE

THEY WERE ON THE VERGE of nailing a killer, several killers, in fact; and Marian Larch was working on a heavy-duty, Guinness-Records-quality blue funk.

"What're you looking like that for?" her partner asked, ripping open a bag of peanuts with his teeth. "We got 'em. Two more and they'll all be here."

My partner. "Yes, we got them."

"So? Why the long face?"

She stared at him a moment before answering. "Doesn't it ever bother you, Foley? The fact that people kill each other?"

His face didn't change expression. "That's a Girl Scout question if I ever heard one. Maybe you're in the wrong line of work, *Sergeant.*" Heavy on the irony.

Marian didn't bother responding. She shifted her weight behind the wheel of the car, trying to get comfortable. She was wearing one of the new half-ceramic, half-aluminum bullet-proof vests; it weighed no more than a heavy coat, but it still impeded movement. And it trapped her body heat— probably a good thing in winter but not the first week of September. To add to her discomfort, the springs in the car seat were broken. The Chevrolet was several years old and in need of a good wash; it had been chosen especially not to attract attention in Alphabet City. They'd been waiting for over an hour, no time at all for a stake-out. Twelve of the girls had made their way into the abandoned tenement; only two to go.

The girls they were watching for were all members of a gang called the Downtown Queens, and they were dangerous. The Queens were different from other girl gangs like the Sandman Ladies or the Five Percenters; those gangs were auxiliaries of male gangs—pushing drugs for the boys, running errands for them, providing sexual favors. The girls joined the gangs for protection, which they almost never got. The boys simply allowed the girls to act tough for a while before settling down to the real function the boys had in mind for them all along: having babies.

But the Downtown Queens were allied to no male group, and they looked to themselves alone for protection. These girls didn't just *act* tough. Fourteen black and Hispanic girls in their mid- to late teens, crossing racial barriers first to survive... and then to rule. The entire neighborhood knew the Queens. The Queens were feared and respected. The Queens were lethal.

"There they are," Marian said.

The taller of the two girls was called Carmen; Marian couldn't make out the face of the other girl even though the light was still good. Foley tossed the rest of his peanuts out the window and reached for the walkie-talkie. "You see 'em?"

A voice crackling with static answered. "Yeah, we got 'em. We move now?"

Marian was already out of the car. "Now," Foley said.

Other car doors were opening silently down a couple of side streets; seven cops in all to capture fourteen teenaged girls. *Two girls per cop; should work.* Marian pulled out her service revolver and held it pointing toward the ground. *Never draw your weapon unless you're prepared to kill,* the instructors at the Academy had said repeatedly. Marian hated this part of her job.

"Give me the walkie," she said to Foley. When he'd handed it to her, she spoke into the mouthpiece. "Remember, easy on the triggers. No shooting at all except to defend yourselves." There was no answer. "Acknowledge!"

"Yes, *ma'am*," a voice said sarcastically. One of the gangs specialists borrowed from Intelligence, thank you very much.

The building had a bombed-out look to it—great gaping holes, most of the roof gone. Being open to the air hadn't done much for the pervasive urine smell, though. Marian watched her step; the floor was littered with broken glass, cigarette butts, beer cans, used condoms. She listened a moment but heard nothing. Good; Foley was being careful. He wasn't, always.

She caught a glimpse through a hole in a wall of two of the other cops, moving parallel to her. She pointed toward the one section of the building that still had a roof; the two cops nodded. The three of them converged on a closed door at the same time. Marian glanced behind her to check on her back-up; Foley was nowhere in sight. Angrily she stepped aside and motioned the other two cops to go in. The room was empty.

"Upstairs," she said into the walkie-talkie.

That was bad luck; it was hard to climb a rotting staircase without making noise. And where the hell was Foley? They'd almost reached the top when they heard a sound behind them. Marian glanced down to see the other three cops starting up the stairway, one of them the sarcastic man from Intelligence. Foley wasn't with them.

Then they had a piece of good luck; angry voices reached their ears. The Queens were arguing about something, energetically and loudly, effectively covering any small sound the advancing police might make. Still, Marian's mouth was dry; one of the first bits of advice she'd been given when she came into the Ninth Precinct was *Watch out for the Queens*. The fact that they were girls made no difference; the number of homicides committed by teenaged females had risen twenty-five percent in just the last five years. The Queens had contributed their share.

The girls were in the one room on the second floor that still had a door; the argument was raging louder than ever. The sarcastic gangs man from Intelligence, whose name was Jaime Romero, didn't wait for Marian's go-ahead. One kick knocked the door in, the hinges pulling easily from the decaying wood frame. "Hold it!" Romero yelled, moving his gun to cover as many of the girls at once as he could. "Don't move!"

"Drop it!" Marian shouted when every one of the Queens drew a blade—small enough to be concealed easily but not too small to kill a careless cop. "Put down the knives!"

The other cops were in the room, guns drawn, yelling instructions and moving out in a semicircle. The Queens gave as good as they got, holding on to their knives and screaming abuse. *White pig bitch* was their epithet for Marian; she'd heard it before and it hadn't sounded any better then. The police were working the Queens, herding them into pairs that could be more readily controlled. But because Foley was still on vacation, Marian found herself trying to restrain four of the girls at once. They started to separate, clearly meaning to encircle her. "Get back there!" she yelled, hoping desperately she wouldn't have to use her gun. "Stay together!" The girls stopped moving, neither circling nor retreating.

"Where's your back-up?" Romero yelled from across the room.

"Wish to hell I knew," Marian snarled. She picked out the one girl of the four she knew best and spoke directly to her. "Carmen, you've got some sense—use it! You're facing *guns*. I fire once, and they all start shooting. You want that? Is that what you want? Don't make it worse for yourself!"

The tall Hispanic girl hesitated. Out of the corner of her eye Marian saw Romero had disarmed his two Queens and was handcuffing them. Carmen saw it too. "Deal?" she asked under her breath.

Marian shook her head. "First-degree, Carmen."

Carmen looked at Romero heading toward them, his gun aimed directly at her, and dropped her knife with a clunk. "We surrender," she said quickly. Three more clunks followed.

Romero covered the girls while Marian cuffed Carmen and another girl; the other two remained free because the police were out of handcuffs. One of the cops started chanting the Miranda warning; "Listen to the man," Romero ordered. Then he glanced toward the doorway. "Well, look who's decided to join the party!"

Foley was in a crouch, arms straight out, gun pointing at no one in particular.

"Where the hell were you?" Marian snapped.

"Checking the back." Foley stood up and holstered his gun. "You didn't tell me you were going upstairs." Accusingly.

"You weren't there to *be* told. You're supposed to stick with me, Foley!"

He stared at her with challenging eyes. "You need a sitter, Sergeant?"

"Children, children," Romero interrupted mockingly, enjoying the row. "Save it for later. Let's get this bunch out of here."

Marian pointed toward the last two Queens. "Cuff them," she told Foley and motioned everybody else out. She put a hand on Carmen's arm and held her back until last. When they were alone in the room, Marian said, "Off the record, Carmen. Just between you and me. Why Mrs. Alvarez? Why'd the Queens go after *her*?"

Anger and frustration seethed in the Hispanic girl's face. After a moment she muttered, "Bitch needed killin'." It wasn't really an admission, but it was all she would say.

Marian was feeling a bit of frustration of her own. She looked at the girl before her: eighteen years old and her life was as good as finished. And why? Why?

Bitch needed killing.

THE PUBLIC DEFENDER'S Office would spare only two attorneys to represent the Queens; both were kids fresh out of law school, learning the ropes until they could land jobs with real law firms. Marian didn't worry about that, but the prosecutors wouldn't be any better—and that she did tend to worry about. Her unit had reported to the captain, and interrogations of the fourteen girls were now under way.

Captain DiFalco, like Marian, was a newcomer to the Ninth Precinct. His predecessor had retired, and the lieutenant in charge of the Precinct Detective Unit was a desk jockey everyone agreed could never run the station. So Captain DiFalco had been brought in to fill a void, just as Marian had. She had to wonder whether his new job was a demotion; she felt her own was. DiFalco seemed at home in the Ninth, though, comfortable in a way Marian never would be. The lieutenant ostensibly running the PDU was on vacation; Marian could see no difference in the day-to-day operation of the station except that now she reported directly to the captain.

Right then he was nodding to her with the closest expression to approval he ever showed. "Nice going, Sergeant," he said. "You got 'em all without firing a shot. That's the kind of report the Zone Commander likes to get. Worked out all right with the Intelligence people, did it?"

"No complaints. They did their job. Only one sticky moment, and that wasn't their fault."

DiFalco's face showed neither sympathy nor disapproval. "Foley."

"This isn't the first time he's failed to back me up, Captain. If Romero hadn't stepped in, I would've had some serious grief back there. I need a partner I can count on."

"Nobody available."

"Get somebody."

"You want a desk job?"

"No! I want you to put *Foley* on a desk. Before he gets somebody killed." *Namely me.*

The first time she'd asked for a new partner, the captain had looked at her with a narrow-eyed expression of disapproval that said she was guilty of breaking one of the primary rules of police work: *Never bitch about your partner.* But DiFalco had had to call Foley on the carpet often enough to convince him that Marian wasn't just playing the crybaby. Right then he unbent enough to say, "I know he's a problem. Going sour right now, but his record says he used to be a good cop. I'll request a replacement so I can move Foley to a desk. But don't hold your breath—the Ninth isn't the only precinct with a manpower problem. Just stick with him for now. That's the best I can do."

Marian knew it was. "Thanks, Captain. Appreciate it." She got up to leave.

"Larch—do the paperwork on this one yourself? And send Foley in."

Foley was on the phone when she got back to the PDU room. He looked up and she jerked a thumb over her shoulder: *Captain wants you.*

He hung up abruptly. "What'd you tell him?"

"The truth."

Foley snorted. "I'll bet." He headed toward the captain's office.

Marian muttered to herself and started rolling forms into the old mechanical typewriter on her desk. She'd just started filling in details when a shadow fell over the paper.

Romero was standing by her desk. "Went all right, didn't it?"

She finished typing a word and said, "Went just dandy."

"Maybe we can do it again sometime."

Marian looked up at him, this sarcastic man from Intelligence who'd done her partner's job for him. "Wouldn't mind," she said. He nodded without answering and went on out.

She was only halfway through the report when Foley came out of the captain's office, his face purple; DiFalco must have given him a real going-over. Her partner stormed over to her desk. "You and your buddy Romero fixed me real good, you did. Proud of yourself?"

So Jaime Romero had backed her up in the captain's office as well. "You fixed yourself, Foley," Marian said. "You can't blame somebody else this time. Too many people saw it."

"Saw what? I didn't do anything!"

"That's what they saw. You not doing anything."

He didn't even hear. "He gave me a warning. Me, a *warning*! I been working this shithouse precinct eleven years and you two virgins come in here and tell me I—"

"Put a cork in it, Foley," Marian said sharply. "Enough! And that's an order."

"Oh, yes, *sir*, Sergeant Larch, ma'am sir! Whatever the *sergeant* wants, ma'am sir!"

Marian lowered her voice. "And it's not my fault you failed the Sergeants Exam. If you'd studied a little harder, I wouldn't be here at all. That's what really burns your ass, isn't it?"

Foley wasn't quite self-destructive enough to say what he was thinking. Rank was rank, and he'd been a cop too long to forget that. He whirled and charged out of the squad room, muttering obscenities under his breath.

Marian let her own breath out. Pulling rank wasn't the most diplomatic way of handling a troublesome partner, but she'd had it up to *here* with Foley. The confrontation had rattled her a little—not as much as facing four healthy teenagers armed with knives, but enough. Locking horns with Foley was nothing new. The first day she showed up at the Ninth, he'd let her know he resented her presence and he'd reminded her of it without fail every day since.

Marian missed her old partner. She and Sergeant Ivan Malecki had worked together for almost four years, and they'd reached the point where they could anticipate each other and even complete each other's thoughts. That kind of rapport wasn't built up quickly or easily, but their partnership had been dissolved in a blink of an eye. Shortage of sergeants, their superior officer had told them. Bunch of retirements coming all at once, along with the lowest median score on the Sergeants Exam in the history of the NYPD. They couldn't have two sergeants working as a team out of Police Headquarters when a couple of precincts were screaming for at least one sergeant.

So Sergeant Malecki was sent to the Thirty-second Precinct and Sergeant Larch to the Ninth, Ivan to Harlem and Marian to the Lower East Side. *It's only temporary*, their captain had told them; *once we get some qualifiers after the next Sergeants Exam, you'll both be back here.* The two sergeants had gritted their teeth and said *Yes sir*, wanting to believe him. Once a week Marian and Ivan got together and debated which of them had the lousier job. Ivan's new partner was a hotshot rookie who saw himself as an irresistible force chosen by destiny to clean up New York's crime scene all by himself; consequently he had to be watched all the time. Marian would gladly have traded Foley for him.

At first Marian had looked on Foley's hostility as just another challenge, but after a month she'd given up on him. She wished to god Foley had passed the exam; the two of them would never find a way of working together. Sergeant Larch *ma'am sir*, he'd called her.

Sergeant Larch. Still *Sergeant* Larch. But Marian couldn't dwell on that; she had enough to be dejected about.

She put Foley out of her mind and re-immersed herself in the life and times of the Downtown Queens; and right away she felt the chronic sadness creeping in that plagued her whenever she arrested someone for murder. This time it all seemed especially senseless. Why had the Queens killed Mrs. Maria Alvarez? A harmless, helpless woman with no connections. What did they possibly have to gain from her death? Mrs. Alvarez was a native Jamaican whose husband had long since disappeared from her life; she was struggling against great odds to make sure her four children stayed clothed and fed. Her English was poor enough to keep her in menial jobs, whenever she could find one—

usually cleaning office buildings at night. She'd been on and off welfare for the past ten years.

Marian had first come across Mrs. Alvarez while investigating a minor scam a paper boss was working. Paper bosses oversaw the distribution of the dailies, dealing with both carriers and newsstands. Unsold papers were returned to the bosses, who cut off the banner and date from the front page to be turned in for credit; the rest of the newspaper was discarded. But one paper boss had gotten the idea of clipping all the manufacturers' coupons from the papers and selling them to grocery store managers at a discount. The managers then sent in the coupons for their full value plus a handling fee and the books showed a little extra profit that week. The arrangement had grown into a big enough enterprise that the paper boss had had to hire Mrs. Alvarez to cut out coupons for him.

But that was the only dishonest venture Mrs. Alvarez had ever been associated with. She'd steadfastly refused to have anything to do with *the* business of the project house where she lived. She'd even managed to keep her four children free of drugs. But Mrs. Alvarez had been found with forty-three stab wounds in her body. Why? She was no threat to the gangs; she was no threat to anybody.

Their tip that the Queens were responsible had come from a male gang calling itself, theatrically, the Symptom of Death. The gang coveted the Queens' turf, and because of that Marian had been inclined to discount the tip at first. But then the Symptom had turned up two witnesses, a ten-year-old boy and an old man, both scared witless. The kid and the old man were afraid of the Queens if they talked, and afraid of the Symptom of Death if they didn't. But eventually the story came out. The Queens had been waiting for Mrs. Alvarez when she came home from her night job; they'd jumped her and stabbed her repeatedly, right there in the street. *It was like they wanted ever'one to know, man,* the kid had said. Yes, there were other witnesses.

Those other witnesses would start creeping out of hiding once it was known all fourteen Queens were safely locked away at Riker's Island. Marian sighed. They had a case. What they didn't have was a reason. All those girls with their colorful names...Denzella, Little Leticia and Big Leticia, Ti-Belle, Guadalupe, Frisky Nell, Encarnaçion (nicknamed "Ree"), Large Marge—they'd all been counting on fear to keep the witnesses from talking to the police. It would have worked, too, if the Symptom of Death hadn't seen Mrs. Alvarez's murder as an opportunity to get rid of a rival gang.

Well, maybe one of the girls would let something slip during interrogation; some of them were very young. Marian finished typing the report and glanced at her watch. Two and a half hours until she met Brian for dinner. If she left right then, she'd have time to wash her hair.

Or, she could go tell young Juanita Alvarez they'd caught the girls who'd killed her mother.

Marian rubbed her eyes tiredly. No real decision. Brian had seen her with messy hair before.

TWO

RUNNING NORTH and south along FDR Drive, the Jacob Riis Projects sat on a windswept lot surrounded by a low wire fence. The tallest building was a fourteen-story pile of mud-colored brick (*shit-colored*, Foley called it), with bars or plywood or chicken wire over the windows of the lower floors. Marian Larch had no trouble getting in; all three locks in the double glass doors were broken. Inside, the ubiquitous stench of urine mixed with the smells of spices and marijuana. Spray-painted gang signs were everywhere—on the peeling walls, the doors, even on the ceiling. The elevator was working for a change. Marian checked the escape hatch before stepping in; someone had nailed boards across it. Kids strung out on speed or blacktar heroin sometimes thought it was a gas to ride on top of elevator cars and blast away with a shotgun at unsuspecting passengers.

The Alvarez apartment was on the eighth floor. The decibel level would have made a deaf man wince; TVs were blaring, boom boxes were booming. Twelve-year-old Juanita Alvarez and her siblings were being cared for by an aunt—who Marian suspected was a neighbor bribed to put in an appearance whenever the cops or the social workers showed up. Juanita was a very self-sufficient child.

Marian's knock was answered by a cherub-faced child of eight or so who had eyes that never quite looked at you. Marian smiled at him and said, "Felipe?"

"Felipe dead," the boy said tonelessly. "I'm Tito."

Marian was taken aback; one of the children was dead too? "Oh, I'm sorry! When did he die, Tito?"

The boy gazed at his shoes, said nothing.

Marian hunkered down to his eye level. "When did Felipe die? How long ago?"

Tito stared past her shoulder at open space. "Mama say don't talk about Felipe and Estella."

Estella as well? What was going on here? Marian gently took hold of the boy's arms. "Tito, is Estella dead? The baby died? How?"

He didn't answer.

"You understand your mother won't be taking care of you anymore, don't you, Tito? You have to tell me so I can help you. Is Estella dead too?"

He nodded, wouldn't meet her eyes.

"But Juanita's all right, isn't she? Is she here? Where—"

A high, shrill scream made Marian jump. She looked up to see Juanita flying through the air at her. The girl landed heavily, fists and feet flailing and her mouth pouring out a stream of curses in Spanish. Marian lost her balance and they both fell across the doorjamb, Juanita screaming and hitting and Marian trying to catch the girl's arms. Three black teenaged boys walked by and laughed. "Thassit, Sugar Doll—you get 'er!" one of them said.

Tito stood by silently watching, or not watching.

Marian finally managed to get the girl turned around and wrapped both arms around her in a restraining embrace. She spoke soothingly into Juanita's ear and rocked her like a baby; the girl's fury gradually dissolved into a kind of crying that wracked her whole body. Marian half lifted, half wrestled her into the apartment and closed the door. She told Tito to fetch a cold wet cloth; he moved silently to obey.

Eventually Juanita had calmed down to the point where she could talk, but she still looked as if she wanted to kill Marian. It turned out Juanita already knew about the arrest of the Queens; news traveled fast in the projects. And it also turned out that that was the reason she'd attacked Marian.

"But why?" Marian asked in bewilderment. "Those girls killed your mother, Juanita! Didn't you want them caught?"

"No! Not the Queens! Not them! Oh, you don' unnerstan' nothin'!"

"I most certainly do not. Explain it to me, Juanita. Why should you care what happens to the Queens?" When she was met with only sulky silence, Marian turned to Tito. "Do you know why she wants to protect the Queens?"

The boy stared at her without blinking. "She ast 'em to kill mama."

"You shut your mouth!" his sister screeched.

Tito's eyes turned inward.

Marian was shocked. Juanita had asked the Queens to kill her own mother? And they had obliged? Juanita looked as if she was getting ready to attack again, so Marian made her voice as gentle as she could. "What did she do to you, Juanita? What did your mother do?"

The girl licked her lips. "She dint do nothin' to me."

To *me*. "To Tito? Did she do something to Tito?"

Juanita's eyes flickered toward her brother and back again. "She dint do nothin' to him neither." And then in a voice so low as to be almost inaudible: "Yet."

Yet. "What was she going to do to him?" No answer. In a firmer voice: "Juanita, what was your mother going to do to Tito?"

"She was goin' to kill him, you dumb pig!"

Slowly the ugly story came out. According to Juanita, Mrs. Alvarez had killed her two younger children—first two-year-old Estella and then six-year-old Felipe. Juanita hadn't been too sure about Estella but she'd actually seen her mother push Felipe out the window...eight floors up. Keeping out of sight, the frightened girl had followed as her mother went down and wrapped Felipe's body in a filthy army blanket. Mrs. Alvarez had carried him away in the middle of the night; two hours later she'd returned with nothing in her arms.

The reason? She couldn't support four kids. The two deaths had gone unreported; and each time a social worker paid a visit, Mrs. Alvarez had borrowed two children from her neighbors so her food stamps and living-expenses assistance wouldn't be reduced. Even so, the welfare checks didn't go far enough, and the salary checks when she was working bought less and less. First she'd disposed of one mouth to feed. And then another. And now times were lean again.

"Tito was next," Juanita said in an old woman's voice.

Oh dear god; what a thing for a twelve-year-old to have to face. "And then you were next after Tito."

"Not me!" Juanita said with scorn. "I bring money in!" She glared at Marian defiantly.

Marian carefully did not ask how. "But why didn't you go to the police, Juanita?"

"I did," the girl said. "I tol' a brownie, but he dint listen."

A traffic cop. Marian's cheekbone was hurting, where one of Juanita's sharp little fists had landed. She tried asking Tito a few questions but got only grunts in reply; she wasn't even sure the boy was still with them. Juanita said she'd told a lot of people, but nobody did anything. So she'd gone to the Queens for help.

"Why the Queens?"

"Because they the only ones 'round here who *take care*, you know, look out for things. I tell 'em what happen and they say don' worry, we take care of it. And now they all in jail—*and it's my fault!*" The body-wracking sobs started again. "They all gone now—because of me!" Juanita's attack on Marian had been some last-ditch attempt to fight off the self-blame that was choking her; but now she'd given in to it.

Oh lord, lord. The Queens were the law in that neighborhood; the murder of Mrs. Alvarez had been nothing less than an execution. She'd been judged guilty of crimes not to be tolerated in even that crime-ridden section of town. Of course Juanita didn't want the Queens in jail; they were her protectors, the ones who'd helped when no one else would listen. The Queens had done her a favor and now they were going to pay a dreadful price for it.

Marian had thought she'd be bringing consolation to the young Alvarezes; yet there she was with a twelve-year-old drowning in guilt and an eight-year-old hovering on the brink of catatonia. Enough of this pretense that an aunt was looking after them; these kids needed help and they needed it fast.

Marian took both children with her when she went looking for a phone to call a social worker to come take them to a shelter.

MARIAN WOULD JUST as soon have skipped dinner, preferring to collapse into bed with a box of sesame crackers and a cold beer. She was tired, tired, tired. But she'd had to cancel their last two dinner dates, and Brian Singleton had been getting antsy enough lately anyway. Besides, if she stayed home alone, she'd just give in to her depression.

A quick shower was an absolute must. She dressed hastily, ignoring the blinking message light on her answering machine. Beneath her left eye a lovely king-sized bruise was blossoming, which Marian covered with make-up the best she could. Taking a cab instead of driving herself saved a little time, but still she was late when she got out in front of the brand-new restaurant on West Fifty-fifth that Brian wanted her to try. Oh lord, the place had a doorman.

Said doorman looked her up and down and autocratically informed her that reservations were required. Marian said she was meeting someone. The doorman demanded her name and that of the "party" she was meeting. After consulting by phone with some unseen guardian of the A-list, he grudgingly granted her permission to enter. Marian did not thank him.

Inside, the restaurant was exactly what she'd expected: a gathering place for trendoids—oversold, overdecorated, and overpriced. It was one of those places where the women tended to wear dresses that cost more than Marian earned in three months. It seemed that more and more often Brian was placing her in situations where she was likely to be uncomfortable; she didn't need a crystal ball to read *that* message. And there he was, looking well-tailored and impatient. As always.

"I know I'm late," Marian volunteered before he could say anything. "I got caught in something that simply could not be put off. Have you been waiting long?"

He didn't answer her question. "Your face is dirty," he said.

Marian was startled. "Oh…no, that's a bruise. I thought I'd covered it up."

"Been in a fight, have you?"

"With a twelve-year-old girl." Marian started to tell him about Juanita Alvarez but stopped after a few sentences when she saw his eyes beginning to glaze. A few months ago Brian would have wanted every detail and would have been oh-so-concerned for her safety. When they'd first met he'd been intrigued by the kind of work she did, and he never seemed to stop asking questions. He wanted to know *everything* about her.

That had changed.

"Let's order, shall we?" he said. "I don't know how much longer I can stand just smelling all this wonderful food." *Your fault; you kept me waiting.*

After the food arrived and they started eating, they both mellowed somewhat. "I'm sorry you were hurt," Brian said. "Is that why you were late? Tell me about this Juanita…?"

"Alvarez. I'll tell you some other time, Brian, if you don't mind. It's a pretty sordid little story, and right now I need to put it aside for a while."

He nodded. "I can understand that. Is there something I can do?"

"You've already done it. You've provided me with good food and good company."

His eyes crinkled at the compliment. "Fine. I was afraid you were working on another depression."

"Not a chance," she lied.

"Glad to hear it. And you won't forget the Bergstrom opening, will you?"

Bergstrom, Bergstrom. "No, of course not." *Who the hell was Bergstrom?* "Ah, that's next Thursday, right?"

"Tuesday. You've forgotten about it."

"I remember, I'd just mistaken the day. I'm looking forward to seeing his paintings."

"Bergstrom is a sculptor."

"A sculptor? Oh my, I mixed him up with somebody else."

"The most exciting new sculptor to come along in twenty years and *I* got him. And you forgot about the opening."

Whew. "No, I remember your telling me—"

"You're lying," he said calmly. "You can't remember, because I never told you about Bergstrom."

Marian's mouth dropped open. "You...set a trap for me?"

"To prove a point." Brian reached across the table and took her hand. "You're not tuned in the way you used to be, Marian. Look at what just happened. You sit there and pretend to remember something rather than admit you don't know what I'm talking about. You're just not *with* me anymore. I watch you being sucked into that cesspool where you work and I feel powerless to do anything about it."

"I'm not being *sucked* into *anything*," she said indignantly.

"You've changed since you were transferred, did you know that? When you were working out of Police Headquarters, you were able to keep your professional life and your private life separate. Life wasn't all police work to you then. You used to want to know everything that was going on at my gallery. You wanted to know everything that was going on with *me*. But now your head is always...Marian, I want you to ask for a transfer. Get yourself out of that place."

"It's only a temporary assignment, you know that." Too defensive. "Is that what's gone wrong with us? My job?"

He looked as if she'd committed some unpardonable breach of etiquette. "I'm not sure anything has gone wrong with us," he said carefully. "I'm trying to stop it before it does. There's more to the world than the Lower East Side. Come back."

Marian took a deep breath. "I'm sorry if you think I'm not paying enough attention to you. But you know, Brian, I don't think you're paying enough attention to me."

They stared at each other without speaking while the busboy cleared the dishes and the waiter brought their dessert. Marian didn't even look at the gingered figs in cream she'd ordered. When they were alone again, Brian said, "I don't suppose you want to come home with me tonight, do you?"

"Well, it's hard to resist an invitation like that, but I think I will anyway." Suddenly she'd had enough of the hurtful game. "Why do you do that? Word invitations in a way that makes it impossible for me to accept? Why not just *not ask*?"

"My wording offends you? Oh, I do apologize. From now on you must tell me exactly how to say things." Brian was ignoring his dessert too.

"You do it to me constantly—this isn't the first time." Marian put her napkin on the table. "Brian, I'm going to leave before I say something outrageous. Have you noticed how often we've been parting on an unpleasant note lately? Of course you have. I suspect you want it that way. Setting that Bergstrom trap for me—sometimes it seems you're deliberately provoking a scene. Is that what you want?''

''What do *you* want?''

''I want to leave.''

He picked up a spoon. ''But I haven't finished my dessert.''

''Then finish it.'' She got up and charged angrily across the room, ignoring the raised eyebrows of the other diners. She felt used, set up, tricked. Maybe she wouldn't be so angry if she weren't so tired. Maybe she wouldn't be so tired if she weren't so angry.

Outside, in a voice not to be argued with, she ordered the patronizing doorman to get her a taxi. He gauged the extent of her anger and hastened to comply. Marian paced up and down impatiently as cab after cab passed the signaling doorman; finally one stopped. She climbed in.

''Have a nice day,'' the doorman smirked.

THREE

SHE WOKE UP the following morning thinking of the woman who'd started killing off her children one by one when she realized she couldn't feed them. What had Mrs. Alvarez felt when she pushed young Felipe out the window? Relief, or remorse? Both? Marian stared at herself in the bathroom mirror. She had a black eye.

Saturday wasn't one of Marian's work days, but she was on standby this weekend. That meant she had to carry a pager with her when she went out, one more thing to load down her handbag. She put in a couple of phone calls, once again ignoring the blinking message light on her machine. First she called the shelter to check on Juanita and Tito. The two children were doing as well as could be expected; a counseling session with a psychologist was scheduled for that afternoon. The social worker asked if a date had been set for Juanita to appear in Juvenile Court. Marian said she didn't know; she hadn't talked to the DA's office yet. She wasn't at all happy about seeing Juanita and Tito go into the city's foster care program. They'd be better off than with their own mother, but only marginally.

Next she called the precinct house to see how the inter-rogation of the Queens was going; Marian herself had put in a couple of wasted hours the day before, trying to get Carmen to talk. But that was before she'd discovered the reason for the killing and called it in. Juanita's story made all the difference; now the youngest Queen had broken down and admitted her involvement in the group killing. Good police work had done the trick. Bullying killer-children, specialty of the house. The desk sergeant reminded Marian she had standby duty and she snapped at him.

Marian didn't like anything about the case. Juanita had done the only thing she knew to do to protect herself and her brother. Yet she could very well spend time in a juvie detention center; an uncompromising prosecutor might argue that the girl hadn't tried hard enough to get police assistance. And Marian didn't like condemning the Queens for this particular crime; if any woman deserved to be punished, it was Mrs. Alvarez. Yet the Queens couldn't be allowed to set themselves up as the law, meting out justice whenever and however they saw fit; those young female thugs were hardly qualified to make life-and-death judgments. What if Juanita had lied to them? They'd have killed an innocent woman. As far as that went, what if they all—Queens and police alike—had simply been taken in by a very clever and quite conscienceless twelve-year-old girl?

It got more depressing by the minute.

Marian pushed the button to play back yesterday's phone messages. The first three were from telephone solicitors, but the next was from a friend. "Marian, this is Kelly. I left your name with the doorkeeper but you haven't shown up *once*! Previews started on Sunday and we're nowhere near ready and I'm going crazy here! This whole place is insane. Look, tomorrow is Saturday and I know you're not working so you don't have any excuse not to come. We're starting rehearsal at eleven in the morning and we'll probably be here until midnight and don't tell me there isn't one hour in all that time when you can't get away long enough to succor a frantic friend! You like that word 'succor'? It's in the play. Anyway, I desperately need someone sane to talk to...you *are* still sane, aren't you? See you tomorrow—don't let me down."

Marian had to smile. She hadn't seen Kelly Ingram for over a month; but even if it had been a year, her friend would still just pick up their conversation wherever they'd left off. Kelly was rehearsing for her first Broadway role and was scared out of her skull. Marian would make a point of finding time to go to the theater, perhaps during the afternoon.

But first, chores. She put in a load of laundry and had just gotten out the vacuum cleaner when the phone rang. It was Brian. Their conversation was brief. Did she want to do anything tonight? No, she thought it better if they both took a few days to cool off. Fine with me, Brian said. Goodbye.

Kelly's phone call had lightened Marian's blackening mood somewhat, but Brian's quite effectively darkened it again. There'd been a time when just the sound of his voice on the phone had given her a lift. The sheer joy of "learning" another person who was *simpatico* had buoyed Marian along for weeks; but now it was getting harder and harder even to remember the good times. There *had* been good times, lots of them. With an effort of will Marian concentrated on one of them: Brian had agonized with her while she was studying for the rarely given Lieutenants Exam, and he'd celebrated with her when she passed. At that moment, the world had never looked better.

But then, with all the subtlety of a volcano erupting, everything had started changing. Marian was passed over for promotion. A man who *was* promoted to lieutenant was no better qualified than she and perhaps less; she'd have been a fool not to suspect sexual discrimination. Absolutely impossible to prove, of course; she'd had to eat it. And it was about then that Brian had started to cool toward her—no, to be fair, it probably began a little before that, when she'd not rushed to move in with him when he asked her to. But it was pretty obvious that her failure to be promoted had dimmed her luster somewhat in his eyes. Then came the unexpected and denigrating transfer to the Ninth Precinct, and Brian withdrew even further.

Brian ran his life the same way he ran his art gallery, she thought; he was a collector. She admitted now he'd "collected'' Marian the way he collected the other people around him. His friends all had something unusual or even unique to recommend them—an art style, an eccentric way of living, a high adventure or two. The thought of having a police detective for his lover must have promised him new kicks; he'd displayed unglamorous, unornamented Marian Larch as a new discovery he'd made that he expected the world—*his* world—to acknowledge with a certain degree of awe and/or amusement. *Nothing wrong with my hindsight*, Marian thought sourly.

But her welcome in that world seemed to be wearing thin, now that her image was tarnished a bit, and the novelty of the relationship had long since worn off. Yet they'd been too close for either simply to dump the other; that would not have fit Brian's image of himself as a civilized man, and Marian had hung on (too long) out of sheer stubbornness. Brian began to show his disaffection in more subtle ways, subtle and a trifle sadistic, such as putting her on the spot and then proclaiming his innocence. Once he'd taken her to a party on Long Island where the guest of honor turned out to be the subject of a Grand Jury investigation for which Marian was a police witness. She'd refused to stay, of course, thus providing Brian with an excuse to act hurt and put-upon. They'd had their first full-out row over that. His motives may have been petty and spiteful, but the consequences could have been quite serious; Marian's presence there would have compromised the investigation. He couldn't seem to understand that. Or didn't want to.

Marian realized she'd been vacuuming the same place in the rug for five minutes. She turned off the cleaner and left it sitting where it was while she collapsed into the nearest chair and stared at the wall. Brian was an aggravation, true; but he wasn't the problem, he was only the excuse. She was blaming him for what was really bothering her. Not for the first time she wondered why she had chosen a profession in which success inevitably meant a debilitating bout of depression.

This always happened to her, this feeling of disappointment in the human race whenever she had to point a finger and name someone a killer. She'd thought she'd grow hardened to it in time, but it hadn't happened; if anything, her perpetual feeling of letdown was getting worse. And yesterday hadn't helped. She played over the scene in her head: Carmen, Donnice, Encarnación, the rest of the gang. Arresting one person for an act of murder was disheartening enough, but fourteen at once...that had to be the Queen of downers.

"YOU'RE THE LADY COP," said the doorkeeper at the Broadhurst Theatre.

Marian ground her teeth. "I'm a police detective, yes. Sergeant Larch."

"That's quite a shiner you've got," he said with a grin. "Well, you just go right in, Sergeant. Miss Ingram said if you showed up I wasn't to let you get away. I think they're taking a break now—she's around someplace."

Marian hadn't made it to the theater in the afternoon; it was almost ten that night before she was able to drag herself out of her lethargy and make the trip to West Forty-fourth Street. She'd waited for Kelly Ingram on television sets before, but this was the first time she'd come looking for her friend in a real honest-to-god theater. The backstage area wasn't any too well lighted; Marian had to pick her way carefully among the cables and the other obstacles that might have been strewn about by some careless giant. A number of people were doing the same thing, looking determined and a bit grim; no one spared her a glance. Someone—the stage manager?—was reading the riot act to a couple of stagehands, who seemed more bored than intimidated; Marian was surprised to see the former had a hook in place of one hand. Just at that moment A Presence moved among them; Marian recognized stage star Ian Cavanaugh, now pushing fifty but still handsome enough to turn heads.

A young woman struggling with an armful of costumes told Marian she thought Kelly was out front talking to Abby.

"Out front?"

"The auditorium. You know—where the seats are?"

Marian smiled. "Yes, I know where the seats are. Thank you."

She edged her way onto the stage, feeling like an intruder, and looked out toward the audience seats. Kelly was standing in the aisle talking to a short, dark-haired woman who listened but said very little—"Abby," the costume woman had said. It must be Abigail James, the playwright responsible for bringing all these people together. The play was called *The Apostrophe Thief*; Marian didn't have the foggiest notion what it was about.

Kelly was getting more and more animated, to the point of waving her arms while she talked. In contrast, Abigail James folded her own arms and stood stolidly, once in a while shaking her head. Then Kelly happened to glance toward the stage. *"Marian!"* she shrieked, in a voice loud enough to carry to the last row of the balcony.

Every eye in the theater was on Marian. Self-consciously she lifted one hand in a weak wave.

Kelly abandoned her argument with Abigail James and rushed toward the stage, graceful as a dancer. "Marian! You've got a black eye!"

"I know."

"Does it hurt? What happened?"

"A twelve-year-old girl gave it to me. I was in no danger."

Kelly clucked over her a minute and then said, "I thought you were *never* coming. I've got a few minutes before we start again—let's go to my dressing room. You won't be-

lieve—oh, Ian, wait a minute, I want you to meet my friend
Marian Larch. Marian, this is Ian Cavanaugh.''

The big, good-looking actor didn't offer to shake hands
but his smile was cordial. He didn't mention her black eye.
''Not the infamous *Sergeant* Marian Larch?''

Marian blinked. ''Did you say 'infamous'?''

''The police sergeant who's going to put us all in jail if we
don't stop hassling Kelly?''

Kelly didn't look the least embarrassed. ''I may have said
that once.''

Cavanaugh laughed. ''Once a day.''

Marian went along. ''And are you hassling Kelly?''

''Never,'' he said, just as Kelly exclaimed, ''Constantly!''

''Seems to be a slight difference of opinion here,'' Marian said, wondering if they were really joking or whether
there was tension between them; they seemed friendly
enough. She asked how rehearsal was going and got answers like *Could be better* and *Still needs work.* Cavanaugh
caught sight of Abigail James gesturing to him and excused
himself.

Marian watched him walk away. ''Attractive man.''

''And a nice one too, I think,'' Kelly said. ''He keeps to
himself a lot—not very outgoing. About the only ones he
talks to are Abby James and the stage manager.''

''That's Abby James?''

''Yep, that's her. An absolutely terrifying woman. Demanding, inflexible, and with a heart of stone. She comes
up only to my shoulder, but I'm *afraid* of her!''

Just then Cavanaugh casually put his hand on Abby
James's shoulder; the gesture was unexpectedly intimate.
''He doesn't look afraid of her,'' Marian observed.

Kelly made a rude noise. ''Those two have been living together for centuries.'' She grinned. ''He won't even *look* at
me. Come on.''

Marian followed her, right past a pretty girl in her late teens that Kelly pretended not to see. In the dressing room, Kelly plopped down and stared at herself in a mirror. "Who was that girl we just passed?" Marian asked.

Kelly made a face. "Oh, that was Xandria. Not *Alex*andria, but *Xan*dria. Did you ever hear such a phony name?"

"She's in the play?"

"My kid sister, can you imagine? We don't look anything alike. She's a little too young for the role, if you ask me. But nobody did."

Oh-oh, Kelly was feeling her age, all thirty-two years of it; change the subject. "When did you start wearing your hair like that? I haven't seen that kind of hairdo since Joan Crawford. Is it for the play?"

"No, I just thought I'd try it out," Kelly answered, patting the sides of her hair. "I don't like it much either. Actually, it doesn't matter how you wear your hair these days," she snickered, "so long as it looks as if you paid someone a lot of money to fix it that way for you." Then in a completely different tone: "God, Marian, I'm glad you came!"

That sounded bad. "Kelly, what's wrong?"

Her friend made a keening sound. "I'm going to blow it! My big chance to prove I can act and I'm going to blow it! It's so much *harder* acting on the stage! If you goof, you have to cover it up the best you can and get on with the next part—you can't stop and redo it for the camera. And I've been goofing a lot, Marian. I'm going to *ruin* this play. I'm going to spoil it for everybody! I thought I was ready for something like this but I'm not!"

"Oh, don't say that! Somebody must have thought you were ready or you wouldn't have gotten the role in the first place, right?"

"That's the strange part. It was Abby who picked me for this role. She saw a TV movie I did and thought I'd be right for the role of Sheila and here I am! I've been trying to get away from those glamour-girl roles I've been stuck in for so long that I practically slobbered on the woman the first time she spoke to me about it. But now . . ."

"Well, then, that should count for a lot—she's never picked a TV star before, has she?"

"No, and she never will again after *The Apostrophe Thief*."

Marian smiled. "Sorry, I just don't believe you're that awful. What you've got is nothing more than good old-fashioned stage fright. What I hear, lots of actors suffer from that all their lives."

"Oh, thanks a lot!"

"What I mean is, there's nothing wrong with *you*. It's just one of the hazards of the profession, isn't it?"

Kelly made a noise that might have been assent. "You'd think Abby'd be willing to help me out, since she picked me. But she's barely spoken to me since rehearsals began."

"Well, maybe that's just her manner."

Kelly sighed. "I suppose. She and Ian Cavanaugh are both like that—kind of stand-offish."

"What do you mean, she should have been willing to help you out?" Marian asked. "What were you arguing with her about?"

"I wanted her to rewrite a line—it's too hard to say without twisting it up. *One* line. But no, nobody meddles with Abigail James's peerless prose! Even the director has asked her to cut it, but she won't. She just keeps telling me to get it right."

"What's the line?"

Kelly thrust a script at her. "This speech here." She pointed. "I absolutely, positively, cannot *say* it."

Marian looked at the line. "'People mean no more to you than a watch battery,'" she read. "'Useful for about a year, then it's time for a replacement.'" She frowned. "What's so hard about that?"

Kelly's face had fallen. "You too? Everybody in the whole *world* can say that line except me! I can say 'Better buy better rubber baby buggy bumpers' and 'He thrusts his fists against the posts and still insists he sees the ghosts'—but I *cannot* say 'People mean no more to you than a batch watery.' There, you see? I always do that—*batch watery*. Read it again."

Marian read the line again. "Try building up to the word 'watch,'" she said. "Don't think about 'battery.'" And immediately felt foolish for giving acting advice to a professional.

But it did the trick. After a couple of tries Kelly got the line out the way it was supposed to be said and did a little dance of triumph to celebrate. She tried it again; and while her delivery wasn't smooth, at least she was no longer spoonerizing. "Ah, *thank* you, Marian! You've saved my life!"

"Didn't your director tell you to do it that way?"

Her friend looked sheepish. "He probably did. John's a good director, but I've been so rattled I don't always remember what he's told me. I don't see how these people do it—remember everything, I mean. In television, you finish a day's work and go home and forget those lines because they're *over*, done, finished, goodbye! But here you've got to remember a whole play's worth of lines and you have to remember them all the time. Plus about a zillion stage directions. And do you know I'm responsible for remembering to check out my props before each act?"

Marian murmured sympathetically. Kelly practiced the line until she could say it without stumbling, beaming broadly the whole time. An intercom on the wall announced Miss Ingram was wanted on stage "immejutly."

"What about you?" Kelly asked as they left the dressing room. "Working on a big case?"

"Just wrapping one up. I made the arrest yesterday."

"Oh . . . was it a murder?"

Marian nodded.

Immediately Kelly looked stricken. "That means you're in one of your notorious blue funks! Oh, I'm sorry, Marian! Here I've been rattling on about my own problems while you—"

"It's all right," Marian stopped her. And, strangely enough, it was; Kelly always managed to cheer her up, even when she didn't know she was doing it. "I'm feeling better already. You're such a *good* distraction."

Kelly laughed. "I'm going to give that the best possible interpretation I can. Do you want to watch from back here? Or from out front?"

"Back here, I think."

"Okay. I've got to go on."

Marian watched as Kelly took her place on the stage as the rehearsal started. Her friend didn't seem nervous, and when the scene started she was quite good at pitching her voice so it could be heard at the rear of the auditorium without benefit of a microphone.

Marian noticed Ian Cavanaugh waiting for his entrance cue. Since he didn't seem to be doing anything Stanislavskian to get himself into the proper mood, she went up and spoke to him. "I wonder if you would tell me something. Truthfully."

He smiled, a little. "I wonder too."

"Kelly's been saying she's going to ruin this play."

"Oh, tush. She exaggerates."

Marian let out a sigh of relief. "That's the truth? I thought she might be overstating, but since this is her first venture in live theater—"

"She's about as insecure as all television actors are their first time on the legitimate stage. No more, no less. Kelly has spurts of brilliance, times when she shows enormous stage presence. Her problem is that she has difficulty sustaining."

"Nerves?"

"More likely it's that she's used to working in shorter units of time. Television scenes run only fifteen lines or so, and here of course we go on much longer than that. What Kelly needs is an audience. Once she starts getting feedback from the people watching, she'll find it easier to sustain."

"You sound very sure."

"I've seen this happen a dozen times, Sergeant. Kelly has the talent. She'll know how to use it better once she has some live-performance experience under her belt. Now if you'll excuse me, my cue is coming up."

Marian stepped back to let him concentrate.

The Apostrophe Thief seemed to be about a widower (Cavanaugh) who was possibly undermining a generations-old family business; Kelly played his sister-in-law, who suspected him of taking kickbacks and skimming off the top. The main conflict was between those two, with Kelly trying to convince the other characters of what he was up to. Those other characters turned out to be "prizes" the two antagonists contended for as they struggled to line up allies, the duel stirring up all sorts of long-dormant feelings that had been kept suppressed for the sake of amity. It was hard to tell from just one scene, but it seemed to Marian that Cavanaugh's alleged cupidity was just the excuse, that the battle was really about something else. In the scene then being rehearsed, Cavanaugh was working on Kelly' younger sister—the "Xandria" who'd evoked such scorn (and fear?) in Kelly. Marian still couldn't figure out what the title meant.

"People mean no more to you than a watch battery," Kelly trilled happily.

Marian wanted to cheer.

The tension was building nicely. The younger sister was torn between Cavanaugh's charm and loyalty to Kelly— loyalty that was somewhat forced, the scene revealed. Kelly kept making protective moves toward the young woman

Cavanaugh kept seducing her with his voice...and Marian's pager started to beep.

Once again every eye in the place was on Marian; she'd never known the blasted thing to be so loud. She turned it off and asked a stagehand where she could find a phone.

"Police business," Kelly explained importantly to her fellow actors.

Marian made her call and got the bad news. *Multiple murder, sorry if it's your day off, no one else available, don't argue, get on it.*

The play's director had taken advantage of the interruption to give a few added instructions to his players. When Marian tried to wave goodbye unobtrusively, Kelly made an attention-drawing dash to the side of the stage. "What is it? You're not leaving, are you?"

"Have to, Kel. Nobody else is available."

"Where are you going? Is it a new case?"

"Brand new."

"Not another murder!"

The stagehands were all listening carefully. "Afraid so," Marian said.

Kelly looked alarmed. "But you can't!" she protested. "You're not over the last one yet!"

On that note of encouragement, Marian left.

FOUR

THE NINTH PRECINCT stretched south from Fourteenth Street for about a mile to East Houston, and east from Broadway to the river. The bulk of the precinct was made up of Alphabet City: the far East Side avenues A, B, C, D, and FDR Drive. The precinct was a disconcerting mixture of crumbling slums and rat-infested empty lots on the one hand, and on the other old buildings that had been renovated and occupied by upscale young professionals. Even the East Village was making a comeback from its notorious days as a focal point of drugs and prostitution. New commercial businesses stood side by side with longtime ethnic restaurants of every persuasion. Sidewalk peddlers still set up outside the old Cooper Union Building, hookers' corner was still Third Avenue and Twelfth Street, Bowery bums still shambled out with dirty cloths to wipe off windshields, and St. Mark's Place was still the drag center of the universe. But new crafts shops, accountancy firms, restaurants, interior decorators, and computer stores had moved in and were settling down for a long stay. Gentrification was progressing nicely.

Separating this mishmash from the river was a stretch of public greenery called East River Park. Marian parked illegally and headed toward the three Radio Motor Patrol cars she'd spotted. She elbowed her way through a bunch of noisy spectators, close to a hundred of them, she estimated, most of them talking in either Cuban Spanish or black "swain" lingo. The uniformed officers had their hands full keeping them back, but keep them back they did

Foley was leaning against the front fender of the first RMP, waiting for her.

He stared at her black eye. "Who gave you the mouse?"

"Juanita Alvarez." She waited for the putdown but he merely nodded and pointed toward some spot in the park.

"In there," he said. "I've been here fifteen minutes. What took you so long?"

Marian started walking in the direction he'd indicated. "What did the first officer say?"

"Didn't talk to him."

"You've been here fifteen minutes and you didn't question the first police officer on the scene?"

"I was waiting for you."

Marian bit back what she wanted to say and merely instructed him to go find the first officer. The excited buzz of the onlookers faded as she moved deeper into the park. She walked up to the yellow crime scene ribbon and stopped.

Four men lay dead on the ground. They were handcuffed together. Each had been shot through the eye.

Jesus.

Marian swallowed and looked more closely. Four men, four individuals. One was fat. One was young and one was old. The fourth was bald. All four were well-dressed. But as well as Marian could make out from her vantage point, none was wearing a wristwatch. Probably all four bodies had been stripped of their valuables before the police got there.

The nearest cop guarding the crime scene was young, not more than twenty-one or twenty-two. He was muscular and well-built, *a high school athlete who'd been recruited from out of town,* Marian thought. She hoped he wasn't going to be sick; his pasty face and clenched jaw made him look as if working the Ninth Precinct had left him in a perpetual state of shock. "You the first officer?"

The young cop shook his head. "My partner." He motioned with his head toward the left.

Marian glanced over to see a black patrolwoman talking to Foley. "Did you call the Crime Scene Unit? And the Medical Examiner?"

"My partner did."

Then where are they? She couldn't even examine the scene until the CSU was finished, and the Medical Examiner was the only one who could remove anything from a homicide victim's body. All Marian could do was wait.

Four dead men handcuffed together. The handcuffs themselves didn't mean anything; they could be picked up in any pawnshop. It was the linking-together that was important, that was the core of the message left by the killers. Had to be more than one; one man couldn't have moved four corpses by himself. And they had to have been moved; the murders couldn't have taken place here out in the open in East River Park. How did they get here? Any witnesses?

Foley had the answer to that; he walked over to Marian and said, "First officer says when she got here there were people all over the place, trampling up evidence—"

"And robbing the victims."

"Surprise. She had to call for back-up just to get the crowd to move away so they could put the ribbons up. The bodies were dumped out of a van, black, late-model—that's all she had time to get. Want me to start on the witnesses?"

Marian told him yes and turned back to stare at the four bodies again. What she was looking at was obviously an execution; there was even something ritualistic about it, with each man shot right in the eye like that. Dumped in a public place like this—was it meant as a warning? To whom? And what had these four men been involved in that had led to such a grisly ending?

She glanced around; the only one looking in her direction was the sick-looking young cop. Marian broke the rules and ducked under the yellow ribbon. A quick search of the four bodies revealed no identification on any of them; she was back outside the ribbon in less than a minute. But that minute of touching the bodies had been enough to bring home their *peopleness*. These four weren't just lumps of trouble unloaded on the NYPD; they were individuals, four people who'd led autonomous lives but shared a common death. One of the bodies, the fat man, was still warm.

"My god," an appalled voice said from behind her. "'If thy right eye offend thee, pluck it out.'"

Marian turned to see a red-haired man carrying a medical bag. She flashed her badge and identified herself; the man from the Medical Examiner's office was named Whittaker. Following his first biblical reaction to the scene, the doctor was all business. "Rigor's started in two of them," he said after a quick once-over.

"The fat one was last?" The warm one.

"Can't tell yet. Some fat people never go through rigor mortis at all."

Marian hadn't known that. "'If thy right eye offend thee'...somebody playing God?"

"Sure looks like it. But that's your department, I'm happy to say. Know who they are?"

"Not without I.D. Give a quick look, will you?"

"Come off it, Sergeant, we both know you've already looked." But he went through the motions anyway. "Nothing."

"Prints first?"

"Sure," Dr. Whittaker said obligingly. "You want to come to the morgue?"

Marian said yes and went off to call Captain DiFalco. She used the radio in one of the RMPs, got some static from the dispatcher for not using a landline, but was finally put through to DiFalco. Police captains were not particularly fond of being disturbed late on a Saturday night, but DiFalco had already been notified of the multiple murder in East River Park. He didn't know any of the details, though.

"Handcuffed corpses?" he said, disbelieving. "Four of them?"

"And all four shot through the right eye. No I.D.—I'm going with the ME to get prints. Foley's interviewing witnesses. Captain, there's no way the two of us can handle it alone. We're going to need help. Are you coming in?"

"Yeah, I'm coming. And I'll get you some help." He pretty much had to agree to that, because of the 24/24 rule. That was the unwritten rule that said the last twenty-four hours of a homicide victim's life and the first twenty-four of the investigation were crucial to nailing the killer. It was hard enough with just one victim, but four would be impossible to investigate with only one two-person team working on it.

By the time Marian got back to the murder site, the Crime Scene Unit had arrived and was busy taking pictures and scouring the ground for evidence. Dr. Whittaker had finished his preliminary examination and motioned her inside the yellow ribbon. "Extensive dental work in all but this one," he said, pointing to the youngest of the four bodies. He lifted the bald man's dead hand. "Expensive manicure. Wrist and finger indentations where he wore a watch and two rings. They've all had watches taken."

Marian nodded. "What about rubbed places on their wrists? I'll need to know if they were all cuffed at the same time."

"I can tell you that better after I get them on the PM table. You want to look some more, or can I take them?"

She said she wanted a longer look. Marian tried studying their faces, but the blood from the shot-out eyes made that difficult. The youngest of the four was about thirty, blond, neither handsome nor homely as far as she could tell. The oldest was gray-haired and probably had been rather courtly-looking in life; Marian put his age at mid-sixties. She could just make out laugh lines on the face of the overweight man, around his mouth and at the corner of his left eye: the stereotypical jolly fat man? The bald man reeked respectability, even in death; he was the most conservatively dressed of the four—he could have been a judge. Marian estimated his age and that of the fat man as late forties, early fifties. She examined their expensive clothes, finding a pair of eyeglasses in a coat pocket of the oldest victim. Everything else had been cleaned out.

Marian watched as two of the CSU men carefully moved the bodies to see if anything of interest was underneath; nothing was. They told Marian the only thing they'd found so far was a part of a tire mark. Even that would probably lead only to a stolen car. There was nothing here to help her.

She told Dr. Whittaker he could take the bodies and went looking for Foley. Her partner had corralled a couple of the uniformed cops into helping him interview witnesses, some of whom had slipped away, he said. "But we got a partial license number on the van—which is either a Dodge Caravan, a Plymouth Voyager, or a Ford Aerostar, depending on which witness you talk to. The only thing they agree on is that it was black."

"How many in the van?"

"They saw only one guy pushing the bodies out the back, but there had to be a driver, right? Two men at least."

"How much time between the dumping of the bodies and the van's starting to move? Did it take off while the guy in the back was still visible or was there time for him to move up to the driver's seat?"

He stared at her. "I don't know."

"You didn't ask," Marian said tiredly.

"Christ, you don't think one guy did all this by himself? That's stupid."

"No, I don't think one guy did all this by himself, but I don't like guessing. Ask them. Did you get a description of the one they did see?"

"Tall and short, bald and curly-haired, clean-shaven and bearded. Dressed in jeans and a business suit, bareheaded and wearing a ski mask." Marian swore. "What did you

expect?'' Foley asked. ''Real help? Look, you feel like giving me a hand here? I got a lotta people still to talk to.''

She told him one of them had to go to the morgue for the
fingerprints and did he want to swap jobs? Foley walked
away without answering.

So she'd be the one going to those cold-storage lockers on
Thirtieth and First, just as she thought. *Down among the
dead men.* Marian checked her watch, thinking of the 24/24
rule: it was getting on toward one o'clock. Twenty-two
hours and counting.

FIVE

MIRACLES STILL HAPPENED, even in the limping last decade of the twentieth century; but lately they tended to be of the technological sort. Marian Larch rarely had occasion to bless the FBI; but by four A.M. that meddlesome organization's Automated Fingerprint Identification System had searched through its digitized images of millions of prints and had come up with identifications for all four of the dead men found in East River Park.

"At least we don't have to bust our butts finding a connection," Foley said, slurping coffee. "Universal Laser Technologies." All four men had worked there, at one of the country's leading designers and manufacturers of laser equipment, heavy into government contract work. And all four men had had some level of government security clearance, automatically placing their prints on file with the FBI. "Universal Laser," Foley repeated, "that's where the answer is."

"Or that's what we're supposed to think," Marian pointed out. DiFalco had put her in charge of the investigation, a job that would normally have gone to the vacationing lieutenant heading up the detective unit; multiple murders usually merited the attention of the higher ranks. "It could be four murders to hide just one," she said. "The other three could be window dressing."

"Yah," Captain DiFalco said glumly, "I was thinking along those lines myself." They were in the captain's office, getting themselves organized. Not one of them questioned the callousness behind the killing of innocents solely to throw a monkey wrench into the police investigation; they all knew the extent human indifference could reach. "Hell, that'll just make everything harder."

Marian didn't answer right away. Then she said, "We've got to consider the possibility of three of them being cover-up killings, but I don't buy it myself. It *had* to be meant as a warning, dumping them like that. The man in the van—"

"Men," Foley corrected testily. His eyewitness hadn't been able to clear up that point.

"Whichever," Marian said. "The *men* in the van were running a terrible risk, bringing the bodies to such a public place. It would have been easier and safer to dump them in the river. No, they wanted those bodies found as quickly as possible and as sensationally as possible."

"Well, they got that," DiFalco remarked dryly. He'd had to face the TV camera crews that managed to get to the crime scene before he did. "Needlessly conspicuous way of disposing of the bodies, all right. Show-offy."

"The whole schmear of handcuffing them together and shooting them through the eye," Marian went on, "all that had to be aimed at getting covered on the news. There's no other reason for it. It was meant as a warning."

"Unless that's what we're supposed to think," Foley said with a smirk.

"But a warning to whom?" Marian asked, ignoring him.

"Yah," the captain said, "and a warning to do what? Pay up? Keep their mouths shut? Toe the line? We've got to find out what our four dead men were up to lately."

The families of the murder victims had been notified. They'd all been awakened in the middle of the night to find a uniformed police officer and a plainclothesman waiting at the door, their terrible news clear on their faces. All but one: the youngest victim had had no family in New York. It had been Captain DiFalco's job to call the young man's mother in Idaho and break the news.

The youngest victim's name was Jason O'Neill. He was twenty-nine years old and had been with Universal Laser

Technologies for two years. Prior to that he'd been employed by a PR firm until Universal lured him away to do the same sort of work for them.

"I asked his mother if she still had Jason's last letter," Captain DiFalco said. "Evidently he didn't write much, but he called every week. Mrs. O'Neill said he hadn't sounded worried about anything the last time she talked to him, which was Thursday. He said he'd just got back from Washington, where he'd met with a congressman from Maine, and he was going back next week for an appointment with Senator Wagner of Wisconsin. The whole conversation sounded to me like a little bragging, a little name-dropping—just the sort of thing to make a proud momma even prouder. She had no idea what he was working on."

"Maybe the answer's in Washington," Foley said hopefully.

So Jason O'Neill was a small-town boy making good in corporate America, meeting with the nation's lawmakers and doing Important Things. "He must have been a real hotshot," Marian said, "if a firm like Universal Laser would send a twenty-nine-year-old to represent them in Washington all by himself. Or did they? What about the others? Were they in Washington too?"

DiFalco didn't know. "That's something we'll have to find out. I want you to contact Universal Laser as soon as you get your team organized, never mind what time it is. Do you want to split this list, or what?"

"Let's see what Universal has to say first," Marian suggested. "What does the FBI have on the others?"

The elder statesman of the four victims had been named Conrad Webb. In sound health at sixty-seven, he'd been with the firm since its founding, always on the business end, and was in fact a principal shareholder. The FBI's list of Webb's industrial and governmental contacts read like a *Who's Who* of shapers and movers.

"*Government* contacts," Foley stressed. "The answer's in Washington, I tell you."

Webb's children were grown and scattered about the country; his sixtyish wife had collapsed when the officers brought her the news, Captain DiFalco said. Mrs. Webb's housekeeper had chased the police away, telling them to come back later. "Send somebody, or go yourself," the captain told Marian.

The wife of the bald murder victim had been more stalwart; she'd excused herself when she learned her husband was dead and then returned a little later, red-eyed but relatively composed, to ask for details. The bald man's name was Sherman J. Bigelow; he was fifty years old and had been the head of Universal Laser's legal department. Mrs. Bigelow was also a lawyer, in private practice; she and her husband had met while arguing opposing sides of a civil case sixteen years earlier. Bigelow had been with Universal Laser for the last seven. The Bigelows had no children.

The last of the victims was Herbert Vickers, the fat man, forty-three years old but looking older. He was the technology man in the group; according to the FBI, his field was inertial confinement fusion.

"What the hell's that?" Foley asked blankly. The others couldn't tell him.

Vickers had been married twice; his first wife had divorced him after two years of marriage. His second marriage was less than a year old. DiFalco said, "The officers who contacted the second Mrs. Vickers say she's a centerfold blonde, at least twenty years younger than her husband. They also say she seemed more aggravated than heartbroken when she learned he was dead."

"Something there?" Marian asked.

"Find out," DiFalco said. "No way this can be a domestic matter, but we gotta investigate just the same." He looked at his watch. "I'm going home—I'll check back with you later, and I want to hear some results, got that? Have a nice Sunday.'' They were dismissed.

"Yeah, rub it in," Foley muttered on the way out.

Captain DiFalco had assigned four additional detectives to the case to help with the legwork. There was much to be covered. Follow-up interviews with Mrs. Webb, Mrs. Bigelow, and Mrs. Vickers; a follow-up phone call to Jason O'Neill's mother in Idaho. Did Jason have a girlfriend? Check finances; Conrad Webb was probably worth a mint, but what of the other three? Who inherited? Try for a make on the black van, as impossible as that seemed; check on stolen vehicles reported for a start. Check with the cab companies; look through every driver's daily record for Saturday and see if anyone picked up a fare near one of the victims' home addresses. Bug Dr. Whittaker for the autopsy report. But most especially, find out if any of the four victims had an enemy so deadly that he'd kill three other people to get to the one he wanted.

Once the other detectives were squared away, it was time for Marian and her partner to approach Universal Laser Technologies. It was almost six A.M. The head of the firm was a man named Edgar Quinn who lived in an apartment on Park Avenue South.

The security guard on duty in the apartment building lobby was reluctant to ring Mr. Quinn's number even when they showed him their I.D. Only Marian's repeated insistence that the matter was urgent finally persuaded him to wake up an important tenant at such an early hour. Upstairs, the door was opened by a man with hastily slicked-back hair who demanded to see their identification before he'd let them in. "Mr. Quinn will be with you shortly," the man said and left them standing in the entranceway.

"He did say 'Have a seat,' didn't he?" Marian asked dryly and stepped into a hallway that opened on to two rooms on either side, with a stairway straight ahead. A two-story apartment.

Her partner didn't answer; he was too busy gawking. The apartment was spacious and luxurious, of the sort Foley probably thought existed only in the movies. Eleven years in the Ninth Precinct could do that to a man.

They were still standing when a man wearing a gray velvet robe joined them. He was surprisingly young, not yet forty, with an oddly triangular face that he emphasized by brushing his dark blond hair upward from the temples. "I'm Edgar Quinn," he said, and waited.

Marian identified herself and her partner. "I'm sorry to tell you this, Mr. Quinn, but we have bad news." And she told him.

Quinn's mouth opened and his eyes narrowed. "All four of them are dead? Conrad's dead?"

"Yes—I'm sorry. They all died quickly, no pain."

Quinn felt behind him for the stairway banister and shakily lowered himself to one of the steps. He sat there stunned-looking. "How? How did they die?"

"They were all four shot. Death was instantaneous." She didn't know that was true, but why make it worse for him?

Quinn buried his face in his hands. Foley cleared his throat and said, "Uh, can we get you something? Call somebody?"

The other man gestured *no* and after a few moments pulled himself together. He stood up slowly and said, "How am I ever going to tell my wife? She loved Conrad as much as I did."

"You were close to Mr. Webb?" Marian asked.

"He was like a second father. Sergeant Larch, Detective Foley—let's go in here and sit down. I have questions, and I'm sure you must too."

Tons of them. Marian noticed he'd gotten both their names right after only one hearing, something most people failed to do when faced with the unexpected appearance of the police. Once the three of them were seated, Quinn wanted to know details. Marian explained what they'd found in East River Park.

He took it hard. "That's insane! Shot through the eye and then handcuffed? Or were they handcuffed first?"

"We don't know yet," Foley told him.

"But why? Why would anyone want them dead?"

"That's what we're trying to find out, Mr. Quinn."

After a while Quinn couldn't think of any more questions and fell silent. Marian asked him how long he'd known Conrad Webb. "All my life," he answered.

Universal Laser Technologies had been founded by the present owner's father. One of the first things the elder Quinn, a physicist, had done was bring in a man he could trust who had a head for business. That was Conrad Webb, who'd stuck with Universal during early hard times and ended up owning a piece of the firm. He'd been CEO for nearly twenty years, before advancing age had prompted him to opt for a less strenuous position in the company. Webb was as much identified with Universal Laser as Quinn's father had been, the younger Quinn told them.

But Webb had eased out of the actual management of the company several years ago. His real value, Quinn said, was in the contacts he'd built up during his life, both in industry and in government. "We called him The Network King," Quinn said with a wry smile.

"Had he been in Washington recently?" Marian asked.

"They all four had—they were our liaison with the Defense Department. They got back last Wednesday."

"You mean like a committee?" Foley asked. "Those four represented you regularly?"

"Yes, that was their job with the company. Conrad was in charge. Sherman Bigelow was along as legal counsel, and Herb Vickers was the technical adviser."

"What about Jason O'Neill?"

"Jason was a sort of trainee." Quinn sighed. "Conrad was getting on in years—he couldn't last forever. When he retired, Sherman Bigelow would have taken over as head of liaison. But we needed someone to replace Conrad's *charm*, I guess you could call it. Jason O'Neill was one of those loose, relaxed people that everybody likes. I've seen him walk into a room full of government dignitaries he'd never met and make himself right at home. He'd go up to someone, anyone, and introduce himself—and five minutes later they'd be laughing and talking like old buddies who hadn't seen each other in years. Conrad could do that too, in a more subtle way. But Jason had the gift of making people like him. We hired him for his personality.''

Marian consulted her notebook. ''Herb Vickers's specialty was inertial confinement fusion, right? What project was he working on? Why were they in Washington?''

''Sorry, I can't tell you that—it's classified information. The military has innumerable uses for the technology of ultrahigh-power laser and particle beams, and the Defense Department has clamped a lid on most of the research going on. Including ours.''

''But it was a military matter that took all four men to Washington?''

''That's right. More than that, I can't tell you.''

Marian and her partner exchanged a look. Top Secret stuff—that meant the FBI would be horning in.

Edgar Quinn had no idea what the four murder victims had been doing on Saturday. He wouldn't even speculate as to why they'd ended up dead in East River Park. He knew of no murderous personal enemies any of them might have; in fact, he insisted that it was Conrad Webb's and Jason O'Neill's stock-in-trade not to have any enemies at all.

Marian was openly incredulous. ''Conrad Webb was in business for over forty years and never made an enemy? Come on, Mr. Quinn.''

Quinn shrugged. ''Maybe in his youth, before he developed his polish? But I doubt even that. He instinctively knew how to make people feel comfortable. And he wasn't a double-dealer or a back-stabber—he didn't have to be. Conrad just didn't make enemies."

"Well, what about the other two—Herb Vickers and Sherman Bigelow?"

Possible, Quinn admitted. Sherman Bigelow had been in private practice before joining the company; he was bound to have made some enemies there—some grudge-holder whose case Bigelow had defeated in court, perhaps? Sherman was a by-the-book person, Quinn said, rather literal-minded, but with a phenomenal memory; he never forgot anything. And he was scrupulously honest. Quinn trusted his judgment implicitly.

Never forgot anything, Marian wrote in her notebook.

As to Herb Vickers, Quinn went on, he didn't really want to be in the liaison group; he'd much rather spend his time in the laboratory. But Herb knew how to explain technological matters so that laymen could understand, and that made him invaluable in Washington. "He would have made a great teacher," Quinn added. "But he could never have lived on a teacher's salary." Herb was careless; he was careless with money, careless with his clothing, careless with people. He could get so preoccupied with his work that he'd forget everything else. He'd once spent four straight days in the lab without remembering to call his wife and tell her he wouldn't be home.

"That his first wife?" Foley asked.

Quinn nodded. "Candy seems much more tolerant of Herb's eccentric ways."

Marian had to smile. "Candy?"

Quinn smiled back. "She's well named."

Marian tried to find out if there were any sort of internal problem at Universal Laser that one of the four victims might have been involved in, but the company's owner insisted there was none. The business was notably free of office politics, Quinn told them; that was because they chose their personnel *very* carefully, all the way from Head of

Research down to the mail room boy. There were no power plays going on, or incidents of jealous rivals trying to undercut each other.

"We just don't work that way, Sergeant," Quinn said. "Anything like that starts to surface, the parties involved are dismissed immediately. That's been our policy since the day my father started the company. We just don't have time for nonsense like that. Only one thing is important at Universal Laser, and that's getting the job done."

Marian sat back and listened as Foley took Edgar Quinn over the same ground again, looking for contradictions, omissions, hesitations. There were none. Finally Quinn himself put an end to it, saying there were things he needed to do now that he'd lost four of his men. Marian agreed immediately; in her judgment he'd just reached his irritation threshold. She thanked him for his help and gestured to her partner that it was time to leave.

Down on the street, Foley asked: "You don't believe that lily-white picture he painted, do you?"

"Not for one minute," Marian replied. "I can't tell if he's hiding something, or if he's just instinctively presenting his company in the best light possible."

"Shit," Foley said in disgust. "Couldn't you tell? Well, I know a snow job when I hear one. The guy was lying in his teeth."

Marian sighed dispiritedly. That probably meant Edgar Quinn had been telling the truth.

SIX

MARIAN BREAKFASTED on coffee and danish at her desk and read a newspaper the desk sergeant had brought in. The headline screamed: HANDCUFFED CORPSES IN RITUAL SLAYING. She'd sent Foley home to get some shut-eye; now she was the only one in the Precinct Detective Unit room. Staying up all night got a little harder every year, but at least the shadows under her eyes made the shiner Juanita Alvarez had given her a little less noticeable. Marian was going to have to grab some sleep soon, but there was paperwork to take care of first. With an effort Marian shifted mental gears back to Mrs. Alvarez and the Downtown Queens.

She typed up a second report; the first had been submitted before she'd learned from young Juanita the reason behind her mother's murder. In the process of typing Marian found she was able to look upon the whole affair a little more dispassionately than before; nothing like a new murder to cure the blues brought on by the old. God.

When she'd finished her report, she opened a desk drawer and took out a notebook. Being careful to use a red-ink ballpoint pen, she copied everything from the notebook she carried in her handbag to the one she kept in the desk. The notebook she carried with her was filled with names, dates, interview notes, crime scene descriptions, all the details every crime generated. Those entries were written in blue ink, pencil, black ink; in abbreviations, in Marian's own special shorthand she'd developed over the years, in key words that would mean something to her but little to anyone else.

Marian printed the information neatly in block letters, making sure the new entries were complete and that everything was spelled correctly. She'd once had a defense counsel ask to see her notebook while she was testifying in court. Without actually accusing her, he'd managed to imply that because the entries were written in more than one color ink, she'd gone back after making the arrest and simply fabricated whatever details she'd needed to make her case. Her testimony was consequently discredited; the jury had bought the trick and the perp had walked. Marian had been furious and humiliated, and she swore it would never happen to her again.

She was just getting ready to go home when a phone call came in from an assistant DA she knew slightly; he told her the DA was taking the position that Juanita Alvarez's "unilateral" act of self-defense was unjustified, since she had other resources available to her. The assistant DA didn't sound too enthusiastic about the case; he asked who was the attorney representing the child in Juvenile Court. Marian shuffled through the papers on her desk and came up with the name of the kid lawyer the Public Defender's Office had assigned to Juanita.

As Marian was hanging up, one of the other detectives Captain DiFalco had transferred to the East River Park murders walked in. Tired-looking half the time and the only other woman detective in the Ninth Precinct, Gloria Sanchez was the offspring of a black mother and a Puerto Rican father, oscillating between ethnic identities as the mood hit her; today she was in her Hispanic mode. "Got something, Gloria?" Marian asked, shifting gears again, away from Juanita Alvarez.

Sanchez plopped down on the nearest chair. "Been talkin' to Candy Gee-Don't-I-Taste-Good Vickers. She dint have nothin' to do with her husband's death."

Marian remembered that Candy was supposed to have appeared more aggravated than heartbroken by the news of

Herb Vickers's death. "You mean it's finally sunk in on her? She's grieving now?"

"Naw, she's still pissed. Mrs. Herbert Vickers is ver' pretty, ver' young, and ver' lazy. She jus' wan's to be taken care of. She thought she was set when Fat Boy married her, but now she's gonna have to go huntin' again."

"But he must have left her money—a sizable amount, I'd guess."

"It's not jus' the money." Sanchez made an effort and sat up straight. "She wan's a man arrangin' stuff for her, makin' decisions, like that. The only thin' she cares about is her looks—which are great, I gotta give her that. But that mirror-kissin' baby couldn't put herself out enough to commit a murder, much less four. And she couldn' handle it physically neither."

"She could have driven the van."

"No driver's license. My partner checked. Believe me, Marian, Candy Vickers is *not* behind the murders. She'd jus' wrinkle up her pretty nose and go *Ooooh!* You know what I mean."

Marian knew. "What could she tell you about her husband?"

Not a whole lot, it turned out. Around noon on Saturday, Herb Vickers had told his wife he had some business to take care of; so she had assumed that meant he'd be in the offices of Universal Laser. But when she tried to call him there later in the day, she got the watchman, who said the place was empty. No, she wasn't worried when he hadn't shown up by dinnertime; Herb was rather careless about keeping track of time. She was a teensy bit put out with him, though; he knew she wanted to go out that night.

"So what did she do?" Marian asked.

So she'd called some friends and complained that she was bored and wanted a night on the town. There were five of them altogether, hitting one night spot after another. "And yes, they alibi her," Sanchez said tiredly, "right up till almost three in the ay em. This one's a dead end, looks like."

Marian nodded, quite willing to accept Gloria Sanchez's evaluation of the situation. The sooner they could eliminate domestic reasons for the killings, the more time they'd have for pinning down the real motive.

She told Sanchez to put it in writing and that she herself was heading home for some sack time.

FOUR HOURS' SLEEP MADE her feel a hundred percent better. There'd been a message from Brian on the answering machine when Marian arrived home. It was a friendly message, rather nice; he'd ended by saying please call him when she felt like seeing him again.

Foley was on the phone when she got back to the stationhouse; he hung up and said, "They found the van, abandoned at one of the deserted South Street piers. Stolen. Bloodstains in the back match two of the victims. No prints."

"Of course not," Marian said with a sigh as she sat down. "When was it reported missing?"

"Saturday afternoon, late."

Shortly after the time Herb Vickers had left home—only to turn up dead in the park eleven hours later. Too big a time spread. "Autopsy report in yet?"

"Not yet."

"Well?"

"Well what? Oh. I suppose you want me to call Doc Whatsisname and bug him."

"You suppose right," Marian said, "and his name is Whittaker."

Foley grumbled but made the call. "He says the gun was a thirty-eight, but he's not ready to say which of 'em died first."

"What about the cuff marks on the wrists?"

"Nothing yet."

Marian nodded, expecting no more. On her desk were reports detailing the follow-up interviews with the families of the victims. She picked up the first one.

Mrs. Conrad Webb had regained her composure by the time the police came again. She'd had several friends with her, offering sympathy and moral support. With trembling voice she'd explained that on Saturday her husband had left for a 1:30 luncheon appointment at the Tavern on the Green, and that was the last time she saw him. When he hadn't returned by seven that evening, she'd grown worried; Conrad was always so conscientious about letting her know when he was delayed. They'd been invited to a dinner party at the Hutchinsons'—both of whom were among the group of friends present during the police interview—and not knowing what else to do, she'd gone to the dinner party alone. There she'd expressed her concern, but her friends had persuaded her there was nothing to worry about. Conrad often got involved in marathon business meetings, they'd reminded her. She'd left the party shortly before midnight. Both the Hutchinsons confirmed her story.

No, Conrad hadn't said whom he was meeting or what the meeting was about. He hadn't seemed tense or worried about the meeting, or about anything else, as far as Mrs. Webb could tell. No, she didn't know what project he'd been working on lately, only that it required frequent trips to Washington. It was the interviewing detective's opinion that Mrs. Webb was reluctant to admit how little she knew about her husband's work.

The Saturday staff of the Tavern on the Green had been contacted; they told the police that Conrad Webb had not been there for lunch on Saturday, nor had he made a reservation. The maître d' was quite positive about it; he knew Mr. Webb well and would have remembered if he'd come in.

So Conrad Webb had lied to his wife, Marian thought, just as Herb Vickers had lied to his. According to Mrs. Webb, her husband had left their apartment shortly after one o'clock; that narrowed the time a little more. The bodies had been dumped around eleven that night; there were still ten hours to account for.

Marian read quickly through Gloria Sanchez's report on Candy Vickers; nothing there Sanchez hadn't already told her. As she was picking up the next report, the phone rang; it was a television reporter wanting to know what progress had been made. Marian said "No comment" and hung up. He must have come up with a pretty good lie to get past the desk sergeant.

The next report was on Jason O'Neill. A phone call to the victim's mother in Idaho had elicited no new information; Mrs. O'Neill was despondent and mystified as to why anyone would want to kill her son. The detectives had found an address book in Jason's apartment and proceeded to interview his friends and a few of his business associates. And yes, Jason O'Neill had had a girlfriend. Two of them, in fact: one in New York and one in Washington. The New York girlfriend was a singer named Amy Camus who'd only recently moved into Manhattan from Brooklyn. Amy told the investigating officer she and Jason had had a date for Saturday night but Jason didn't show. She'd been furious with him until she learned why he hadn't kept the date. Wasn't she worried when he didn't show up? Well, they hadn't been getting along too well lately, and she thought he'd just stood her up. Did Jason do things like that often? No, but there's always a first time, isn't there?

Marian smiled wryly; there was a lady with her feet on the ground. When was the last time she'd talked to Jason? the detective had asked. Friday, Amy supposed, but she had heard from him on Saturday. He'd left a message on her answering machine while she was out, saying he'd pick her up a half hour later than they'd planned. The machine had a timer, and the call had come at 3:05 P.M. The message had not yet been erased so the detective was able to verify both the content and the time. Amy had spent the night, from about ten o'clock on, with a woman friend of hers who'd been recently divorced; the two women had sat up most of the night talking. The detective got a confirmation of the story from the friend.

So now they were down to eight hours, Marian mused. Jason O'Neill had died between three in the afternoon and eleven at night. If the autopsy report said he was the first to be killed, that would narrow the time for the others as well.

There was no detective's report on Mrs. Sherman Bigelow—only a note saying she hadn't been home all day and no one knew where she'd gone. The detective said he'd keep trying.

Marian was fairly well satisfied with what they'd found. As far as she was concerned, they'd eliminated two wives and one girlfriend as possible suspects, and she had no doubt that Mrs. Bigelow would soon be joining them. Two of the victims had lied to their wives about what they'd be doing Saturday, and one—Jason O'Neill—had had no one at home to lie to. Marian told Foley to keep two of the detectives on background checks; they still had finances and personal enemies to look into as well as the delayed interview of Mrs. Sherman Bigelow. But the other two detectives were to concentrate on trying to track the victims' movements Saturday afternoon.

The first twenty-four hours of an investigation *were* important. They wouldn't have the murderer (murderers?) by eleven that night, but most of the machinery for tracking him/them was set up and operating. Just a few loose ends yet to take care of—

A uniformed officer stopped by her desk. "Captain DiFalco wants you two in his office pronto." Then he added out of the side of his mouth: "FBI."

At the next desk Foley groaned, but Marian was pleased. That was one of the loose ends that still needed tying up.

SEVEN

THE TWO FBI MEN couldn't have been more different. One was affable without being pushy; the other was aloof and somewhat condescending. Captain DiFalco introduced them as Trevor Page (the affable one) and Curt Holland (the other one). Page, fortunately, was the senior of the pair, both in years and authority. Neither man was dressed in the standard FBI uniform, i.e., conservative suit and tie, with or without trenchcoat. They both wore pullovers of some sort, not really sweaters since they were made of expensive-looking woven material instead of knitted. The FBI was trying to change its image? Or maybe they'd just gotten tired of being called The Suits.

Trevor Page was saying, "I'm aware relations between the police and the Bureau haven't been too smooth in the past, but we'd like to change that. You know as well as I that we'll have a better chance of catching the East River Park killer if we share information. We'd like to make this a cooperative investigation."

"Sharing information," Captain DiFalco said. "That's a two-way street."

Page smiled. "Right now we're running security checks on everyone employed at Universal Laser Technologies. The results will be made available to you."

"That's a promise, not information," DiFalco rumbled.

"It will *be* information, as soon as we've finished. Universal's not a small company—it'll take some time. But I assure you, we're not going to hold anything back."

"That'll be the day," Foley growled, low.

"Did you say something, Detective?" Curt Holland challenged.

Foley was brave enough to stand up to someone outside the police hierarchy. "Yeah, I said something. We've heard this song and dance before. Cooperation and sharing—that's bullshit. *We* do all the cooperating."

"Not this time," Page answered, unperturbed. "Since Defense Department secrets may be compromised by these killings, we have every legal right to take the case out of your hands. But we don't want to do it that way. We need your help, and we're quite willing to offer the resources of the Bureau in exchange. This case has too many ramifications for either one of us to hog it."

Marian asked a question. "In your security checks on Universal Laser personnel, what do you look for?"

"This time, primarily for connections with individuals or groups that would benefit from acquiring Defense secrets. Terrorist groups, other governments. Armaments manufacturers."

"Industrial espionage?"

"Possibly."

Marian thought that over. "You're convinced that's what these killings are about? Laser weaponry?"

It was Holland who answered. "They're about dominance," he said sharply. "Everything is always about dominance. Money and power? Means to an end."

Everyone except Page looked startled. Captain DiFalco said, "You care to explain that?"

"I should have thought it was obvious," Holland replied stiffly. His speech was clipped, precise, like an actor's. "Those in possession of secret knowledge have an advantage over those who don't. Whatever deposited four corpses in that park, you can be dead certain a power play was at the center of it."

DiFalco snorted. "Yah, well, that doesn't get us very far, does it? What I want to know is, what are you doing in Washington?"

Marian wanted to know the same thing. The FBI, Page told them, was checking every one of the Universal Laser liaison group's contacts, whom they met with, why, for how long. They were also running "in-depth" security checks on those contacts, looking for any possibility of leaks or secrets-smuggling.

"But why kill the liaison group?" Marian asked. "What would that accomplish, to be precise?"

"Oh, by all means do let us be precise," Holland said, making no attempt to soften the derision in his voice.

Marian stared at him. This guy wasn't out to win any popularity contests, that was sure. "Why would someone in the secrets-smuggling business want a mere liaison group dead?" she repeated.

"To shut them up?" Page suggested. "Maybe they learned something in Washington that threatened whoever is after Defense secrets."

Holland made a sound of exasperation. "In which case they would have passed on their information to Universal Laser immediately. Even if they forgot how to use the telephone, they'd been home for three days before they were killed."

Good point, Marian admitted reluctantly.

"Perhaps they didn't know they knew something," Page said, to which Holland responded with a sarcastic laugh. "It's just a possibility, Holland," Page said mildly. "That's all we have now—possibilities." He turned back to the police. "We know the person we're looking for doesn't have to be government-connected. It could be someone from the personal life of any one of the liaison group, and that's where we can save time. There's no purpose to be served in conducting separate investigations. We'd just duplicate each other's efforts. If there's anything you can give us now, we'd appreciate it.''

DiFalco cocked an eyebrow at Marian. ''Why, certainly,'' she said silkily, and gave them the name of Jason O'Neill's Washington girlfriend.

The five of them spent the next fifteen minutes talking over what had been done and what still needed to be done. They agreed to share information and work together, and the first step toward that end would be for the two FBI men to read all the police reports that had been submitted so far—which showed a great leap of faith on the part of the NYPD, Marian thought. As they were leaving the captain's office, DiFalco said, ''Larch—hang on a mo.''

She waited until the others had left and then closed the door. ''Something?''

''I want you to make this work,'' DiFalco said urgently. ''I want you to see to it that we're *glued* to the FBI, so tight that nothing can pry us loose. Make those two feds dependent on us—on you, on me, even on Foley. Can you do that?''

She looked a question at him.

DiFalco sighed. ''The Major Crimes Unit wants to take over the case.''

''No,'' Marian said, appalled.

''Yes. I just got a tip from a buddy in the Chief of Patrol's office, who found out from—well, that doesn't matter. But the MCU wants this case, they want it bad.''

Marian sputtered, ''But, but, they, they—''

''The only thing that's holding them up,'' DiFalco went on, ''is that they're having a little manpower problem of their own right now, just like everybody else. But they'll be back at full strength in another two or three days. You've got that long to turn this circus into a joint Ninth Precinct/ FBI investigation, a *real* one. Lead Page and Holland by the hand, if you have to. Give 'em whatever they want. Hell, take 'em along on stake-outs, if you got any.''

"I got the picture. As a matter of fact, the FBI can be a help. I was wondering how we were going to handle the Washington end."

DiFalco grinned. "If they're right about military lasers being at the bottom of this, they may just end up solving our case for us. But whatever happens, I want *you* to make the collar, you or Foley."

"Right."

Then, surprisingly, Captain DiFalco clenched his fist and slammed it down on the top of his desk. "Those bastards aren't going to screw me on this one. Not this time!" Marian watched in astonishment as his face began to turn purple. He waved her away.

She closed the door behind her as she left, wondering what the Major Crimes Unit had done to DiFalco in the past to earn that kind of resentment. She didn't know the captain very well, no one at the Ninth Precinct did; he'd been on the job only a couple of weeks before Marian herself had transferred there. But clearly the man was ambitious, playing departmental politics for all he could get. He actually had a private pipeline to the *Chief of Patrol*'s office, for crying out loud. The Chief of Patrol was God; every precinct commander, every zone commander, every borough commander in the city of New York was answerable to the Chief of Patrol. If DiFalco had a connection that high up the chain of command...Marian wondered why he'd come to the Ninth in the first place. To prove he could handle anything?

When she got back to her desk she found the two FBI men reading reports that Foley had given them. Page asked, "No follow-up interviews with Mrs. Sherman Bigelow?"

"She's missing," Marian said. "We're still looking."

"Do you think she's involved?"

"I doubt it. She's probably just staying with family or friends."

Holland was examining the black-and-white glossies the Crime Scene Unit's photographer had taken. "If thy right eye offend thee, shoot it out. Did they all die at the same time?" He passed some of the pictures to Page.

"Don't know yet," Marian answered. "Autopsy report hasn't come through." She took a moment to study the FBI agents as they in turn studied the photographs. Trevor Page seemed friendly enough, but cautious—the sort of man who was willing to meet you halfway but no more. Light brown hair, hazel eyes, a good face. Curt Holland must have been good-looking once, with his black hair and eyes and strong features. But the deep shadows under his eyes and the scowl lines around his mouth spoiled the effect; even in repose his expression was one of... arrogance? Resentment? Arrogant resentment? Whatever it was, something was off-kilter there.

Holland dropped the last of the photographs on her desk. "Two-man job at least, perhaps three. But however many took part in the actual killing, transporting, and unloading of the four bodies, *one* man was behind it all. He's the one we look for."

Foley threw a triumphant look in Marian's direction. "Told you there was more than one guy in the van."

Marian gritted her teeth. "I never disagreed with you, Foley."

"A superior sort of man," Holland went on, ignoring them, "or at least he thinks he is. Never questions his convictions, always positive that he is right. He feels qualified to pass judgment and dispense justice. Arrogant. But a little jealous of his authority, I would say—thus his 'signature' on the killings. The ritualistic shooting out of one eye, the linking of four together to demonstrate their equal culpability in whatever happened to arouse our killer's god-like ire."

Interesting, Marian thought, that it was the arrogant one who spotted the arrogance behind the killings. "Are you a psychologist?" she asked him.

He gave her an ironic smile. "In a murder investigation, I am whatever I need to be."

Oh my. "I'd say the killings were meant as some kind of warning."

Holland spread his hands flat on her desk and leaned his weight on his arms, staring her straight in the eye. "*Of course* they are a warning."

Marian stared right back. "So *glad* you agree."

"Why else bother with the 'signature' if not to convey a message to someone else?"

"Exactly. You don't have to convince me."

"I'm delighted to hear it."

Page had watched the exchange with mild amusement. "So how did our judge and jury manage it?" he asked, bringing them back to the point. "Gather them together and kill them all at once? Kill them at different times and places?"

"The autopsy report ought to tell us that," Marian remarked. "We'd be better off—"

"Larch—pick up." Foley was on the phone, gesturing at her.

Marian punched the number two button and lifted the receiver. She heard Gloria Sanchez's tired voice on the other end. "Bingo," she said without enthusiasm. "We been checking the cab companies and got something." Sanchez sounded as if she was in her black street-smart mode today. "We found pick-ups near three of the victims' addresses on Saturday," Sanchez went on, "all of them after noon, around one o'clock, like that."

"Which three addresses?" Marian asked.

"All but Jason O'Neill's."

"Where'd they go?"

"You ready for this? They went to Jason O'Neill's place."

"Jesus," Foley said. "They were holding a meeting!"

"Looks like," Sanchez agreed. "Here's the good part. None of 'em took a cab afterwards. At least, there's no record at the cab companies of pick-ups near O'Neill's address."

"Because there wasn't any 'afterwards,'" Foley growled. "That's where they were killed—in O'Neill's apartment."

"Whoa, wait a minute," Marian said. "Our detectives have been in that apartment—when they got O'Neill's address book? They'd have seen evidence—"

"Not if the killer cleaned up, they wouldn't," Foley insisted. "We gotta get the Crime Scene Unit to check the place."

"What's going on?" Page asked.

"We'll need a search warrant," Marian said. "I'll get on it."

"Can I go home now?" Sanchez asked wearily.

Marian said everybody could go home. Foley was out of the room before she'd hung up the phone. Marian held up a finger to tell Page and Holland to wait and punched out Captain DiFalco's number. She told DiFalco—and the two FBI men—what Gloria Sanchez had found at the cab companies. "We'll need a warrant to search Jason O'Neill's apartment."

"I'll start making calls right now," DiFalco said. "It's too late for a warrant tonight, but with luck it'll come through sometime tomorrow. What the hell were they all doing at Jason O'Neill's apartment?"

"He was the only one of the four who lived alone," Marian pointed out. "Whatever they were meeting about, they wanted it kept secret. Conrad Webb and Herb Vickers both lied to their wives about where they were going. Sherman Bigelow probably did too."

DiFalco was silent a moment. Then he said, "I want you to get on to the Crime Scene Unit first thing tomorrow morning. Make damned sure they understand we're looking not only for evidence that a murder—or four murders—took place in that apartment, but anything else they can find that might give us some hint as to what that meeting was about."

"I'll see to it."

"Things are beginning to break, Larch. Stick with it." He hung up.

"Yes, sir," Marian said to the dead phone. She grinned happily at the two FBI men, pleased with what had been accomplished during the first twenty-four hours of the investigation. "Did you get all that?"

Page nodded. "The killer must have found out about the meeting…and decided he'd never have a better chance? All four of them were together."

Holland raised an eyebrow. "And four grown men just stood there obediently and let themselves be shot one by one? How very considerate of them."

"The killer would have had help. You yourself said it was a two-man job, possibly three."

Holland shook his head. "Too convenient. Our murderer just *happens* to find out about the meeting? And when he shows up uninvited with a sidekick hit man or two, the victims don't suspect a thing and ask them in for beer and munchies?"

"Don't be so quick to dismiss it," Page said sharply. "For all you know, that could have been exactly the way it happened. *You don't know,* Holland."

Holland's smile had a touch of menace in it. "Nor do you."

Marian started to say something but then clamped her mouth shut. Their problem, let them get themselves out of it. Page and Holland were glaring at each other, some long-simmering conflict between them bubbling to the surface. Marian could taste the tension in the air. The cause was more than Holland's acerbic personality; these two obviously had a history.

It was Page who put an end to it. "There's no point in arguing about something we'll know for certain in the next day or two. The autopsy report will tell us if they all died at the same time. I don't see that there's anything more we can do until then." He looked a question at Marian.

"No, we're finished here," she said. "For now, at any rate. Once we learn what the Crime Scene Unit finds in Jason O'Neill's apartment, we'll have a better idea of what to look for next. Are you coming in tomorrow?"

"Probably," Page said. He put a card on her desk. "If not, you can reach me there. I'd appreciate a call. And now, why don't you come have dinner with me?"

"Yes, we'd like you to come," Holland added dryly— more to include himself than her, Marian thought.

Page didn't even blink. "Is there a place around here you like to go?"

"Oh," Marian said, "I thought I'd just go home—"

"One hour. You can give us an hour, can't you? I'd like to talk about something other than corpses and murder for a while. We should get better acquainted if we're going to be working together." He smiled—a big, open smile. "Besides, we're on an expense account."

The smile was infectious; Marian smiled back. "Well, I'm not. One hour, you say? You're on. And thank you."

She cleared her desk and left with the two FBI agents, well satisfied with the day's work.

EIGHT

THEY WENT to an Oriental restaurant two blocks from the precinct stationhouse; Marian told the two men she'd never eaten there but had heard the food was good.

"The word 'Oriental' has multitudinous meanings in the restaurant business," Holland said. He peered in through the window. "It looks like the sort of place that would fix you a moo goo gai pan pizza if that's what you wanted."

Page sighed. "I'm sure it's just fine." He opened the door.

The restaurant's only window was in the front, next to the door. The subdued lighting helped hide the smallness of the place, and a smiling waitress seated them at once. Marian ordered Mandarin, Page Cantonese, and Holland Szechuan—the latter making his selection by pointing a finger at the menu without looking at it. *Très* bored. Marian and Page chatted easily while waiting for their meal; Holland was brooding about something, wrapped in his own thoughts. He sat absolutely still, his head held high; Marian wondered if he was posing, showing his profile to the world. She rather enjoyed having dinner with two attractive men, even if one of them was a bit of a snot.

When the food came, conversation stopped as they all three dug in. Marian had taken only three or four bites when a smiling elderly Chinese appeared at her side wanting to know if her dinner was all right. She told him everything was fine; still smiling, he left without asking the men whether they were equally well satisfied.

"Like it or lump it," Marian said with a smile.

"I guess we'll have to," Page answered. "Fortunately, it is very good. Not at all greasy."

Holland abruptly put down his fork, stood up, and headed toward the men's room.

"What a moody man," Marian said. "Is something bothering him? Or is he always like that?"

Page smiled wryly. "He's always like that. Holland's all right—you just have to get used to him. His problem is that he doesn't want to work for the Bureau."

"Then why doesn't he quit?"

"He can't." Page turned the conversation in another direction, not wanting to talk about his partner behind his back. They kept to neutral topics, steering clear of both personal questions and the crime they were investigating. Page tended to be conservative in his politics, hardly surprising in an FBI agent; there were very few liberal cops. Page was a casebook hard-liner when it came to protecting the security of America; he was a little more casual about the use of force than Marian was. But by the end of the meal that was all she'd learned about him. When Holland returned to the table, he still kept his distance—as if refusing to waste his energy on inconsequential dinner talk. These two really played it close to the vest.

"Well, that was good," Marian said. "I'm glad you talked me into—ahhhhhh *yeah*!"

"Ah yeah what?"

"Ah yeah I just thought of something. About the case, the meeting the four victims held Saturday. Hell, why didn't I think of that before? Jason O'Neill called his girlfriend at five minutes after three Saturday afternoon—the girlfriend here in New York, not the one in Washington. The meeting must have started at one-thirty or two—"

"So it was over by three?" Page interrupted. "Mm. Then the others had probably left by then, is that what you're saying? If that's the case, your Crime Scene Unit isn't going to find anything in O'Neill's apartment."

Holland came back from wherever he'd been and focused on what they were saying.

"So we still won't know where the murders took place," Marian concluded glumly. "Damn. But none of the other three took a cab when they left O'Neill's place. And I can't see Conrad Webb riding the subway."

"Could they have walked home?" Page asked. "Started walking, I mean. How far did they live from Jason O'Neill?"

Marian closed her eyes and visualized the addresses in her mental file. "The only one who lived within reasonable walking distance was Herb Vickers, but he was so out of shape he'd never try it on foot. No, they all had to have some form of transportation—if they left O'Neill's apartment alive."

Page grunted. "Maybe the killer showed up in his car and offered them a lift."

Holland held up a hand to get their attention. "There is one other possible interpretation. What was it O'Neill called his girlfriend about?"

"He left a message saying he'd be late picking her up that evening," Marian answered.

"How late?"

"Half an hour, I think. Why?"

"He knew at three in the afternoon that he'd be late picking her up at…seven? Eight, nine? At least four hours ahead of time, he knew he was going to be thirty minutes late."

"What are you getting at?" Page asked.

"I'm saying they may have planned something, the four of them. Something that couldn't be done until several hours later, running close to the time O'Neill would normally have been picking up his girlfriend."

"They got together a second time on Saturday?" Marian thought that over. "Or just stayed together until it was time to do whatever it was. You know, that sounds pretty good."

Holland gave them a mocking smile. "Unless, of course, O'Neill made his phone call while the meeting was still going on. Perhaps he saw they wouldn't be finishing until late and he made the call as a not-too-subtle hint that they were taking up too much of his time."

"He *could* have made the call during the meeting," Marian said, ignoring the mockery and fixing on the content. "Depending on when the autopsy report says they died."

"So we're right back where we started," Page said. "Without the results of the autopsy and the Crime Scene Unit's examination of O'Neill's apartment, all we can do is guess."

But Marian wasn't quite ready to give it up; she looked at Holland. "If they were planning something for later, what could it have been? Dinnertime, Saturday night. What could they do then, besides eat?"

Holland frowned. "Something they couldn't do when they met earlier? Universal Laser is closed on Saturdays, isn't it?"

"Yes. But the watchman could have let them in."

"Then he could have let them in earlier as well. Why wait?"

Page cleared his throat. "At the risk of sounding like a broken record, may I again suggest we wait for the autopsy report? The right explanation may be something we'd never think of in a millions years, no matter how elegant our theorizing gets. Let's put it away until tomorrow."

Marian smiled. "That's right—we weren't supposed to talk about the case over dinner."

"*I* never agreed to that," Holland said dryly.

At that moment the ever-smiling waitress returned and did her best to persuade Marian to indulge in an after-dinner sweet. Lichee? Honey sesame banana? Ice cream? When Marian had said no for the tenth time, the waitress's face fell and she sadly placed the bill on the table between the two men. "Pay please to cashier." She left.

Page laughed. "She didn't even ask us." He fished out a credit card and they got up from the table. The cashier turned out to be the same old man who'd showed such concern over Marian's dinner. "Hold on a minute," Page said, looking at the bill. "There's a mistake here—you charged us for only two dinners."

"No mistake, no mistake, is right!" The old man all but snatched the bill and credit card out of Page's hand. Page turned and signaled to the waitress, who hurried to join them; when he tried to point out they'd been undercharged, she too denied there was a mistake.

It was Marian's dinner that had been left off the bill. "They know I'm a cop," she said with a sigh.

"I thought you'd never been in here before," Page remarked.

"I haven't. And don't ask me how they know." By then the charge slip was made out and was smilingly presented to Page for his signature. "Go ahead and sign it," Marian said, taking a twenty out of her billfold. "I hope this covers it." She placed the bill on the cash register and was immediately met by a stream of rapid-fire Chinese and much shaking of the head. The cashier thrust the twenty back at her while the waitress started plucking at her sleeve. "I wish to pay," Marian said loudly and distinctly. She was answered with more Chinese, more head-shaking.

"Amazing, how quickly they've forgotten their English," Page said with a smile.

Finally Marian made the two Chinese understand she could not accept a free meal from them; she did so by speaking in the voice she normally reserved for *Stop or I'll shoot.* "Let's get out of here," she muttered to the men.

Outside, Holland raised an eyebrow and said, "Well, well, well. An honest cop."

"Well, well, well," she shot back, "a cynical fed. Now which is the rarer bird, do you suppose?"

One corner of his mouth lifted. "Sor-ry," he drawled, not looking or sounding the least bit sorry.

Marian refused their offer to walk her to her car, thanked them for the dinner she'd paid for herself, and said good night.

THE FOLLOWING MORNING Marian found that her black eye had faded considerably; only a slight bruise remained. Just as well, she thought wryly; nobody had felt particularly sorry for her anyway. Except Kelly. Kelly had worried.

When Marian arrived at the stationhouse, the desk sergeant gave her a phone message from Trevor Page. He would be in Washington today, the message said. Curt Holland had something to check out in New York, but if needed he could be reached through the phone number he (Page) had left with her last night. Marian was just as glad to have them out of her hair for the day, but that did make it a mite hard to follow Captain DiFalco's order to stick to them like glue. She wondered what it was Holland was checking out; Page had given no details. And that, Marian thought, was the FBI's idea of cooperating and sharing information.

Foley wasn't in yet. Marian put in a call to the Crime Scene Unit, telling them a search warrant would be coming through for them to give a thorough going-over to Jason O'Neill's apartment. They were to look not only for evidence of a crime but also for anything that might provide a clue as to why the four murder victims had found it necessary to meet together surreptitiously Saturday afternoon. Search for notes, Marian said, torn-up papers, anything that looked as if it wasn't part of O'Neill's regular possessions. And for god's sake call the minute they had anything.

Foley strolled in, eating a jelly doughnut. "Grab a pencil, Foley," Marian said. "Things to do today."

"I can remember," he said, mouth full.

"Write it down."

He glared at her and stuffed the rest of the doughnut in his mouth. He sat down at his desk and made a big show of picking up a pencil and pulling a note pad toward him. *Satisfied?* his body language asked.

"First, get a copy of the watchman's records at Universal Laser Technologies," Marian said. "We want to know everyone who went in on Saturday, day and night both. Second, as soon as the banks open, get a balance statement for all four of the victims—look for unusually large deposits or withdrawals, that sort of thing. Third, put a one-man stake-out on Mrs. Sherman Bigelow's apartment. She's got to come home sometime."

"*Maybe* she does," Foley mumbled.

"Fourth, contact the limousine services and see if Conrad Webb, Sherman Bigelow, or Herb Vickers ordered a private car anytime after three Saturday afternoon. Fifth, find out where Jason O'Neill kept his car. Look for a garage attendant who might tell us if O'Neill took his car out during that period—after three, Saturday."

"Jesus, Larch, this'll take forever!"

"Then you'd better not waste any time. And there's one more thing. We still haven't pinned down whether any of the four victims had personal enemies. *Real* enemies, the kind that hate deeply enough to commit murder. We've got to go into that more thoroughly."

Foley threw down his pencil. "Shit. You sure don't mind wasting other people's time, do you? You know damn well it wasn't a personal enemy that killed 'em."

"I know it and you know it," Marian replied soberly, "but the Major Crimes Unit doesn't know it. Or at least they'll say they don't."

"Major Crimes? What the hell do they have to do with it?"

"DiFalco told me the MCU wants to take over this case. The first sign of sloppy police work on our part, they'll be all over us and it's bye-bye to the East River Park murders.

So we're going to cover *everything*, and then we're going to go back and cover it again.''

Foley nodded slowly, understanding. "Jesus, they wouldn't take it away from us now? Forget that, sure they would! Let us do all the legwork and then grab the collar for themselves.''

"So you see why we have to be doubly careful? Foley, I want you to make all these arrangements yourself. Everyone is to report to you. Do whatever shifting or adjusting you think necessary. You're in charge.'' The one thing Marian had never tried in her dealings with her troublesome partner was giving him a little authority—for the simple reason that she didn't trust him. But this time he wouldn't be in a position to get someone killed by not being where he was supposed to be.

Besides, she intended to check on him every step of the way.

Foley was sitting up straighter. "And where will you be?'' he asked importantly.

"I have to check with DiFalco, and then I'm going to Universal Laser.''

On her way to the captain's office, Marian heard Foley yell, "Sanchez! Roberts! Get your asses over here! I've got a job for you.'' A real take-charge kind of guy.

She opened DiFalco's door and saw the captain waving a large envelope at her. "Autopsy report—just in. They all died at the same time.''

Marian slid the report out of the envelope and started reading. "Time of death between six and nine o'clock, estimation based on the stage of rigor mortis in the bodies of Webb, Bigelow, and O'Neill at time of examination.'' Herb Vickers excluded; Marian looked up. "Dr. Whittaker told me some fat people don't go through rigor at all.''

"Yeah, I knew that,'' DiFalco said.

She read on. "He says the abrasions on the wrists were made before death—all four men were handcuffed while they were still alive. Death in each case was caused by a thirty-eight-caliber bullet through the right eye. Lividity indicates the bodies were moved after death."

"Hell, I knew that too."

"Between six and nine," Marian mused. "Did they stay in O'Neill's apartment all that time? From one-thirty or two on?"

"They must have. Maybe they were waiting for the killer—not knowing he was a killer. Then when he got there, he and the van driver handcuffed them together...why? Just to get 'em in the van?"

"Wouldn't that be rather noticeable? It's still light at six o'clock."

"So he just killed them there? And then waited until dark to move them? Then why the handcuffs?"

Marian licked her lips. "I don't think they were killed in O'Neill's apartment. I think they went out somewhere together, to do something."

"And got caught by the killer?"

She shrugged.

DiFalco tapped a forefinger against his chin. "It's possible, I guess. Did you talk to the Crime Scene Unit?"

"Just a few minutes ago. They know to look for evidence about the meeting as well as the murders."

The captain nodded. "What's your next move?"

Marian explained what she had Foley and the others working on. "If we can't trace their steps after they left O'Neill's apartment, we're going to have to abandon that line of inquiry and go at it from another direction. We'll have to try to pin down the motive."

DiFalco made a rude noise. "Needle in a haystack."

"Not really. We know the reason's connected with Universal Laser Technologies and Washington."

"Two pretty big haystacks, if you ask me. Speaking of Washington, where are the two feds?"

Marian told him about the message from Trevor Page. "They're cutting us out already, Captain. I don't know what Holland's working on in New York and I don't know why Page went to Washington."

DiFalco swore. "Larch, sometime today I want you to get hold of the one who stayed here—Holland, that the one? Get him to meet you, make up some excuse. Don't let those sonsabitches forget that this is a *joint* investigation! Goddammit, we open our files to them and the first thing they do is pull a vanishing act! Well, I won't have it! Do you hear what I'm saying? *Do you hear?*"

She was sitting four feet away. "Yes, sir. I hear."

"You get hold of this Holland and you—which one is he, by the way?"

"The cynical one."

"Oh, him. Go call him now."

"Excuse me, Captain," Marian said, "but I think I should go to Universal Laser first. This is their first workday since those four men were killed, and it might be a good chance to pick up something."

He thought that over. "Yah, you're right—it might be at that. Well, what are you sitting there for? Get a move on!"

"On my way," Marian said.

NINE

UNIVERSAL LASER TECHNOLOGIES had factories in New Jersey and Pennsylvania, but its corporate headquarters were in the West Fifties near Fifth, about as high-rent as the local real estate could get. Marian was most curious to see this paradigm of American industry, where office politics were not tolerated and no one had ever made any enemies. Even if Edgar Quinn had not said *that*, she would have suspected him of having a fondness for hyperbole, simply from his reaction to the news about Conrad Webb's death. Webb had been like a second father, Quinn had said. The latter had had a few bad moments, but then he'd recovered quickly enough to answer Marian's questions lucidly and articulately. Quinn had obviously been fond of the old man and his death had shaken him—but a second father? Marian doubted it.

Building security was tight. Marian had to show her badge in the lobby even to be allowed on the elevator, and again on the eighteenth floor, where she was issued a visitor's badge by a receptionist. Universal Laser wasn't exactly what Marian had been expecting. For one thing, *Dress for success* didn't mean much there; she saw more jeans and sneakers than she did neckties and high heels. The offices themselves disclosed a pleasant-enough working environment, but there'd been no attempt to turn them into a showplace. On her way to Edgar Quinn's office, Marian spotted an arrow sign pointing to the legal department. On impulse she turned in that direction.

The legal department was a small complex of offices off to itself. Two women were standing in the middle of the reception area, talking; they looked distraught and nervous. Marian cleared her throat and they both jumped. She asked for Sherman Bigelow's secretary; in Mr. Bigelow's office, she was told, over there.

Marian knocked on the door and was invited in. The woman sitting behind the big desk had been crying; she made a visible effort to pull herself together. "May I help you?" she said automatically. The secretary's theme song.

Marian identified herself and learned the secretary's name was North. She asked her, "Did you just hear of Mr. Bigelow's death?"

North shook her head. "It just hit me all over again, when I came in to check Mr. Bigelow's calendar and see if he'd made any notes for what he wanted done this week." Her voice was high and tense. "Normally he'd leave them on my desk, but now..."

Marian asked to see the calendar. The secretary got up and walked around the desk to hand it to her. She turned out to be on the plump side and wearing baggy slacks and espadrilles; not the usual picture of an executive secretary, but she looked very comfortable. Marian glanced at Bigelow's calendar. Business meetings, a doctor's appointment, dinner engagement Thursday night. "This appointment with Dr. Greenberg...was Mr. Bigelow ill?"

"No, he just needed new glasses. Dr. Greenberg's an ophthalmologist. Would you like me to make you a copy of the appointment sheet?" the secretary offered, thus saving Marian from having to ask.

"Thank you. Did Mr. Bigelow seem to be acting normally when he got back from Washington last week?"

"Normally?" A high squeak.

"Did he appear to be worried, distracted? On edge?"

North paused long enough to get her voice under control. "I noticed nothing, Sergeant. Everything appeared quite as usual to me."

Marian studied the woman, wondering what was going on. "Ms North, what are you afraid of?"

Her eyes grew huge. "Four people in this company are murdered and you ask me what I'm afraid of?"

"You think you are in danger?"

"Me? No, ah, why should I be in danger? I never said anything!"

"Never said anything? About what?"

"About anything! I don't talk outside these offices. I keep the company's confidentiality."

Marian stepped closer to her. "I think you just told me that you do know something."

"No I don't! I mean, I know my job, but that's all! I don't know why Mr. Bigelow was killed! Sergeant Larch, I'm trying to cooperate—please don't bully me. We're all very distressed, and this is difficult for me."

"Of course it is," Marian said soothingly. "I know it's not easy and I want you to understand I do appreciate your cooperation. Especially since we can't locate Mrs. Bigelow—anything you can tell me will be a help."

The other woman looked surprised. "Mrs. Bigelow? She's at their place in Connecticut."

It was Marian's turn to look surprised. "She told you she was going to Connecticut?"

"I talked to her on the phone yesterday," the secretary said, obviously relieved at the change of subject. "I heard about Mr. Bigelow on the news and tried calling their apartment. But when I got the answering machine, I simply assumed she wanted to get out of the city and I called their weekend place. Mrs. Bigelow just wants to be by herself for a while. She said she can't even make arrangements for the funeral until the Medical Examiner releases the body."

"That'll probably be today. Do you have an address in Connecticut, and a phone number?"

North wrote them down for her. Marian borrowed a phone and called Foley to tell him where he could find Mrs. Bigelow, while the secretary photocopied the appointment sheet. Marian didn't press her any further; she wanted first to see whether North's reaction was characteristic of the Universal Laser employees as a whole or not. The woman was *very* nervous.

Marian tracked down the secretaries of Conrad Webb, Herb Vickers, and Jason O'Neill. All of them tried to conceal the fact that they were afraid. Webb's secretary was a man, and Marian asked him why he didn't resign if working there made him so nervous; he stammered something about good jobs being hard to find and changed the subject. The tension wasn't limited to just the secretaries, Marian found; everyone she talked to was keyed up and edgy— a receptionist, a researcher, a couple of managers, a procurement agent. She spent a little time in the advertising department; even the air there was charged with the same edgy electricity.

The morning was almost gone. Marian sat at Jason O'Neill's desk and tried to get a fix on the situation. In a group of people this size, there ought to have been a few otherwise decent people who got a pleasurable excitement out of what had happened—the gleaming-eyed, lip-licking, *Oh-how-terrible-tell-me-about-it* reaction that had surfaced in every murder case Marian had ever investigated. But none of the Universal employees she'd talked to had reacted like that. Not one.

Marian spread out the four murdered men's appointment sheets she'd collected and studied them. They had only one appointment in common, a meeting scheduled with Edgar Quinn on Wednesday. Time to go see the boss.

Quinn's secretary seemed to know her and ushered her right in; Quinn himself was waiting for her, in an office considerably larger than all the other offices she'd been in. Marian saw immediately where the company's casual style of dress came from: Quinn was wearing a loose Armani shirt and faded jeans, no tie or jacket. And sandals—holding on to summer as long as he could, clear into September. Not your typical president of a big company. "I was wondering when you'd get around to me," Quinn said with a dry smile.

Marian looked at the triangular face and the upswept hair; the man's face was unreadable. She told him they had a time of death for the four victims now, and asked him where he'd been on Saturday night.

His face became readable very quickly; he didn't like being asked such a question. "My wife and I went with some friends to see a show, an experimental thing in one of those dreary little SoHo theaters. Then we hit a few clubs afterward."

"What time did the show start?"

"Eight." He gave her the name of the show and of the friends he and his wife had been with.

The murders had taken place between six and nine; close timing. Could a man commit four murders and then calmly go out for a social evening with his wife and friends? Marian had no reason to think Quinn was behind the killings; it was just that her list of suspects was nonexistent. "You were expecting me, Mr. Quinn—you know I've been talking to your employees. Or trying to talk to them. These people here are afraid."

Quinn made a *huh* sound. "I'm not surprised. What did you expect? *I'm* afraid. Four of our people have been murdered, for god's sake."

"Why does a middle manager who had nothing to do with the liaison group keep looking over his shoulder? An artist in your advertising department who didn't even know three of the four victims—what's he so nervous about? What's going on, Mr. Quinn?"

He ran his fingers through the sides of his hair, sweeping it up even more. "Sergeant, maybe you're used to this sort of thing, but we're not. Conrad Webb's death alone would have rattled everybody, but when his three teammates are killed with him . . . well.''

''What will their deaths to do the company?''

''They'll hold up business with the Defense Department for one thing, until they can be replaced. Even then, we'll lose some time—the replacement team will have to be briefed almost from scratch.''

''Who's going to be the new liaison?''

''I don't know yet. I'll have to go to Washington myself in a day or so, but I haven't had time to work up a permanent group. I may ask Elizabeth to take over—Elizabeth Tanner, our vice president in charge of production. She's been in on it from the beginning.''

''In on what?''

Quinn shot her a sharp look. ''The project we're working on for the Defense Department.''

''Is that the Top Secret one you can't talk about?''

''That's the one. And I still can't talk about it.''

''What about the meeting you had scheduled for Wednesday? The one with all four murder victims?''

''A briefing for their next trip to Washington. And I can't tell you about *that*, either.''

Marian took a deep breath. ''Mr. Quinn, the NYPD is working with the FBI on this case, on an equal information-sharing basis.'' *Hah.* ''Whatever your project is, we'll learn about it eventually.''

He shook his head. ''Then you'll have to learn it from the FBI, not from me. We could lose the contract if I shoot off my mouth. There's a reason for all this hush-hush stuff, Sergeant. Over the past forty years every single new development in technology has been immediately followed by another designed to neutralize it. So any edge we might have is lost once specifics of the new development are known. We once built a device for Israeli tanks to detect a particular laser-targeting weapon the Syrians had—*before* the Syrian lasers were ready for use. All because of leaked information."

"Aren't you giving something away?" Marian asked wryly.

Quinn smiled. "No, both those devices are obsolete now. But you do see my point, don't you? Each new generation of technology has only a short life span. Its period of effectiveness is determined solely by how long it take for countering devices to be developed. And once that happens, new technology is needed to counter *those* devices—and on and on ad infinitum. That's not ever going to change."

Marian scowled. "What a depressing thought. About this leaking of information—could Mr. Webb and the others have learned anything in Washington that made them a danger to someone?"

"I'm sure they didn't. They would have informed Elizabeth Tanner or me immediately if they had. Unless it was something one of them didn't want to pass on?"

What's this? "Didn't want to? You mean one of them might have deliberately kept something from you?"

Again the fingers through the hair. "Dammit, Sergeant, I don't *want* to think that! Do you think I like suspecting one of my own people of working against me?"

"Working against you how? Selling secrets?"

"What else could it be? Maybe the deal went sour, and the buyer felt cheated or was afraid his source would talk—I don't know."

"Then why kill all four of them? Could they all have been in on it?"

"Impossible!" Quinn looked offended by the question. "Conrad Webb would no more sell out this company than he'd slit his own throat. I don't know why they were all killed. As a precautionary measure?"

"Some precaution," Marian remarked. "If one of them did sell you out, which one do you think it was?"

"I have no idea."

"Guess."

He shrugged. "Jason O'Neill."

"Why him?"

"He was the youngest, he hadn't been with us as long, Jason hadn't had the time to build up a sense of company loyalty like the others."

"And that's your only reason for picking him? The fact that he hadn't worked for you as long as the other three?"

"That's my only reason."

It wasn't much of one. "Did you tell all this to the FBI?"

"No." Quinn sighed deeply. "And frankly I'm already regretting saying anything to you. I don't really *know* anyone sold me out. It's just that I can't think of any other reason they'd be killed. Speaking of the FBI, did you run into them? They're here now."

"No, I didn't know. Where—"

"Five of them. Four accountants and a computer man, looking for irregularities in the books or hidden files or whatever. Tying up five computers and wasting everybody's time...as if the answer to why Conrad and his team were murdered can be found in a data base."

Marian asked for directions to Elizabeth Tanner's office; Quinn's vice president in charge of production would probably say the same things her boss had said, but her name should go on the no-stone-unturned list. On her way Marian mulled over what Quinn had said...or had not said. He'd seemed more concerned about the possibility that one of his men had sold him out than he was about the murders themselves. His insistence that the tension in the company was understandable considering the circumstances—well, that was entirely reasonable, Marian had to admit.

The sight of Elizabeth Tanner made Marian sigh with relief; she hated having her favorite preconceptions about big business demolished all at once. Elizabeth Tanner was one of those people who at first glance could be anywhere between thirty-five and sixty; second glance put her in her early to mid-forties. But more importantly, she looked exactly the way Marian somewhat cynically thought a woman business executive had to look: fashionably anorexic, carefully made up with not one hair out of place, and wearing a suit so expensive that it went past sinful into some unique monied realm of its own. Tanner looked like a movie star *playing* a businesswoman.

Also, she fairly oozed self-confidence. "Sergeant Larch? I hope you can tell me the police are close to finding the killer. It's been a day and a half now." Taking control of the interview from the outset, just the way she'd been taught in management seminars.

"We have a few leads," Marian answered noncommittally. "Ms Tanner, Edgar Quinn—"

"Mrs. Tanner."

"Mrs. Tanner." Whatever happened to *Ms* as the catch-all female honorific? "Edgar Quinn tells me you've been in on the Defense Department project since the beginning. I know you can't tell me what the project is, but did any of the liaison men come back from Washington with anything unusual? Any kind of information at all that you weren't expecting?"

She didn't have to think about it. "Nothing. I wondered the same thing myself, so I went over all my notes of our meetings, looking for some clues as to why they were killed. There was absolutely nothing out of the ordinary."

"What about outside the meetings? Casual talk, something mentioned in passing?"

Tanner pursed her lips. "I believe Conrad Webb was the only one I saw outside a meeting. He and Edgar and I had lunch on Thursday. It was casual talk mostly. The only Washington-related bit I remember is a rather naughty story Conrad told about a certain senator from the Midwest." She closed her eyes to think. "No, there was nothing."

"Edgar Quinn thinks one of them may have sold him out," Marian suggested.

The other woman shot her a sharp look. "Does he, now? I suppose you mean selling industrial secrets to a competitor?"

"To anyone willing to pay, I imagine."

"That widens the field of suspects considerably, doesn't it? Do you think he's right?"

"You're in a better position to know that than I am," Marian pointed out.

"Then I'd say he's wrong. Sergeant Larch, none of those men would have sold the company out. It just wouldn't have been smart. They all owned a piece of Universal. It was a policy Edgar's father started, to assure loyalty. Nearly half this company is owned by its employees."

"Including you?"

"Of course. Conrad held the largest number of shares, Herb Vickers and Sherman Bigelow less but still sizable amounts. But even Jason O'Neill was given the opportunity to buy in, six months after he was hired—an opportunity he took advantage of immediately, I might add. Selling company secrets would have hurt each one of them, in varying degrees. No, whatever's behind the murders, it isn't that."

Marian thought that over. "So if the killer isn't someone outside the company trying to buy privileged information...?"

Elizabeth Tanner turned her head away. "Then perhaps you should start looking closer to home?"

"The killer is inside the company?"

"I didn't say that." Cautious.

"Why is everyone here so afraid?"

"Are they? I hadn't noticed."

Nothing there. "I have to ask this. Where were you Saturday night?"

"I? Oh, good lord." Tanner didn't like the question any more than Edgar Quinn had. "My husband and I spent the weekend as house guests of a friend in Glen Cove. We left the city late Friday afternoon and got there in time for dinner." She gave Marian the name and address of their host.

The interview had a finished feel to it, so Marian mechanically thanked Elizabeth Tanner for her help and left, and as if on cue her stomach started to growl. It was past lunchtime, but she had one more thing to do before she could leave Universal Laser. She fought down visions of a juicy gyro sandwich with extra sour cream and set out to discover what the FBI was up to.

TEN

UNIVERSAL LASER'S accounting department was more crowded than the rest of the offices Marian had seen, and not solely because the FBI agents were taking up so much room; there wasn't all that much space to begin with. Partitioned cubicles instead of real offices, circling a slightly large open area filled with desks, computers, and mountains of paper. A worktable had been taken over by the FBI agents, four men and a woman, all tapping away at computer keyboards. One of the men, surprisingly, was Curt Holland.

Marian pulled up a chair and sat down. He didn't take his eyes from the screen, but he knew she was there. He did have a good profile, Marian noticed. "Feel the tension in this place?" he asked.

"It's hard to miss," Marian said. "These people are scared."

"Understandably so. I might even be a wee bit disconcerted myself, in their place."

"Are you one of the accountants or are you the computer man?"

The corner of his mouth lifted, briefly. "I'm 'the computer man'—is that my label here? I'm looking for electronic hidey-holes, if that's what you're going to ask. Floating files, coded directories, buried treasures of any species, legal tender or otherwise."

"Find anything yet?"

"Not a thing. In fact it's all rather tediously straightforward. Standard commercial software, very little in the way of original programming. Boring. A stupid and unimaginative use of a good system." He touched a key and the screen changed. "In case you haven't noticed, Sergeant, I do not tolerate fools gladly. In fact, I don't tolerate them at all."

Marian's stomach growled. "Excuse me. What's Trevor Page doing in Washington?"

"Checking on the investigation into our four victims' activities last week," Holland said, biting off his words. "Tracing their footsteps through the hallowed corridors of power. Sniffing out senatorial indiscretions and probing for shady meetings with Bad Companions. A job Page is eminently suited for, by the way." His tone was contemptuous. "Sworn to uphold the law, Page is, but much more than that. Committed to seek out sniveling traitors, tired Communists, and all the misguided souls who profess political creeds at some degree of variance with the current criterion of ideological acceptability. Pledged to do his duty to God and his country, to help other people at all times—"

"That's the Boy Scout oath."

"Is it? I always did get those confused."

Marian was amused. "You're not exactly reverent, are you? You don't talk like any FBI agent I've ever known."

Holland turned his eyes from the screen and looked at her for the first time. "Why, thank you, Sergeant." He smiled.

Marian didn't know what to make of that. "Why do you dislike Page so much?"

"My, you are full of questions, aren't you? Very well, I'll tell you. I do not include myself in his cheering section because Trevor Page is one of the most dangerous men I know."

"Dangerous? Page?"

"Dangerous. Even after his forty-three years of observing evidence to the contrary, Page still believes people can be coerced into behaving decently. Goodness by force of arms. An immaculate society protected against its own dark impulses by the ever-vigilant among us, of whom Page numbers himself first and foremost. An idealist—and therefore dangerous.''

"I suspect you have a fondness for hyperbole," Marian said, unimpressed. Her stomach growled again. "All these wonderful things Page is finding out in Washington—of course you're going to share them with the police?"

The FBI agent raised an eyebrow in mock offense. "Do you doubt it for a minute? After all, we gave you our *word*. Now if I may make a suggestion, go get something to eat. It's hard for me to concentrate with that growly stomach of yours only three feet away."

"Good idea." She stood up to go, and then remembered Captain DiFalco's instruction. "Why don't you join me? There are several good places to eat near here."

Holland was back to tapping instructions to the computer. "I'm right in the middle of something—I don't want to stop."

"I could use the company."

"And your captain told you to stick close to us."

Marian laughed. "Is it that obvious?"

"A lucky guess."

Since Holland didn't seem to be one for hellos or good-byes, Marian left him to his work and went in search of her too-long-delayed lunch.

"WHERE THE HELL HAVE YOU BEEN?" Captain DiFalco roared the minute Marian walked into his office.

"In court," she said. "The Downtown Queens were arraigned this afternoon."

"Oh." He'd forgotten. "What'd they plead?"

"Justifiable homicide."

The captain snorted. "Fat chance. All fourteen of them?"

"Only thirteen, turns out. One of them was in the hospital getting her appendix out the day Mrs. Alvarez was killed."

"Which one?"

"Large Marge. Looks to me as if the DA doesn't want to bother trying to prove prior knowledge. They just kicked her loose."

"They can always pick her up later if they want. Large Marge? What's her last name?"

Marian couldn't think of it. "I can check the reports."

"Don't bother. Something came in while you were gone. Webb, Bigelow, Vickers and O'Neill—all four of 'em went to Universal Laser late Saturday afternoon."

"No! Why, that's too good to be true!"

"But true it is. The night guard's sign-in sheet shows they checked in at a quarter to six, never checked out again."

"Ah. Didn't that make the guard wonder?"

"He just thought they were staying all night," DiFalco said. "That happens a lot there, evidently. Then on Sunday the watchman came down sick and has been in bed ever since. He didn't even know the four men had been killed."

Marian frowned. "How did they get out of the building without going past the guard?"

"That's your next little problem. So how'd it go at Universal Laser? Find out anything?"

Marian brought him up to date, including the fact that Curt Holland was there searching their computers for whatever he could find. "The main thing is that the two people at the top have different ideas as to what's behind the murders. Edgar Quinn suspects one of the liaison team sold him out and got killed in a screwed-up deal. The others may have been shot simply because they were with him at the time the killer caught up with him. Elizabeth Tanner, on the other hand, isn't buying any of it. All four men owned a piece of Universal Laser, and Tanner says there's no way they'd sell *themselves* out. She thinks no outsider was involved at all."

"Meaning somebody at Universal Laser is responsible? Who? Edgar Quinn?"

"She isn't saying."

"If Quinn thought somebody sold him out . . . yah, that's a motive I could live with. Did you check his alibi?"

"It's being checked now. Elizabeth Tanner's too."

DiFalco told her to keep him posted and waved her out. Only one man was in the Precinct Detective Unit room—not one assigned to the East River Park murders. Foley had left a pile of reports on her desk with a note on top: *Nobody available to check Quinn's and Tanner's alibis, so I'm going myself.* Marian found the note heartening; normally Foley wouldn't bother telling her what he was doing.

The reports wrapped up a lot of loose ends, starting with Mrs. Sherman Bigelow. She'd fled to the seclusion of their weekend place in Connecticut upon hearing of her husband's death, but had returned to New York just a few hours ago. The Medical Examiner had released her husband's body and she was now in the process of making funeral arrangements. As for last Saturday, Bigelow had told her he had a meeting with another lawyer representing one of Universal Laser's clients. They had some contractual matters to be worked out, he'd said, and it had to be done right then because the client's lawyer was leaving for London at midnight. At the time Mrs. Bigelow had thought it odd that her husband hadn't given her a phone number where he could be reached; they'd always been quite careful to keep each other informed as to their whereabouts. A check with Bigelow's secretary indicated no contract meeting had been scheduled, either for Saturday or any other day.

Bigelow's secretary—that would be Ms North, Marian remembered, the one wearing espadrilles. But the interesting point was that Bigelow too had lied to his wife about where he was going; all three married men had lied. And Jason O'Neill had not confided in his girlfriend. Marian couldn't think of a stronger indication that the murders had nothing to do with the victims' private lives than that. They didn't want the women involved in what they were up to, they didn't want them to worry, they didn't want them even to know what was going on. That suggested that what they were doing was either dangerous or illegal, or both. And whatever it was, they had to do it at Universal Laser Technologies.

But why wait until the afternoon was over? Were they trying to avoid somebody? Marian shuffled through the papers on her desk until she found the photocopy of the night guard's sign-in sheet. Only one other person had been in on Saturday; someone named Brown had showed up around noon and had left again fifteen minutes later, probably just picking up something he'd forgotten. No Edgar Quinn, no Elizabeth Tanner.

How did the liaison team get out of the building without being spotted? There was only the main exit; no delivery door opened into the alley because there was no alley. No private elevator; the boss rode the same elevators as everyone else. Did the guard take a nap? Was only one man responsible for the security in the building? Marian scribbled herself a reminder to check. The real question, of course, was whether the four men were still alive when they left, whenever and however they did leave. She would have liked to send the Crime Scene Unit to give the place a good going-over, but she knew she'd never get a warrant for that. Universal Laser was just too big, for one thing; she'd need to have a specific location in mind—and a specific reason for thinking so—before she could get the expert help she needed.

The Crime Scene Unit. She looked through her papers for a report and found only notes from a telephone call Foley had taken. The CSU was waiting for lab reports on fibers and hairs taken from Jason O'Neill's apartment, but the preliminary conclusion was that no murder had taken place there. *A little late,* Marian thought wryly. The CSU reported finding fingerprints for Conrad Webb, Sherman

Bigelow, and Herb Vickers. They were there in O'Neill's apartment, all right.

Marian got up and went to the wall-mounted map of New York City on the other side of the room. Universal Laser was in the West Fifties, and Jason O'Neill's place was only three short blocks plus one long block away. An easy stroll. That's why there'd been no record of anyone's taking a cab after three; they'd simply walked over.

Marian returned to her desk and finished going through her papers. Reports on finances—all four victims were in good shape financially, some more than others. Herb Vickers had perhaps less in investments and savings than Marian had expected, but Edgar Quinn had said Vickers was careless with money. Even so, he wasn't exactly hurting. Nothing there.

Write-ups of interviews with the victims' friends and co-workers pretty well scotched the possibility that any of the four had made a private enemy so deadly as to be out for blood. Herb Vickers's occasional bull-in-the-china-shop ways had been an irritant at times, but on the whole people were fond of the fat man. Sherman Bigelow was too cautious a man to leave any outright enemies in his wake. And Conrad Webb and Jason O'Neill were both professional diplomats, domestic variety. The investigators had turned up a few people who didn't like one or another of the men, but it was never anything serious.

As far as Marian was concerned, that closed the book on the personal angle of the investigation. Even the Major Crimes people couldn't pretend there was, say, a domestic motive behind the killings. (If there were, Major Crimes wouldn't have been interested in the first place.) But now Marian could concentrate her entire investigation on Universal Laser; all the process-of-elimination work was done.

When she next looked up from her desk, she saw she was the only one in the room. Marian glanced into Captain

DiFalco's office; even he had gone home. *What a good idea,* she thought.

AT HOME two messages waited on her machine. The first was from Kelly Ingram.

"Marian, I'm leaving two tickets for you at the box office for the opening, that's Friday night, F-r-i-d-a-y, don't you *dare* forget it. I'm counting on you, Marian—don't let me down! And be sure you and Brian come backstage afterwards and say all sorts of nice things to me—I'll need a friendly face or two by then. But please please *please* don't come back *before* the show because I am going to be a NERVOUS WRECK. Half the people in that audience are coming only to see me fall on my face and I'm already snapping at everybody just thinking about it." There was a pause. "Well, I guess that's all, unless you know a good prayer or two. Oh—I meant to tell you, I haven't said 'batch watery' once since you were here! 'Bye, Toots—see you Friday.''

Batch watery? Then Marian remembered: *watch battery.* She laughed and tapped out her friend's number—and got *Kelly's* machine. Marian left a message that was as supportive and encouraging as she could make it, promising to be there Friday night with bells on, further promising to come backstage afterward, declaring she wouldn't dream of intruding before the play started, etc. After she'd hung up, she said, "But Brian won't be there."

The second message was from Brian Singleton himself. "Marian, I wanted to remind you of the Bergstrom showing tomorrow night. I know you're none too eager to see me, but I thought this might make it easier for both of us. Lots of people around—we won't fight in public, will we? If you don't come, I'll understand. But I do hope you'll be there. I don't like this bad feeling between us, and I miss you. Please come."

Marian sighed. "Then again, maybe he will."

ELEVEN

TUESDAY MORNING was the time Marian had tentatively earmarked for getting chewed out by Captain DiFalco, but the hours passed and nothing happened. DiFalco had a set speech he liked to use when an investigation wasn't proceeding as rapidly as he'd like; and once he got going, he could make the rafters ring. DiFalco liked the sound of his own voice and he liked making that speech, which consisted mostly of imaginative variations on *Get your ass moving*. Marian had expected at least a pep talk by now, coach-to-player stuff, but DiFalco was leaving her alone. She couldn't figure out why.

The only chewing-out that morning had been the one she'd given her partner. Foley's checks on Edgar Quinn's and Elizabeth Tanner's alibis had been less than thorough. Both suspects, if they were suspects, were backed up by other people to a point, but there was leeway in the time schedules of both. Quinn could have squeezed in the murders before going out for the evening, and Tanner could have made a quick trip back from Glen Cove early Saturday night. But that presumed both people were operating on a split-second schedule, and who could time four homicides that closely? And was it likely that either or both Quinn and Tanner could calmly go off for a social evening after such a gruesome business without giving themselves away? Not very, Marian had to admit.

She also admitted there was absolutely no reason to suspect Elizabeth Tanner of anything. Marian was investigating her only because she was *there*. Nobody else was.

A mountain of computer printouts plopped down on her desk. "Oops!" A pleasant voice laughed. "Sorry, they got away from me."

Marian looked up to see Trevor Page smiling down at her. "Have a nice time in Washington?" she asked.

If he caught the irony in her voice, he didn't let on. "I had a frustrating time in Washington. None of our four victims was up to anything out of the ordinary. It was business as usual, except for Jason O'Neill's quick visit to his Washington girlfriend's place."

"What about her?"

"Straight from Vassar to her job as a congressional aide. Squeaky clean. We'll keep looking, but so far we've found nothing that wasn't strictly on the up and up."

Marian pointed to a chair and Page sat. "This Top Secret stuff they were meeting about," she said, "do you know what it is?"

Page said he did. "New technology requires constant progress reports, and that's all this last trip was about. Updating, explaining. Making sure everybody on both sides understood what was expected and what was being done. I can't give you any details, but that's the gist of it."

"No secret meetings with bad guys, no suspicious phone calls in the middle of the night? No scraps of paper with coded messages left behind?"

He looked at her in mild exasperation. "Why do I get the feeling you're not taking this too seriously?"

"Because I'm not," Marian said bluntly. "Spy stuff! There's no international intrigue behind the East River Park murders. The cause is right over there in the Universal Laser offices."

Page propped his elbows on her desk, rested his chin in his hands, and grinned. "I'm all ears."

Marian told him what she'd been doing while he was off gallivanting around Washington, and her reluctant conclusion that the only one so far who showed any signs of qualifying as a suspect was Edgar Quinn. "He thinks he was betrayed. *His* interpretation is that something went wrong with the deal, and whoever the traitor was dealing with killed him—possibly to shut him up, perhaps for some other reason. But if enough was riding on it, Quinn himself could have killed whoever sold him out."

"But why kill the others?"

Marian was silent a moment. "Maybe he didn't know which one it was. Maybe he killed them all to make sure he got the right one."

To her surprise, Page burst out laughing. "And maybe pigs have wings. Edgar Quinn? Murder four people?"

"You know him personally?"

"Not personally, but I'm the one in charge of running security checks on the Universal Laser personnel. I know them all on paper, and I've had a few face-to-face dealings with the people at the top. I knew Conrad Webb and Sherman Bigelow too."

"Were they friends?"

"I didn't know them that well." He winked one eye. "Besides, we're not allowed to make friends with people we're investigating."

"Of course not," Marian said soberly.

"Does Quinn have an alibi for Saturday night?" Page asked.

"He has a partial. He and his wife and another couple went to a play and then out on the town, according to Quinn. His wife backs him up, but that's to be expected. The other couple is out of the city and can't be reached." Foley had made no attempt to try to trace them, or even to confirm that the Quinns had indeed gone to a play. But Foley was trying to confirm it now—oh, yes, Marian had seen to that.

"What about Quinn's wife?" Page asked. "Did you believe her?"

"My partner talked to her. He claims she'd probably say anything Quinn told her to say. But my partner thinks everyone in the world is a liar."

"Your partner is probably right," Page remarked blandly. "So we're left with a questionable motive and a sort-of alibi. Not too sterling a case."

Marian placed a hand palm-down on the printout paper piled on her desk. "What's this stuff?"

"Results of our most recent security check. I can save you some time—there's nothing new, nothing helpful. But I promised you we'd share what we found, and there it is."

Marian started pawing through the paper. "What are you looking for?"

"Elizabeth Tanner. These in alphabetical order? Ah, here she is." Marian read silently for a moment. "Married three times?"

"Widowed twice," Page said. "First husband killed in a traffic accident, the second died of a heart attack. Or was it the other way around? Anyway, both times she waited exactly six months and then remarried. The lady doesn't like being single. One son, from her first marriage—just now starting college."

The three marriages were the only remotely unusual things in the report on Elizabeth Tanner. Everything else could be a textbook lesson on how to succeed in business by trying hard all the time. The right schools, the right degrees, the right contacts. Carefully timed career moves followed by rapid promotions. No drugs, no "subversive" activities, no connections with any criminal elements. Generous donations to both political parties. Mrs. Clean. And it had paid off; Elizabeth Tanner was as high at Universal Laser as she could get without actually taking over Edgar Quinn's job.

"I'd like to have another go at Mrs. Tanner," Marian said.

"Any particular reason?" Page asked.

"She's a late starter and I don't have a fix on her yet."

"Sounds like a good reason to me," he said. "I'll go with you."

"I thought you might." Marian looked at the stack of printouts with distaste. Page undoubtedly knew what he was talking about when he said there was nothing helpful there, but police procedure wouldn't allow her to take his word for it. Someone was going to have to plow through all those sheets of information, most of it undoubtedly useless. She looked around the room. One of the other detectives assigned to the East River Park murders was talking on the phone; his name was Roberts and he was the youngest detective in the Ninth Precinct. Long-standing police tradition decreed that the new kid was the one who got stuck with boring detail work as often as possible; it was a tradition of which Marian heartily approved.

She dumped the printouts on Roberts's desk and ignored his squawk of protest. "Let's go," she said to Page.

ELIZABETH TANNER WAS in the process of moving into Conrad Webb's office—or rather she was directing traffic while other people did the actual moving. Marian and Page trailed after a maintenance man pushing a file cabinet on a dolly into an office the same size as Edgar Quinn's. Marian remembered one window in Tanner's old office; here there were two. Clearly a step up.

When Tanner caught sight of them, a big smile appeared on her face, much to Marian's surprise, until she realized the smile was for her companion. "Trevor!" Tanner said with genuine pleasure. "I didn't know the FBI was investigating—unless you're here for another reason? Whichever it is, it's nice seeing you again."

"Hello, Elizabeth," Page replied neutrally. "Yes, we're cooperating with the New York police on this one. You've met Sergeant Larch?" He spoke with the same mixture of courtesy and caution Marian had noticed the first time they'd met.

Tanner acknowledged Marian with a polite hello and turned back to Page. "I haven't seen you since the time we all went out to dinner at the Tavern on the Green. You were here investigating...one of our design engineers, that was it."

"I remember. And I remember the dinner. Conrad and Edgar had some disagreement about the gazpacho, as I recall."

"Why, so they did. Imagine your remembering that. But I suppose you don't forget much, do you?"

"I try to remember everything."

Marian rested one arm on top of the file cabinet the maintenance man had brought in and settled herself to enjoy the show. Elizabeth Tanner wasn't exactly coming on to the FBI agent, but that would have been the next level up in her approach. It was more as if she were sussing him out, probing to discover how receptive he might be to a more direct approach. Page, on his part, maintained his usual level of courteous attentiveness without ever encouraging a more personal note...or without being so gauche as to imply Tanner was crossing some line of acceptable behavior. Marian liked the way he was handling the situation, and she had to admire Tanner's poise and skill in the game she was playing. All in all, two very professional performances.

Page was finally able to work in a sentence about her new office.

"It is nice, isn't it?" Tanner said with a smile. "Much roomier than my old one. That place seemed to shrink a little more every week."

Marian decided it was time she joined the conversation. "It's as big as Edgar Quinn's office, isn't it?"

"Same size exactly. When Edgar's father first leased this space, he made sure Conrad had as good an office as he did. Then when Conrad stepped down from the CEO position, no one suggested he move to a smaller office. He'd been in this room as long as Universal Laser has been here, you see.''

''Who replaced him as Chief Executive Officer?''

''Edgar's acting in that capacity,'' Tanner said shortly. ''His father's idea.''

A note of disapproval? Marian threw a glance to Page; he picked up on it. ''Big shoes to step into,'' he said. ''I'd hate to follow Conrad Webb in a job.''

Tanner sighed. ''Poor Edgar. He's expected to replace both Conrad *and* his father. That's a lot to ask of anyone.''

''Too much for him to handle?'' Marian asked innocently.

Tanner hesitated just the right amount of time before speaking. ''No, I wouldn't say that. It's just that Edgar isn't...the dynamo his father was. I don't mean he's resting on his father's laurels—he isn't. But Edgar Senior was a true man of vision, one of the few I've ever met. Edgar Junior,'' she laughed apologetically, ''is junior.''

That was twice she'd undercut her boss, both the times Marian had spoken to her. ''Do you still believe he's wrong in suspecting one of the liaison group of having sold him out?''

This time Elizabeth Tanner waited several moments before she answered. ''I believe no one sold him out,'' she said slowly. ''But I also believe Edgar is quite capable of *thinking* someone did. Not that's he's paranoid—I'm not saying that. But the son can't expect to command the same sort of loyalty the father could. And Edgar knows that. I've heard him remark on it on occasion.''

''Elizabeth,'' Page said quietly, ''what do you think happened?''

''I'm not accusing anyone,'' she said quickly.

''I know that. But do you think he's capable of killing?''

She spread her hands. ''I honestly don't know. Edgar sometimes allows himself to be led. I don't know whether that makes him more likely to kill or less.''

"But you must have given it some thought."

"I'm afraid it hasn't gotten me very far," she said brightly, unwilling to commit herself further. "I just meant Edgar's suspicions about the liaison group's loyalty are in character. He sees himself as constantly being compared to his father and found lacking, you see. Naturally he's going to be a little suspicious."

Marian wondered if Page caught that one last little dig Elizabeth Tanner got in at Quinn even while seeming to exonerate him. She also wondered if this was the way the assistant to the CEO spoke of all her co-workers. A test question. "Did Conrad Webb have that trouble too? He'd stepped down as CEO before Edgar Senior died, didn't he?"

The other woman's face changed, to what Marian thought was honest regret. "Yes, he'd stepped down before Edgar Senior died, and no, he never had to worry about employee loyalty. Conrad was special. He was the perfect man for getting this company off the ground and moving, and old Edgar was one smart cookie for knowing that. Those two made a perfect partnership—that's one of the things that attracted me to Universal Laser in the first place. But now, what with both of them gone..." She trailed off, leaving the obvious unstated.

So was she sincerely concerned for the company's future, or was she just out after Edgar Quinn's job? Marian couldn't tell. Right at that moment another maintenance man showed up, pushing a platform truck loaded with computer equipment; and Elizabeth Tanner's whole attention was given over to deciding where she wanted things set up. Page motioned to Marian with his head; they left without saying goodbye.

In the elevator on the way down, Marian asked, "Just how well do you know Elizabeth Tanner? Enough to make any sense out of that?"

"I know her well enough to see she's trying to edge Edgar Quinn out of his father's company."

"By throwing suspicion on him? But how would that help her, if he didn't commit the murders?"

Page shrugged. "By rattling him? By undermining employee confidence in him? She's looking for anything that'll make him look bad."

"You seem pretty sure," Marian remarked. "How do you know she's not just worried about the company?"

"Because the only thing Elizabeth Tanner worries about is Elizabeth Tanner. No, Sergeant, that was just plain old office politics we got a taste of up there."

"Edgar Quinn assured me there were no office politics at Universal Laser," she said with a smile.

Page didn't even bother answering that.

On the street, they headed uptown, both of them wrapped in their own thoughts. After they'd gone several blocks, Marian said, "You know, don't you, that Edgar Quinn is the only suspect we've got? His motive may be on the puny side—accusing one of the liaison group of having betrayed him. But that's more motive than we've been able to come up with for anyone else."

"Tell me something," Page said to her. "How did you first learn that Quinn was suspicious of the liaison group?"

That was easy. "Quinn told me himself."

"And would a murderer voluntarily hand the police a motive where none had previously existed?"

"Sounds farfetched, I know."

"Damned right it does. You know, Sergeant, the more I think about it, the more I like Quinn's notion that one of that group was involved in a deal that went sour. The sheer methodicalness of the way they were killed smacks of a pro doing his job, don't you think?"

Marian had to agree. "It's hardly the method an amateur would attempt for his first killing. What are you going to do?"

Page pointed to a hot dog vendor on the corner. "Have lunch. How do you take yours?"

"Mustard only."

They took their hot dogs to one of the benches outside the wall around Central Park. "One thing bothers me," Marian said between bites. "Edgar Senior doesn't sound like the type to be blinded by paternal pride. If he was shrewd enough to see he needed a Conrad Webb to run his company, why didn't he know Edgar Junior wasn't up to the job when his time came?"

Page laughed shortly. "Because Edgar Quinn isn't anything like the incompetent boob Elizabeth Tanner painted him to be. Old Edgar knew what he was doing."

Marian finished her hot dog and licked a spot of mustard off one finger. "You seem awfully sure Edgar Quinn is innocent."

The FBI agent let the air out of his lungs with a *whoosh*. "I'm not, really. He could be guilty as hell. I'm just afraid we're zeroing in on him because we can't find anyone else."

Marian knew the feeling. "Have you ever seen his apartment?"

"No—what's it like?"

"Beautiful place, and rather formal. Quinn himself is so informal, even in his office . . . he and that apartment don't seem to go together."

"It was his father's. He inherited it along with the business."

"Ah, that explains it."

They sat in companionable silence for a few minutes. Marian couldn't help but think what it would be like having this man as her partner instead of the one she was saddled with. Page would be a real *partner* instead of a resentful, foot-dragging—no, better not get off on that. She was stuck with Foley and that was that.

Page cleared his throat. "If you're right that the East River Park murders were some kind of warning, then whatever's been going on isn't over yet. I wasn't going to tell you until the warrant came through, but we're going to put a tap on Quinn's phone. Maybe we'll get something.''

Quite an admission. "So you do think he's guilty?''

He grinned, wryly. "Frankly, we couldn't think of anything else to do. FBI rule of thumb—when you're stuck, plant a bug. We should be set up by tonight. Do you want to listen in?''

"Not tonight. Tonight I'm doing one of those things cops periodically do to remind themselves they do indeed have personal lives.''

"Oh, sorry—I didn't mean to intrude.''

"You didn't. It's just that I'm committed to attending a showing tonight, a sculptor named Bergstrom.''

"Bergstrom?'' Page looked at her with interest. "You like his 'liquid configurations'? I think that's what he calls them.''

"I never heard of him before last week,'' she admitted, a little piqued that he had. "The gallery owner is a friend of mine, and he's been rather...''—*insistent* was too strong—"...persuasive,'' Marian finished.

"I see. Well, enjoy yourself.''

"I'm sure as hell going to try,'' she said with determination.

TWELVE

FOR ONCE MARIAN GOT HOME in time to wash her hair before going out. She was a little edgy about seeing Brian again and began to wonder if a public reconciliation was such a good idea after all. She put on a red dress she'd worn only once before—to a party she'd gone to with Brian, she suddenly remembered. Brian had liked it. The thought occurred to her that she was dressing to please him; quickly she looked through her closet but couldn't find anything else dressy enough to suit the occasion. So, the red dress it was.

She found a parking space on East Seventy-eighth, only a couple of blocks from Brian's gallery. The night air had turned chill, as if suddenly recalling it was September. The walk back toward Madison served to increase her jitters, for it was then that Marian finally admitted she *wanted* to see Brian again. Why had they fought? Best not to remember.

The gallery was crowded, noisy, and so brightly lighted that Marian had to squint at first, coming in from the dark. Scores of ultrastylish people with drinks in their hands moved to an intricate dance of their own devising, totally unrelated to the taped music booming from the concealed wall speakers. At the same time these ostensible patrons of the arts all engaged in a speedtalking contest, those that weren't waiting for their turn to compete. One or two of them were actually looking at the sculptures. *Cliché in living color,* Marian thought. She didn't see Brian.

She accepted a glass of champagne from a morose-looking young man bearing a tray and edged through the crowd toward the nearest sculpture. The piece looked like an old-fashioned TV antenna that was just starting to melt.

What was the phrase Trevor Page had used? Liquid configurations. Well, it did look rather liquid at that. Marian knew she was supposed to be overcome by the aesthetics of the piece, but all she could think was *How did he do that?* She wondered which of these people was Bergstrom.

Ten minutes passed and still no sign of Brian. Marian knew he had to be here somewhere; the gallery wasn't all that large, but the constantly moving crowd made it difficult to see more than a few yards. She put down her empty champagne glass and started a systematic hunt.

In a matter of seconds she caught a glimpse not of Brian but of another face she knew. Black hair, black eyes that bored into you like drills, downturned mouth, condescending air. He was dressed all in black, as he had been the first time she'd seen him, in Captain DiFalco's office. In his slightly decadent way, Curt Holland looked right at home among this artsy crowd.

When he saw that she'd spotted him, he made his way over to her. "Well, well, if it isn't Maid Marian."

She was angry. "I don't believe in coincidence."

"Nor do I."

"Page was the only person I told I was coming here. Did he send you to spy on me?"

"Page didn't send me at all. He mentioned you were coming to the Bergstrom showing so I decided to take a look myself."

Marian grunted. "So suddenly you're interested in sculpture? I'm supposed to believe that?"

"I'm interested in what you're up to. You found something that brought you to this gallery—I want to know what it is."

She stared at him in disbelief. "I do have a personal life, you know."

He gave her one of his cynical smiles. "Page may have bought that, but I myself am inclined to be a trifle more skeptical when it comes to what the local police choose to tell us. You wouldn't be holding something out on us, would you, Sergeant?''

"Butt out, Holland. This has nothing to do with the FBI. Go away.''

"I think not.''

They were interrupted by a loud burst of laughter. As it died away, Marian could hear Brian's voice calling, "Marian darling! *There* you are! Stay right where you are—I'll come to you.''

Marian "darling"?

He was with three other people, two men and a woman. Marian knew the men, both sycophantic social butterflies whom she couldn't stand. But the woman—the woman was new. Tall, chic, with hair so blond it was white, hanging straight to her collar bone where it had been cut to razor-edge sharpness. Younger than Marian. The blonde was clinging to Brian's arm with a familiarity that made it plain the two had not met tonight for the first time.

"Hello, Brian,'' Marian forced herself to say, and nodded to the others.

"Ah, you're wearing your red 'power' dress, I see—I've always like that one,'' Brian said with an insincere smile. He shot a glance at Holland. "And you brought a friend—how nice. Or is our little opening so threatening you felt you needed moral support?''

Marian couldn't believe her ears; she'd never heard Brian be so...*bitchy*. She pointedly did not introduce Holland, who stood silently watching and listening.

Brian said, "Diane, love, I want you to meet Marian Larch. *Sergeant* Marian Larch.''

The blonde's eyebrows rose. "Sergeant? Uh, like in the army?''

So she didn't know who Marian was. "Police.''

"Oh. That's nice.'' The other woman's smile was friendly.

Brian disengaged Diane's arm so he could put his own arm around her waist, dropping his hand so that it was resting low on her hip. "Diane is a model. Isn't she lovely?"

One of the male butterflies snickered. "Don't they make a *super* couple?"

That was why Brian had wanted her to come? To see her replacement? *He set me up again,* Marian thought, stunned. *The son of a bitch, he set me up again!* "Brian," she said wonderingly, "I had no idea you could be so petty."

Brian and the butterflies all laughed as if she'd said something wonderfully witty; Diane joined in, although it was clear she had no idea of what was going on. The same butterfly who'd spoken before said, "You're not going to make a scene, are you, Marian?"

Don't you wish. Marian ignored him and spoke to Brian. "You didn't have to do this. Does it make you feel taller? You could have just let it go."

"Oh, I'm never one to let things go," he answered airily. "I firmly believe in tying up loose ends. You don't mind being referred to as a loose end, do you, Marian?" He smiled at his own double entendre.

Even Diane caught the insult; something like comprehension was beginning to dawn in her face. She looked from Brian to Marian and back to Brian again. *That's right, honey,* Marian thought; *if he did it to me, he can do it to you.* She looked her ex-lover straight in the eye. "Now that I've seen what I was meant to see here," she said evenly, "there's no point in my staying any longer. Goodbye, Brian." She put a finality into the last two words that no one could possibly misunderstand. Without waiting for an answer, she turned and left with as much dignity as she could muster.

"Oh, don't go away mad!" a butterfly voice wafted after her.

Outside, Marian walked rapidly back toward her car, her face burning. How dare he? How *dare* he? She didn't even know the Brian she'd just left; he wasn't the same man who'd given her so much joy in the past. Marian cursed herself for a fool, for allowing herself to be set up again. People lied to her all the time in her job and she could almost always tell when; but she'd not once questioned the seductive lies on her answering machine. She should have anticipated something like this, she should have been able to see through Brian better—she certainly had enough to go on. But no, she'd hung on, trying to make a go of it, unwilling to admit she'd made *that big* a mistake in judgment.

"I apologize," a voice said beside her. Startled, Marian jerked her head around; she hadn't even realized Holland was walking with her. "You were right," he said. "I had no business being there."

Marian sighed. "Holland, couldn't you just discreetly disappear?"

"I intend to. But first—are you all right?"

"That's a dumb question," she muttered. They'd reached her car; she unlocked the door and climbed in.

Holland tapped on the glass and she rolled down the window. "Just one thing," he said. "You must have really gotten to him—otherwise he wouldn't have gone to such extremes."

"Stand back," she ordered. When he did, she started the car and drove away. The last thing she needed was commiseration from the man who'd witnessed her humiliation.

MARIAN HAD A HARD TIME making it into work the next morning. She'd stayed up too late and she'd had a few drinks. Last night she'd just driven around for a while, yelling at other drivers now and then to let off steam. Then she'd spotted a parking place a few doors down from a bar and it seemed only natural to pull in. Marian wasn't a heavy drinker, and drinking alone had never been much fun. She wanted company, but it had to be someone who would listen indulgently and let her gripe until she got it out of her system. That let out the entire Ninth Precinct. Kelly Ingram? No: preview performance tonight. In the end Marian had called her old partner from better days and got him to come join her in the bar. On the whole Ivan Malecki had listened sympathetically, but then he took a stern-uncle line with her.

"You're better off without that Brian," he'd said, pouring himself a beer.

"You're telling me something I already know," she'd muttered.

"So why did you stay with him?"

"I must have had a reason. I just can't remember what it was."

Ivan's comfortably familiar face had smiled sympathetically. "You should have walked away yourself, long ago. You musta seen signs he was the kinda man who could pull a stunt like that. Why didn't you walk away then?"

Marian didn't know.

When she finally dragged herself into the Precinct Detective Unit room the following morning, it was to find four men she didn't know taking up what little space the crowded office had. They were all reading from the reports on the East River Park murders.

"Who are you?" she demanded. "What's going on?"

"Major Crimes Unit," one of them said without lifting his head.

Marian whirled and charged into Captain DiFalco's office. He lifted a hand to stop her before she could say anything. "No, they haven't taken over the case...yet. But you can be damned sure they're looking for gaps in the case we're building. Your police work had better be rock solid on this one, Larch."

"It is, Captain. We didn't leave any holes."

"Because if you did, because if they find *one little thing* we've forgotten, we can kiss that case goodbye. I've given you a lot of leeway, Larch, because I thought you'd function better without me breathing down your neck. But if you screw this up for me, I promise you, you're going to regret the day you ever set foot in the Ninth Precinct.''

I already do, she thought. ''We've covered everything,'' she said firmly. ''And what we couldn't get to, the FBI took care of. Major Crimes isn't going to find anything.'' Marian wasn't at all sure that was true, but it was death to appear uncertain when reporting to a superior; she'd learned that lesson her first year on the force.

DiFalco dismissed her and she went back to her desk, one corner of which was being used by one of the Major Crimes men. Her head hurt. Foley was in one of his sullen moods and wasn't speaking; that suited Marian fine. The FBI was nowhere in sight. The memory of the ugly trick Brian had played on her the night before kept running through her head; with an effort she pushed the scene out of her mind, took a Nuprin, and pulled out the glossies taken at East River Park.

Conrad Webb. Sherman J. Bigelow. Herbert Vickers. Jason O'Neill. Webb was the heart and soul of the liaison group, and probably its mind as well. Two men would have been needed to take his place: Bigelow for his know-how and O'Neill for his ''charm,'' as Edgar Quinn put it. And the group was rounded out by overweight, disorganized Herb Vickers with his talent for explaining high-tech matters to laymen. If any one of them had been involved in selling secrets, surely the FBI would have found at least traces of the deal by now. Probably Quinn just wanted the killer to be someone outside Universal Laser. Or wanted the police to think so, if he himself was guilty.

How can you have four murders and NO suspects? The only reason she had for even considering Edgar Quinn a possible suspect was something that Quinn himself had said, that one of the four victims might have been selling Universal Laser secrets. Sheer supposition on his part, if he was playing straight; an attempt to misdirect the investigation if he was not. That was all they had on him, that and an iffy alibi. But Elizabeth Tanner's alibi wasn't absolutely airtight; a further check had revealed a time early Saturday evening when she, her husband, and their Glen Cove host had not been together.

"Got something," Foley said from the next desk. "Put it in writing," he said to his phone and hung up. "Security at Universal Laser was one man short on Saturday. Regular man and two back-ups were sick, a fourth man couldn't be located. They like to keep two men on the monitors, so one's always watching while the other's doing rounds upstairs. But only one was manning the monitors Saturday."

Marian grinned at him. "So that's how they got out of the building. It's also how someone else could get in."

"Yeah, they just snuck by when the guard was taking a crap."

"Elegant, Foley. But would there be enough time to get four *bodies* out? They must have still been alive when they left." She noticed all four men from Major Crimes listening intently.

"Shit," Foley said. "We still don't have the scene."

Marian thought a minute. "Yeah, I hate to give up on Universal Laser. That guard still sick? Get somebody to pin him down as to exactly when he left his post and for how long. And we don't take 'I can't remember' as an answer."

Foley reached for his phone, and Marian sifted through the papers in her desk drawer until she found the card Trevor Page had left. Her call was transferred three times but she finally got him on the line.

"Sergeant Larch," he said with a lift in his voice. "Anything new?"

"Maybe. I want to know if Holland's finished his check of Universal Laser's computers."

"Yes, he wrapped it up yesterday."

"And?"

"And nothing. All the erased files Holland recovered were records of ordinary business transactions that are no longer current. And the only hidden files were restricted ones accessible only to certain key personnel for security reasons, or else they were ordinary DOS system files. You were counting on something?"

"Did Holland read all the files?"

Page laughed, ruefully. "It would take a year to read the correspondence alone. Holland has access to the restricted files, of course, but they all have to do with the Defense Department project and we already know about that."

"*You* already know about it."

"Believe me, Sergeant, if there were anything to be found, Holland would have found it. But I'm glad you called. There's something here you might be interested in—I don't know whether it's related to the killings or not, but there's a chance. Can you come here?"

"I'm on my way." She hung up and told Foley she was off to Federal Plaza. As she left she saw the Major Crimes men watching her and openly wondering if she was on to something. She exited with a flourish, doing nothing to spoil the impression.

THIRTEEN

THE FBI OFFICES at Federal Plaza had the impersonality all government offices have to some degree, slightly forbidding at first but then quickly forgettable. Trevor Page was waiting at the main doors and led Marian to an office that had no name or number on the door.

"Sorry I had to ask you to come here," Page said, "but we uncovered some information I couldn't print out because it's in one of our classified files. You'll have to read it from the computer screen."

That struck Marian as odd; she didn't have any sort of government security clearance. Page must be bending the rules for her benefit. "What kind of information?"

"Did you ever hear of a man named Evan Christopher?"

"No. Who's he?"

"An arms dealer. When we struck out on Universal Laser's people, we decided to run a check on their suppliers and customers. Christopher has dealt with Universal in the past, twice. But here's what turned up—Christopher was at Harvard the same time Jason O'Neill was enrolled there."

Marian perked up. "A connection?"

"Not that we can prove. They may not even have known each other. We compared their class schedules and they took no courses together—which proves nothing one way or the other. But look at this."

Marian read the computer screen; it was a list of names and affiliations Evan Christopher did business with or was suspected of doing business with. The names were foreign and unfamiliar to Marian, and she said so.

"Watch." Page moved the cursor to one of the names and pressed the return key.

The screen changed to a personal data record, and suddenly it all made sense. "PLO," Marian said with a sinking feeling.

"Exactly. The Palestine Liberation Organization gets most of its money from wire-transfer theft—intercepting the transfer of funds and diverting them to their own accounts. They steal American money and use it to buy American weapons, illegally, from venal dealers like Evan Christopher."

"Why haven't you arrested him?"

"The agents assigned to his case went to his home in Baltimore Sunday to bring him in. They found him dead."

Oh boy. "Murdered?"

"Evidently not. He just tripped and fell down a flight of stairs—and broke his neck. The Baltimore police are satisfied it was an accident. Christopher was alone in the house, for one thing. Our men on the scene accepted it as an accident."

Marian thought a moment. "So this Evan Christopher was a sort of middleman...buying weapons legally here and selling them illegally to terrorist groups like the PLO? Did he ever sell anything other than weapons? Like information?"

Page sighed. "His file doesn't say so. But there are a lot of things about Evan Christopher that we don't know. Such as, how does a young, clean-cut MBA from Harvard get involved in the arms-dealing business in the first place? We have a lot of gaps to fill in."

"And his only connection with the East River Park murders is that he attended the same school Jason O'Neill went to?"

"It may not be as thin as it sounds. We've cracked cases before by following up flimsier connections than that. But in situations like this the rule of thumb around here is 'Follow the money.' Holland is working on that right now, starting with Christopher and trying to trace some financial trail to Jason O'Neill. If he can find a link, then your case is solved. But even if he can't find one, you still have to consider Evan Christopher a suspect."

"A dead suspect." Marian walked aimlessly about the office. "I'd give a ton of money to know what went wrong—assuming it was Christopher who did the killing, I mean. Did O'Neill get scared before the deal was consummated and threaten to blow the lid off the whole thing?"

Page nodded. "I'd say that was a good guess. Otherwise why would Christopher cut off his source of supply? O'Neill must have gotten cold feet."

"Someone at Universal Laser may have found out."

"Someone else on the liaison team? Possibly. That would account for the murderer's killing another member of the team in addition to O'Neill, but why the other two?"

"Maybe they all knew. Maybe the killer was just playing safe. Maybe a lot of things. Maybe I'm through investigating the East River Park murders?"

Page grinned at her. "Could be. Disappointed?"

Marian laughed. "Oh, sure, *real* disappointed. Look, I'm going to have to tell all this to Captain DiFalco."

"I know. Just ask him to keep it under his hat for the time being. No paperwork, Marian, since this is still classified material."

"Okay. How long has Holland been trying to trace the money?"

"He just started. Unless he gets lucky immediately, we won't know anything for a while."

Marian wondered how long *a while* was. "Is he working on it alone?"

"No, he has help. Perhaps you'd like to work with him, to keep track of his progress?"

"I'd rather kiss a Klingon."

Page looked started, and then laughed. "You're not too fond of Holland?"

"Let's just say he's not one of my favorite people. What I want to do now is go see Edgar Quinn."

"Oh? Why?"

"To find out if he knew this Evan Christopher himself. Or whether the sale of Universal Laser weapons was arranged by someone else, and if so, who. I'd like to pin this down."

Page nodded. "Good idea. I'll go with you. But let's call first." He went to the desk and used the phone. After a minute he hung up. "Quinn's leaving for a business lunch in about twenty minutes—we won't have time." He checked his watch. "Speaking of lunch, are you hungry? I promise I'll do better than a street vendor's hot dog this time. I've been trying to buy you a meal ever since we met."

"You talked me into it," Marian said. "Where are we going?"

THEY TOOK A CAB to Le Rivage on West Forty-sixth. The theater district had seen a blossoming of new restaurants in the past few years, but Page ignored them and chose a long-time favorite instead. Marian almost said no; she and Brian had shared a number of meals there when things were still good between them. But she couldn't spend the rest of her life avoiding places that reminded her of Brian, so she said Le Rivage would be just fine. Lunch was long and leisurely, and Marian was able to fight down any feelings of guilt that threatened to surface over taking so much time; after all, Captain DiFalco had ordered her to spend time with the FBI. The fact that this particular representative of the Bureau was attractive and good company to boot had nothing to do with it. Orders were orders.

At the same time, the ticking of the clock kept nagging at her. All the time Curt Holland was searching for a money connection between Jason O'Neill and some stranger named Evan Christopher, back at the Ninth Precinct the Major

Crimes Unit was closing in on Captain DiFalco...and on *her* case. And there was nothing she could do to speed up the one or slow down the other.

"Just how good is Holland with a computer anyway?" she asked Page. "Does he have a real chance of finding what he's looking for?"

Page didn't answer right away. Then he said, "How good is he? To be blunt, he's the best I've ever seen. Admittedly I'm no expert, but I've yet to see him fail." He considered a moment and then said, "I'll tell you something, but it has to remain confidential. Not cop to cop, but me to you. All right?"

"Sure. What it is?"

"Do you know what Holland was doing before he joined the Bureau? He was a bill collector."

"A *bill* collector?"

"A most extraordinary one, believe me. He took only those cases in which the debtors had the money to pay but were welshing on legitimate debts. Holland had the access codes to more banks than probably any other single person in the world. After he found a hidden account, he'd simply transfer the amount owed to the account of whoever hired him—after first deducting a fat commission, of course. The debtors always knew what had happened because Holland never took one cent more than what was owed, but all they could do was scream about it. They could never prove anything."

Marian stared at her lunch companion aghast. "The man's a criminal!"

"Yes, he is, technically. But he never helped himself to other people's money, and he never accepted cases in which there was some question about the legitimacy of the debt. Holland has his own strange code of ethics."

"And the banks couldn't stop him?"

Page laughed. "The banks were his best customers! But the whole venture was so typical of Holland—setting himself up to correct inequities the law could do nothing about."

"Just like the Downtown Queens," Marian muttered. "Where did he get all the access codes?"

"Bought some, swapped for others. There's a whole subindustry out there dealing with access codes. And some security systems can still be cracked without the codes. Who are the Downtown Queens?"

She told him about the Queens and how they too took it on themselves to execute "justice." Marian and Page finished their lunch and reluctantly agreed it was time to get back to work. Outside, Page looked around for a taxi, but Marian stopped him. "Let's go down to Forty-fourth Street first," she said. "There's something I want to take a look at. Short walk."

Page had no objection, and they set out. The midday crowds were especially heavy in that section of town; people seemed determined to walk as long as the weather stayed good. Marian and Page endured the jostling and turned onto Eighth Avenue.

"What you just told me about Holland," Marian said, "that scares the hell out of me. To think that a creditor could just walk into my bank account and 'collect' money whenever he felt like it—that is truly frightening. But I don't understand why the FBI took him in if you knew that was what he'd been doing."

Page vocalized a sigh. "We took him in *because* that was what he'd been doing. Or one man did, rather, the man who was my superior at the time. He told me that a talent like Holland's mustn't be allowed to go to waste. I'm not sure we could have proved in court that Holland was behind this eccentric approach to debt-collection, but we knew enough to make trouble for him. So my superior told him to join the Bureau or face prosecution."

"You blackmailed him into joining?"

HOW TO PLAY:

1. With a coin, carefully scratch off the 3 gold areas on your Lucky Carnival Wheel. You could get as many as three FREE books and a surprise mystery gift, depending on what is revealed beneath the scratch-off areas.

2. Send back this card and you'll get brand-new, first-time-in-paperback, Mystery Library™ novels. These books have a cover price of $3.99 each. But THEY ARE TOTALLY FREE; even the shipping will be at our expense!

3. There's no catch. You're under no obligation to buy anything! We charge nothing—ZERO—for your first shipment. And you don't have to make any minimum number of purchases—not even one!

4. The fact is thousands of readers enjoy receiving books by mail from the Mystery Library Reader Service™. They like the convenience of home delivery and they love our great prices!

5. We hope that after receiving your free books you'll want to remain a subscriber. But the choice is yours—to continue or cancel, anytime at all! So why not take us up on our invitation, with no risk of any kind. You'll be glad you did.

No Cost! No Risk!

"That's what it amounts to, yes. We sent him to Quantico for training, where he immediately endeared himself by demonstrating he knew more than the instructors. My superior is dead now, but he had me memorize details of Holland's more flamboyant forays into other people's bank accounts—no written records, you understand, since my superior's method of recruitment is not exactly recognized as Bureau standard. Remember I once told you Holland wanted to quit the Bureau but couldn't? That's why. He's afraid of what I might do. That's also why he hates me," Page finished simply.

That was quite a story. Marian mulled it over a moment or two and then shot a glance at Page's face; it was devoid of expression. "How can you stand to work with a partner who hates you?" she asked.

He looked at her. "How can *you*?"

That brought her up short. "My God, is it that obvious?"

Page smiled ruefully, said nothing.

They'd reached Forty-fourth Street. "This way," Marian said and turned toward Broadway.

"What is it we're going to look at?"

"The Broadhurst Theatre. It's one of these along here—there it is."

Marian wanted to see the billboard advertisement out front. Abigail James got top billing, name above the title. Then below the title was a line drawing of two profiles, facing off against each other. The one of Ian Cavanaugh was slightly glamorized, making him look a little younger than he appeared up close. The other was...just Kelly, vibrant with life and energy even in a line drawing.

"Aha, the new Abigail James play," Page said. "It ought to be a good one. Do you plan on seeing it?"

"Opening night," Marian replied. "Friday."

"Opening night, hm? You must have connections. I hear this play is sold out for months."

"Kelly Ingram arranged it—she's a friend of mine." Marian hoped that didn't sound like name-dropping.

Page grinned delightedly. "The star of the show, no less! Well, I envy you. I haven't been to a Broadway opening in more years than I care to remember."

On the spur of the moment Marian invited him to go with her. "I'll have an extra ticket," she explained.

"I'd love to," he said without hesitation, "and thank you!" Suddenly he looked contrite. "I wasn't hunting for an invitation."

"Yes, you were," Marian kidded.

"Yes, I was," Page admitted. "Ah me. Am I still invited?"

"Of course."

He was reading the billboard. "Marian—the title, what does it mean? *The Apostrophe Thief.*"

"Haven't the foggiest. I'll ask Kelly."

"I did some acting in college, believe it or not," Page said. "Mostly period pieces, because I was pretty good with a sword."

And your timing ain't bad either, Marian thought wryly as they turned away to look for a cab.

FOURTEEN

AT UNIVERSAL LASER they learned Edgar Quinn had not yet returned from his business lunch, so Marian and Trevor Page went their separate ways for the time being. Marian took the IRT to Astor Place and walked the few blocks to the East Fifth Street stationhouse.

Upstairs in the PDU room she found Gloria Sanchez sitting elegantly on her desk, wearing what she called cooldude duds. Heavy eyeliner, a few ringlets of hair carefully placed; today she was Michael Jackson. But she, Captain DiFalco, and Foley were all three of them grinning like apes. "What? What?" Marian demanded.

"Major Crimes bailed out," DiFalco told her, still grinning. "They read the evidence we'd assembled, mumbled something about still being understaffed, and split."

"Hallelujah!" Marian cried.

"One of 'em told me it was a shitcan," Sanchez said.

An unsolvable homicide. "I hope you didn't agree with him," Marian said soberly.

"Oh, you better believe it! I said we'd be happy for Major Crimes to take it off our hands. That boy couldn't *wait* to get outta here."

Marian laughed and sank down on her chair; that was one obstacle out of the way, at any rate. "You know, I wouldn't have minded if they'd taken over right at the start, but now—"

"Now that case belongs to us," Foley interrupted. "We're the ones been bustin' our ass."

DiFalco's grin disappeared. "I hope to god that guy isn't right and it *is* a shitcan. We're all out of leads, in case you people hadn't noticed. We've got to come up with something new, and fast."

"How about the name of an illicit arms dealer who went to school with one of the four victims?" Marian asked, and enjoyed the looks on their faces. She told them about Evan Christopher and his tenuous connection to Jason O'Neill. She explained how Christopher had died last Sunday in an accident and how the FBI was trying to uncover a money trail that led from Christopher to O'Neill.

"Tempting," Captain DiFalco said, musing. "Very tempting indeed. Pin it on a dead arms dealer and call the case closed."

"He had to have an accomplice," Foley said. "We could still go after him."

"Hey, put on the brakes," Sanchez growled. "This guy went to the same school as Jason O'Neill? That's all the FBI has?"

"I know, it's not much," Marian admitted. "But if the FBI is willing to try to establish a connection for us, what have we got to lose? It's their time they're using." She turned to Foley. "By the way, we should have heard by now. Did the Crime Scene Unit turn up anything in Jason O'Neill's apartment?"

While Foley looked blank and started pawing through the papers on his desk, DiFalco answered her. "They swear no homicide was committed there. They found note pads with various doodles on them which they say were made by different hands, but no notes or anything that could tell us what the four victims were meeting about Saturday afternoon. Foley, did you talk to that night guard at Universal Laser yet?"

Here Foley was on firmer ground. "Yeah, he's just getting over some virus. That's why they were shorthanded on Saturday—the same bug hit 'em all. And the guy says he left his monitors a lot on Saturday night because he was already sick and couldn't stay away from the can for long. He says the whole Russian army coulda marched through and he wouldna known. And when he wasn't on the can, he was trying to get the chief of security on the phone, to send him some relief—haw, *relief*."

"Get on with it," DiFalco snapped.

"Anyway, he couldn't get hold of the security chief and stuck it out until his regular replacement showed up at midnight. By then me and Larch were already on the scene in East River Park."

DiFalco was nodding. "So getting in and out of the building unseen was never a real problem. Glass doors on the ground floor?"

"Yeah," Foley said.

"Anyone wanting to sneak in could just watch from outside until our diarrhetic guard made one of his periodic dashes to the men's room. And anyone wanting to leave without being seen could watch from...where?"

"The stairwell?" Marian suggested. "It's right next to the elevators."

"Good enough. So our killers follow the liaison group in—"

"Or they're already in there, waiting," Sanchez suggested casually.

"That's a possibility," DiFalco conceded. "So they're either in there or they follow the four victims in. Then what?"

"They kill 'em," Foley said unhelpfully.

"Where?" Marian asked. "Not in the Universal Laser building."

"Why the hell not?"

"And then try to carry four corpses out while the guard is away from the monitors? And then put all four into the stolen van without anyone's noticing? No way, Foley. That'd be risky enough with just *one* body. Four would be impossible."

"You're saying they left alive?" DiFalco asked.

"They had to. Either the killers were waiting for them when they came out of the building, or they marched them out at gunpoint." Foley hooted. "Difficult, yes, but easier than carrying four dead bodies out."

DiFalco considered that. "The killers were waiting for them? The liaison team made an appointment with them, not knowing they were walking into a trap? Damn! If only we knew what they were up to on Saturday!"

"Yeah," Foley echoed, "if we only knew."

DiFalco stood up and straightened his tie. "Well, we're not going to find out sitting around here. The answer's buried somewhere at Universal Laser. Larch, how many of the personnel there did you interview?"

"Only a handful," Marian answered regretfully. "It's not a small company."

"Okay, I want you to try again. You three and the others as well when they come in. Talk to as many people as you can. Start at the top and work your way down. If something is going on, that means a lot of people must know about it. A whole group of people trying to keep a secret? There'll be cracks somewhere. If you think you're on to something, don't back off—keep at 'em until they start threatening to file complaints."

"I want to talk to Sherman Bigelow's secretary again," Marian said. "She may know more than she told me. And I thought I'd ask Edgar Quinn what he knew about this Evan Christopher."

"Divide 'em up however you like, but get started on it now." DiFalco went back to his office, leaving them to it.

Marian remembered the way Gloria Sanchez had gotten a quick fix on Candy Bigelow and asked her to interview Universal Laser's vice president in charge of production, Elizabeth Tanner. "What am I looking for?" Sanchez wanted to know.

"See if you can figure out what she's after. Try to pin her down as to what she thinks is behind the murders. She hinted to me that the killers are probably Universal Laser people, but she wouldn't go any further. Get her to go further.''

"Oh joy," Sanchez said.

Marian asked Foley to interview O'Neill's, Vickers's, and Webb's secretaries. "Find out what their new jobs are. Concentrate on Conrad Webb's secretary. He was very tense when I talked to him. Make friends with him if you can, take him out for a drink, get him to relax.''

Foley snorted. "What's a man doing working as a secretary?''

Marian sighed. "On second thought—"

"I'll do it, I'll do it! Jesus, relax, willya?''

The three of them set out, not planning to return to the stationhouse that day.

MARIAN RAN into a roadblock on her first try: Edgar Quinn had gone home after his three-hour business lunch instead of coming back to the office. Sherman Bigelow's secretary first, then. Marian looked through her notebook and discovered she didn't have Ms North's first name. She asked one of the other secretaries and found out it was Rachel.

Rachel North was wearing ordinary flats instead of espadrilles this time, and her chubbiness was better concealed this time by a loose jacket she wore over her slacks. She still looked comfortable. When Marian walked in, a maintenance man was unloading a set of wooden file cabinets from the same sort of platform truck that had been used to move Elizabeth Tanner's computer equipment into Conrad Webb's old office. The workman pulled the protective mats from around the files, and the secretary ran a hand appreciatively over the wood surface of the nearest file.

"Nice file cabinets," Marian said, making them both jump.

"Oh, hello, Sergeant, ah . . .''

"Larch."

"Sergeant Larch. Yes, they are nice, aren't they? Mr. Emory ordered all new cabinets for the office."

"Mr. Emory? Is he Mr. Bigelow's replacement?"

"That's right. He's been promoted to head of the Legal Department."

"Is he also taking Mr. Bigelow's place on the Washington liaison group?"

The secretary said yes. "In fact, he's in Washington right now. But he'll be returning tomorrow if you want to come back then."

"No, you're the one I came to see. Is Elizabeth Tanner heading up the group?"

"Temporarily, except that it's only a 'group' of two so far. No one from Research has been appointed to replace Herb Vickers yet."

And no young "comer" singled out to take Jason O'Neill's place. The maintenance man had finished unloading the file cabinets and placed them where Rachel North indicated. He piled the protective mats on the platform truck and pushed it out of the office.

Rachel North waited until he was gone and asked, "What did you want to see me about, Sergeant? I've already told you everything I know."

"Well, that's just it. I don't think you did. I think something was going on here before those four men were killed and you know about it... and you're keeping it to yourself."

North's face closed; even her voice changed. "I asked you once before not to bully me, Sergeant."

"You call that bullying? I haven't even got started yet. This is a *murder* investigation, Ms North! What could possibly be more important than that? Some company secret that'll be obsolete and forgotten by this time next year? If you're deliberately withholding something that might help me find the killers, then you're condoning the killings."

"*Condoning* the killings!" The secretary was horrified.

"That's what it amounts to," Marian pushed on. "You're helping the killers when you should be helping the police. There's no way to rationalize your way out of that." North was near tears; this was one of the times Marian hated her job. "When I spoke to you before, you blurted out something about not talking of business matters outside the office. Is that what happened? Did somebody give away company secrets? Was it your boss?"

"Mr. Bigelow would never do that!" the woman gasped, stricken. "He was probably the most dependable man in the company!"

"Then why did he end up dead?"

That did it; that's what made the woman crack. North sank down into a chair and buried her face in her hands, sobbing quietly. Sometimes Marian *really* hated her job. In a choked voice, the secretary said, "He shouldn't have died. He shouldn't have died!"

Captain DiFalco had instructed Marian and the other detectives not to back off when they found something, to keep pushing. Marian looked at the woman huddled on the chair before her; Rachel North was no hardboiled secretary standing like an armed guard between her boss and the rest of the world. She was a woman under great stress, not knowing what to do and wanting only for it all to end. DiFalco would say she was ripe for the kill. "Come on," Marian said with a sigh. "Let's go to the rest room and wash your face—you'll feel better. Come on, Rachel."

They went to the ladies' room and the secretary bathed her face with cold water. Marian asked if Universal Laser had an employee cafeteria or a snack room or some such place they could go. Rachel led her to a room filled with comfortable chairs and low tables; the walls were lined with food and drink machines. One coffee machine was lying on its side on a platform truck, while two men worked busily at installing a new one; the room was otherwise empty. "Do you want coffee or something cold?" Marian asked.

"Diet cola, please," the secretary said; she filled two glasses at the ice machine while Marian got them both sodas. They sat and sipped at their soft drinks, waiting for the men to finish their job. Marian stared at the discarded coffee machine lying on its side. It appeared shrunken, somehow, now that its days of usefulness were ended; or maybe the platform truck that held it was just an extra large one.

The service men completed their installation and wheeled out the dead coffee machine. Immediately Rachel North said, "I don't know anything about the murder of Mr. Bigelow and the others."

"I know you don't," Marian replied. "It's what came before that that I'm trying to find out about. There was a leak of some sort, wasn't there?"

"I'm pretty sure there was. The whole company was buzzing with the rumor. But I'm even more sure that Mr. Bigelow didn't have anything to do with it." She was firm about that.

Marian wondered about something. "You were fond of Mr. Bigelow, were you?"

"Fond of him?" The secretary considered. "No, not really. Mr. Bigelow wasn't a very open man. He liked things kept formal in the office." She smiled sadly. "He couldn't stand the casual way Mr. Quinn ran the company. But I did come to respect Mr. Bigelow—I respected him enormously. He was a good man, and I'm sorry he's gone."

"Then help me find his killers. Tell me about the leak."

"But I don't know anything definite! Only that something got out and all the top brass were extremely agitated about it."

"Including the Washington liaison team?"

"Yes! Those four knew . . . and then those four are murdered? That's no coincidence."

"No. I'd think the Defense Department would send someone to investigate, but they seem to be depending on the FBI."

"The Defense Department? Oh no, the leak had nothing to do with Project Soundbender, I'm sure of that." Rachel North misinterpreted Marian's look of surprise and hastened to add, "It's all right, Sergeant Larch, I have security clearance. I have to type all Mr. Bigelow's papers for him. Had to, I mean."

Project Soundbender. "How can you be sure it has nothing to do with Soundbender?" Marian asked, trying to appear as if she knew all about it.

"Because business was proceeding as usual. For the last week or so Mr. Bigelow was preoccupied with this...this other thing that was going on, and he treated Soundbender in an almost offhand manner. No, whatever was leaked had to do with some new product or process in development, not the Defense Department project. And I honestly don't know what it was."

Marian believed her. All along she'd been going on the assumption that the cause of the trouble was connected to the Defense Department project—which now had a name, thank goodness. But evidently they'd all been following the wrong trail. Something new in development, Rachel North had said, something kept secret even within the company? "Who would know about this new development? Quinn, Tanner, who else?"

The secretary shrugged. "The people in Research working on it, certainly. The other vice presidents? I don't know."

Marian couldn't resist the temptation; North had evidently assumed Marian had security clearance too since she was investigating the case. "You say it's been business as usual with Project Soundbender—that's good to hear. It's my understanding they've finally licked the problem that's been holding them up so long."

"The earth-curvature limitation? Yes, that was the las big obstacle. They're working on refining the final version now."

Earth curvature? "Well, I want to thank you for your help." She stood up to leave. "Are you going back to your office?"

"No, I think I'll stay here a few more minutes. Sergeant Larch?"

"Yes?"

"In no way do I *condone* those murders."

Marian smiled at her. "I never thought you did. You did the right thing, talking to me." The secretary returned her smile weakly, still not sure.

Marian set out to find the elevators but got turned around somehow; she walked down a corridor she didn't remember seeing before. Then she spotted the arrow pointing toward the Legal Department and knew where she was. Her route took her past Elizabeth Tanner's new office.

"Sergeant Larch! Would you come in here please!"

Immediately, your highness. Tanner had glimpsed her through two open doors; Marian walked through the reception area into Conrad Webb's former office. Gloria Sanchez sat relaxed in a chair in front of Elizabeth Tanner's desk; she rolled her eyes at Marian.

Tanner herself was steaming. "Sergeant, I want you to confirm something Detective Sanchez has just told me. It seems that this company was virtually without security last Saturday. Is that true?"

"During a certain time period, yes. Only one guard on the monitors instead of two, and that one was sick. He had to run to the men's room a lot."

"Leaving us unprotected while he was throwing up?"

"Other end, I think, but yes. He did the best he could. He says he tried to get someone to come in and replace him but he couldn't get hold of your chief of security."

Tanner's eyes were fiery. "And I have to learn this from the police! Anyone could have just walked in here last Saturday?"

"Someone did, Mrs. Tanner."

She pressed her lips together. "Thank you, Sergeant."

Marian was dismissed. She winked at Gloria Sanchez and started out, but stopped when she heard a phone being picked up.

"Get Emmett Yellin in here," Tanner said. "Immediately."

Marian turned in the doorway. "Who's Emmett Yellin?"

"Our chief of security. I'm going to fire him."

Marian nodded and went on out. She took the elevator down to the lobby where she used a pay phone to call Captain DiFalco. Marian asked him to get a warrant to have all of Universal Laser's truck platforms and protective mats checked for bloodstains.

FIFTEEN

THE SAME MANSERVANT who'd let her in before answered the door of Edgar Quinn's apartment. But this time he was more affable, not having just been routed from bed at six in the morning. "Mr. Quinn's taking a shower right now, Sergeant. If you'll have a seat, he'll be with you shortly."

"Thank you." Marian followed him into the same room where she and Foley had talked to Quinn before. She decided to try one of the sofas this time.

The manservant surprised her by getting down on his knees at the other end of the sofa. "If you'll excuse me, I'd like to get this finished before Mr. Quinn comes down, and wine stains are so hard to get out." He squirted a foam on the spot on the rug.

"Impossible, I'd heard."

"Well, the label on the can promises miracles. When this dries, I'll brush the residue away and then we'll see. I do wish people would be more careful in other people's homes."

"Then Mr. Quinn didn't spill it?"

"No, it was Mr. Page. Neither Mr. nor Mrs. Quinn drink wine."

"Trevor Page? FBI?"

"The same. He's never spilled anything before, but somehow he managed to dump half a glass of claret on the carpet."

"Are you English?"

"How did you know? I thought I sounded very American."

"You do. But you said claret instead of Bordeaux."

"Ah. I'll remember." He gave her a friendly smile and left just as Edgar Quinn came in.

Quinn was wearing loose gray trousers and an open-necked white shirt. His hair was still wet from the shower, and he had it slicked back against his skull, making Marian think of a 1920s ballroom dancer. He offered her a drink and then sat on a chair facing the sofa when she declined. "Do you have some news for me?"

"Possibly. Do you know a man named Evan Christopher?"

"Christopher? I've met him—once, I think. He's a client. Why?"

"He purchased laser weapons from you?"

"Yes, but I don't remember off the top of my head what. Never a big consignment, as I recall."

"Do you know he resold the weapons to terrorist organizations?"

Quinn blinked. "No, I did not know that. Are you certain?"

"The FBI is. Evan Christopher has even dealt with the PLO. And you knew nothing about it?"

"Of course not!" He jumped from his chair and started to pace. "Good lord, that's all I need! The Defense Department could cancel our contract!"

"For Project Soundbender? When you're so close to completion? Not very likely."

"Maybe not. They'll take Soundbender first and then put me in jail. Evan Christopher! Does he admit it?"

"He's dead." Marian told him about the accident that broke the arms dealer's neck. "The FBI were on their way to arrest him."

"Wonderful. That's just wonderful."

"Surely the Defense Department wouldn't hold you accountable for what Evan Christopher did."

"You don't know the Defense Department." Quinn ran his fingers through his wet hair. "Hoo. Defense is so damned prickly. Normally I'd send Conrad Webb to Washington to straighten it out, but now..." Abruptly he sat back down. "You think I'm overreacting, don't you? I hope to god you're right. So. Page told you about Soundbender, did he?"

Marian tried to look innocent. "To tell you the truth, I didn't really understand that part about the earth-curvature limitations."

"Oh, it's simple enough when you consider Soundbender's just an extension of current technology. Information-gathering agencies use lasers to amplify window glass vibrations and convert them into audible sounds. But the Defense Department got it into its collective head that depending on spy satellites alone was too risky, so they want to operate the lasers from regular aircraft—much closer to the ground, you see. The idea is to keep the planes safely in American air space but still have them listen in all over the world. But the surface of the earth curves, and lasers travel in a straight line. The problem is obvious."

"So an airplane flying over Tucson can eavesdrop on a conversation in Beijing? No privacy at all left in the world, is there? Anyone with the right computer knowledge can enter a bank account and help himself, and now no conversation anywhere will be safe from being overheard. The next thing you know, even our thoughts will no longer be private."

"Yes. That's coming." Quinn didn't seem the least bit perturbed by the idea.

"And as important and earthshaking and all-consuming as Soundbender is," Marian said casually, "it still doesn't have doodleysquat to do with the East River Park murders."

"What?"

Marian uttered a silent prayer that Rachel North knew what she was talking about. "Nobody sold any Soundbender secrets, Mr. Quinn. The leak had to do with an entirely different project. And you must have known that all along.''

''What are you saying?''

''You know what I'm saying. Universal Laser has something else on the burner, something even more dangerous than a supereavesdropping system. Why don't you tell me about it?''

Quinn spread his hands. ''We have a dozen projects in development.''

''But only one of them significant enough to get four men murdered. Which one, Mr. Quinn? And how did you find out about the leak?''

''You're mistaken, Sergeant Larch. Nothing like that is—''

''Stop it!'' Marian commanded angrily. ''Stop lying! Your whole company knows that leak led to the killings, and it's got them scared to death. But only key personnel know what the connection is. One of you is going to talk eventually—we're going to find out, one way or another. It would be better if it came from you.''

Tiny beads of sweat had appeared on Quinn's upper lip. ''I repeat, you are mistaken. And I don't take kindly to being called a liar, Sergeant. The biggest project we have going is Soundbender and—''

''Liar. Get used to it, Quinn, because I'm going to keep on calling you a liar until I get the rest of the story. You know what's going on and you're keeping it from the police. As I see it, that makes you an accessory. And we will prosecute, you can bet your ass on that. So why don't you just cut through all the bullshit and tell me *what the hell is going on*?''

''Get out,'' Quinn said hoarsely. ''I want you out. Right now.''

Marian stood up slowly. ''Okay, you can throw me out, but you can't stop the entire NYPD from doing its job. Talk to me, dammit! Get your lawyer over here if you like, but *talk to me*."

"I said get out! Lewis! Lewis!" The manservant appeared immediately. "Escort the sergeant out. *All the way* out."

"This way, please," Lewis said without a flicker of expression.

Marian followed him out to the entrance hall. She glanced back to see Quinn standing in the doorway of the room she'd just left, watching tensely. Did he think she was going to hide behind a chair and then pounce out on him? She stepped through the door the manservant was holding open.

Lewis had a disapproving look on his face. "You put him on the spot, you know," he whispered, and closed the door silently behind her.

FRIDAY MORNING the light was a peculiar color...storm brewing? Not a very good omen for Kelly's opening night, when the Critics from Hell were expected in force. Marian would have to give her friend a call later during the morning, when she was sure Kelly was up; *you can do it, enjoy yourself,* something upbeat and positive. Marian knew she was not supposed to say *good luck*; for some reason that was *bad* luck. And she didn't think she could say *break a leg* without giggling. But she did want to talk to Kelly, on this most important day of her friend's life.

Marian checked over the clothes she planned to wear that night, her thoughts full of Kelly and what she must be going through right now. The waiting must be torture. Would they be squeezing in a last-minute rehearsal, or would the actors have the day off to prepare themselves? A whole day to think about all the things that could go wrong. To worry about forgetting their lines. To build up an intense fear of the critics. *Will they like me? Will they boo me off the stage?* "Thank god I'm not an actor," Marian said aloud.

She was still thinking of Kelly while she got ready for work. Marian was excited about that evening; she was excited for her friend and she was excited for herself. An opening night. A Reaffirmation of Civilization within a Savage World. An Oasis of Creativity in the Desert of Destructiveness. Marian laughed at herself and pulled on new black slacks and a soft white sweater she'd been saving for a special occasion. Today *felt* special. She took a raincoat down to toss in the back seat of the car and drove to the East Fifth Street parking lot across the street from the station.

Upstairs in the PDU room, Trevor Page was sitting at her desk drinking coffee. He got up when he saw her come in and pointed to a brown paper bag. "Eat your breakfast."

The bag contained fresh pineapple and a brioche, still warm in its aluminum foil wrapping. "What are you doing here so early?"

"Your boss wants a show-and-tell. Someone called me at six to make sure I'd be here." He went to get her some coffee.

The pineapple was tangy and cold, just right with the buttery brioche. Foley and three of the other four detectives assigned to the East River Park murders were sipping at their own cups of coffee and helping themselves to a bakery box full of danish. Gloria Sanchez hadn't come in yet. Marian wondered where Curt Holland was; she hadn't seen him since Tuesday night, after that humiliating scene at Brian's gallery when she'd told him to disappear. He'd certainly taken her at her word. She asked Page.

"I didn't want to pull him off his search for the money trail," Page said. "Holland gets a bit tetchy when his concentration's broken. Besides, only one of us needs to be here."

"He hasn't found anything yet?"

Page shrugged. "He says he has a couple of lines to follow. It's a complicated business."

Marian had finished her breakfast and thanked Page for it. "What time did Captain DiFalco want to start?"

"The androgynous voice on the phone said eight o'clock," he said.

She looked at her watch, but saw only a blank silver face. "Oh-oh. I need a new batch watery."

"A new what?"

"I mean watch battery." She told him about Kelly's spoonerism. "It must be catching."

"How'd you and Kelly Ingram ever meet?"

"A case I was working on. A friend of hers was killed."

Gloria Sanchez came in and lowered herself gently into her chair, looking half asleep and hung over. Marian could get no clues from her clothing whether was she black or Hispanic—no ethnic self-parody today? A first for Sanchez. Right on cue Captain DiFalco joined the rest of them, perching on Sanchez's desk. "Okay, folks, let's get started. I want to make sure that every one of you knows what everyone else is doing. I'm especially interested in what you learned at Universal Laser yesterday. But first, I'd like to hear from the FBI about this arms dealer who died Sunday."

Page nodded and told them everything he knew about Evan Christopher, which wasn't much. "We're still looking for a money link between Christopher and any member of the Universal Laser liaison team, concentrating on Jason O'Neill. Without that link, we've got nothing. But as things now stand, Evan Christopher is our best hope."

Marian cleared her throat. "You put a tap on Edgar Quinn's home phone, didn't you? Anything there?"

"Not a damned thing. Mostly personal calls, some legitimate business stuff. But Mrs. Quinn uses the phone the most at home." Page smiled faintly. "The manservant plays the ponies."

Lewis, a gambler? "And that's all?"

"That's all. As far as we're concerned, Edgar Quinn is clean."

"All right," said DiFalco. "What about Universal Laser? Larch, you first. What did you get yesterday?"

"I found out what Universal Laser's hush-hush project is," Marian said with an apologetic glance at Page, "and I also found out that it most likely has nothing to do with the East River Park murders." She told them about Project Soundbender and Rachel North's conviction that the killings were connected to a different project, one the secretary had no firsthand knowledge of.

"That's what all the fuss is about?" Foley said with disgust. "Some eavesdropping machine? I'da thought they had the ultimate weapon, the way everyone was carrying on."

Marian couldn't believe her ears. "Foley, don't you understand what it means?"

"Later," Captain DiFalco stopped her. "All you've got to go on is what this one secretary told you, right?"

"That's all so far, but the others will start talking now that someone else has opened up. And Rachel North is in a position to know, Captain. She handled all of Sherman Bigelow's business for him, typed his papers. And she's positive there's no connection between whatever was leaked and Project Soundbender. Soundbender was just business as usual during all the panic about the leak."

Page was groaning audibly. "Marian, you're not supposed to know about Soundbender!"

"So what do we know?" she asked him reasonably. "The name of the project and the fact that it has to do with converting vibrations into sound. No state secrets are out."

"You can never be too careful," he insisted. "I don't think you understand how many terrorist groups are watching this country every minute for any little slip we make, just waiting for a chance to attack in any way they can. What are we supposed to do about them?"

"Nuke 'em till they glow?" Gloria Sanchez suggested lazily.

"Look, I know you all think the Bureau is paranoid and I can't do anything about that," Page said earnestly, "but I must ask you to forget you ever heard the word 'Soundbender.' Never say it again, even among yourselves."

"Sure, sure," DiFalco said impatiently. "If it's not behind the East River Park murders, we're not interested anyway. Larch, you got anything else?"

She told them about her subsequent interview with Edgar Quinn and her own conviction that Quinn was lying when he denied the "secret" project story. "The FBI may consider him clean, but I don't—sorry, Trevor. Certain key people at Universal Laser are working on something they don't want us to know about, they don't even want the rest of the *company* to know about." Marian said she'd leaned on Quinn as much as she could until he threw her out.

One of the other detectives had a question. "That word we're not supposed to say—it was just a red herring? Nothing more?"

"It was a red herring handed to us by Edgar Quinn," Marian said. "He wants us to think the killings are connected to you-know-what, which is another good reason to keep him on our suspects list."

"A list of one," DiFalco grumbled. "And another secret project, just what we need. But Quinn says not?"

"Quinn is saying as little as possible," Marian replied.

"Maybe you shouldn't have challenged him," Page suggested.

"Maybe not," Marian acknowledged, "but I wasn't getting anywhere with nice and polite."

"Okay, what about the rest of you," DiFalco said. "Get anything?"

Sanchez was the only one with something to report. "What I got backs up Marian, in a way. Elizabeth Tanner was telling me general stuff about Universal Laser, and she started to say 'weapon' but changed it to 'project.' The first time it happened, I didn't pay much attention. But when she did it *four more times*, I got the message. Also, she made a point of telling me twice that Universal was working on a new technology with no Defense Department contract to underwrite it. And here's the kicker. This new technology? She kept calling it 'Edgar's project.'"

DiFalco actually smiled. "Conclusion?"

"Conclusion—the lady wants us to know Edgar Quinn is using his company to develop a weapon that even the government doesn't know about. She wants us to know *real bad.*"

Page frowned. "That's just supposition."

Sanchez gave him a big smile, all flashing white teeth. "Yeah. But it's *good* supposition."

"But why would she give all that away?"

"She wants Quinn's job," Marian said. "Another thing. Remember the 'message' aspect of the murders? The handcuffs, the bullet through the eye, as if the killings were a warning? These people at Universal who're working on this new weapon—I wonder if they're the ones who were being warned. Keep your mouths shut or look what will happen to you."

DiFalco whistled. "That must be some weapon. And the liaison group had talked? All of them?"

Marian shrugged. "More likely just one. If Quinn's behind this—and he must be—then he and his accomplice might not know which of the four had been telling tales out of school."

"So they just killed them all?" DiFalco said. "That's one way to make sure." There was an uneasy movement in the room; whether the killer was Quinn or somebody else, he had to be one ruthless son of a bitch. "I want a tail on Quinn."

Page coughed discreetly. "That won't be necessary, Captain."

"The FBI's tailing him? Well, I do thank you for keeping me informed, Agent Page!" Heavy on the sarcasm.

"Surveillance is just starting today. Merely a precaution, since we don't think he's involved."

DiFalco grunted and turned back to his detectives. "Okay, listen up. You're all on call all weekend. By tomorrow we should have the lab report on whether the platform trucks they have at Universal Laser were used to move the bodies or not."

"Platform trucks?" someone said.

"Larch's idea," DiFalco answered. "If they find bloodstains, we've got the scene of the crime at last. In the meantime, I want you all to hit that company again. Talk to as many of the employees as you can. Tell 'em we know about the new weapon, make 'em understand somebody has already talked—that might loosen a few tongues. But don't mention the secretary's name. No need to make things hot for her. Find out who's actually working on the weapon, who else knows about it, like that. I want you to come back with *names*. Got that?"

"There's one other thing I ought to mention," Page said. "If we're able to prove a money link between Evan Christopher and one of the murder victims, that will put this case into the realm of international secrets-dealings and the CIA is going to want to move in. So we've got to wrap this thing up."

DiFalco scowled at the thought of even more federal agents horning in on a Ninth Precinct investigation. "What are you all waiting for?" he snarled. "Get going!"

Page said, "See you tonight" to Marian and left. She gathered up her raincoat and handbag and joined her fellow detectives for another day of badgering the already nervous employees at Universal Laser Technologies.

SIXTEEN

MARIAN WAS regularly scheduled on the day shift, from eight to four; but in the six months she'd been at the Ninth Precinct, she could have counted on the fingers of one hand the number of times she'd been able to leave when her shift ended. But on the Friday of Kelly Ingram's Broadway debut, she got away at four on the dot. She even had time to stop at a Radio Shack on the way home and pick up a new batch watery.

Her day of hassling Universal Laser employees had turned up exactly one name, that of a young engineer who was described to her as hyperactive, frighteningly inventive, and totally nuts. If anyone at Universal was involved in the development of some hush-hush weapon that even the Defense Department didn't know about, he'd be the one. It was only a supposition on her informants' part, but it was all she had.

The other five detectives on the case had come back with the same name plus six other possibles. Nobody was admitting they knew anything, but the middle-management-and-lower employees were now willing to play guessing games, once they'd been reassured someone else had already let the cat out of the bag. But the police had brought none of their possibles in for questioning, because shortly before three o'clock Edgar Quinn had been able to pull enough strings to get them all kicked out. The order had come from the Borough Commander's office.

So they'd all trooped back to the Ninth Precinct station-house, where they were surprised to find Captain DiFalco not particularly upset by the Borough Commander's interference. He reminded them they still had another iron in the fire. DiFalco said if the lab found traces of any of the victims' blood on just one of Universal Laser's platform trucks, there was no way in hell Quinn could keep them out then. The Borough Commander himself couldn't ignore evidence like that. All in all, DiFalco was pleased with what they'd learned, and they'd spent the last hour of their workday checking the names they'd brought back against the FBI security investigation printouts Trevor Page had brought them. Their seven possibles were all designers and technicians, and Marian was satisfied in her own mind that they were the target of the warning broadcast by the East River Park murders.

DiFalco had put his detectives on call for the weekend, but Friday night was hers, or Kelly's, rather, and Marian meant to enjoy it to the hilt. While she was getting out a new bar of soap, she came across some aftershave that belonged to Brian and realized with a start that she hadn't thought of him all day. In the shower the fatigue of the week's labors fell away as if by magic; and then she was dressed, ready, and rarin' to go.

She and Page had agreed to meet for a drink before the play, so at seven o'clock Marian took a cab to a bar on West Forty-sixth, a couple of blocks away from the Broadhurst. The bar was noisy and packed, filled with playgoers seeking a quick pre-curtain libation. Marian spotted Page and squeezed through the crowd to join him.

Once they had drinks in front of them, they tried to talk without shouting. Page asked, "How's your friend Kelly doing? Did you talk to her today?"

"Twice," Marian replied. "The woman is a nervous wreck. She's imagining all sorts of disasters, everything from the audience's laughing at her in a serious scene to the curtain's closing during her biggest dramatic moment. She told me she'd dreamed that she showed up tonight only to find the rest of the cast doing Shakespeare. Ian Cavanaugh s supposed to have said, 'Oh, didn't anybody tell you? We decided to switch.'"

Page laughed sympathetically. "That is a *bad* case of nerves. Is she worrying about that line you said she spoonerized?"

"She didn't mention it. But you see, Kelly's never performed in front of a live audience before this play—all her acting's been done in front of a camera. If you goof before a camera, you just reshoot the scene. Kelly doesn't have that safety net tonight. If she goofs, she could ruin it for everybody. And that's what she's thinking about right now."

Page took a swallow of his drink. "Don't you imagine that's what all stage actors go through before a performance?"

"Oh, I suppose so. But Kelly has so much riding on tonight. Most of her career she's played sex-object roles, because of her looks. Tonight is the first chance she's had to break the mold."

"Do you think she can do it?"

"Yes," Marian said without hesitation. "Kelly has backbone. She can do it."

Page smiled. "She also has a good friend."

They decided they didn't have time for another drink and left the bar. The cracked and broken sidewalks were filled with playgoers rushing to their various theaters, and Marian felt her own sense of excitement growing. They hurried the two blocks down to Forty-fourth; twice as they approached the Broadhurst they were stopped by people wanting to buy their tickets. Marian picked up their passes at the box office.

The seats were excellent, almost at the exact center of the theater. Marian looked at her program: *The Apostrophe Thief*, a play by Abigail James. The characters were listed in the order of their appearance; leading off was Ian Cavanaugh, whose character name was Richard. The fourth name on the list was that of Sheila, Kelly's character. The

audience was noisy and talkative, buzzing with expecta-
tion. The air was electric. Marian loved it.

"Did you ask Kelly what the title means?" Page said.

"Oh lord, I forgot. Well, the play should make it clear."

It was time. Marian felt the rush of anticipation that ran
through the audience as the house lights dimmed and the
curtain opened. Ian Cavanaugh stood on the stage alone, big
and handsome and authoritative. The audience clapped with
enthusiasm and affection. *That must really be something,*
Marian mused, impressed. *To reach a point in your career
where you get applause just for standing on a stage. Just for
showing up.*

Cavanaugh was looking through what appeared to be a
small leather-bound notebook. Voices sounded offstage;
Cavanaugh quickly locked the notebook away in an old-
fashioned writing desk and was smilingly facing the door
when a man and a woman came in. And they were off and
running.

Marian had trouble concentrating on the dialogue, worrying about Kelly's entrance instead. She wanted it to be
soon; the tension was getting to her. *Get out there, Kelly,
and do your thing!*

She must have heard her. The upstage door opened and
there stood Kelly Ingram, one hand resting lightly on the
door frame, not acknowledging the smattering of polite
applause that arose from the audience. She looked like a
million bucks. The Joan Crawford hairdo she'd been trying out during rehearsal was gone, and her posture was erect
without being stiff. Kelly looked straight at Ian Cavanaugh
and said, "Has anyone seen my address book? It seems to
have grown legs and walked away." Her voice carried, the
words were clear, and the line didn't sound rehearsed. Marian wanted to bounce up and down.

After another couple of minutes, Marian began to relax
for the first time that evening. Worry about Kelly? Nonsense; the play's female lead obviously knew what she was

doing. She wasn't going to trip over her own feet, she wasn't going to forget her lines. Belatedly, Marian began to pay attention to the *play*. The tension between Kelly and Cavanaugh was tangible from the moment of Kelly's entrance; they engaged in some subtle verbal fencing that the other two characters on the stage never caught on to.

People came on the stage, people left the stage. Kelly disappeared and made a costume change. Young Xandria showed up, playing Kelly's (Sheila's) kid sister. Then only the two sisters and Cavanaugh were on the stage, and Marian realized they'd come to the *watch battery* scene. She tensed up all over again.

Here it comes.

"People," Kelly said to Ian Cavanaugh, "mean no more to you than a..." She trailed off.

Marian held her breath.

"Than a *watch battery*!" Kelly shouted at the top of her lungs.

Marian exhaled. "That's one way of doing it!" Page whispered in her ear.

"Useful for about a year, then it's time for a replacement," Kelly finished scornfully.

Marian was so happy she wanted to cry. The play moved on, picking up its tempo and building to a climax. By the end of the first act, the fencing between Kelly and Cavanaugh was over. Their enmity was out in the open, and war had been declared. The stage was set for the battle to be fought in Act II. Applause erupted like an explosion.

Intermission.

"I don't think I ever want to come to an opening night again," Marian told Page. "Too exhausting."

They got up and went outside, where the sidewalks and street were jammed with people grabbing a between-the-acts smoke. "I feel the same way," Page said, "and I don't even know Kelly Ingram. She's great, Ian Cavanaugh's great, and the play is great. Whoo! What an evening."

"Which one of them is going to win, do you think? Sheila or Richard?"

"I have no idea. It could go either way."

A couple of TV camera crews were there, looking for celebrities. All around them, the other playgoers were making the same speculations as Marian and Page. Did Richard really do all the things Sheila thinks he did, or is she guilty of a horrible mistake in judgment? Maybe she's doing it deliberately, and *she's* the villain? Neither is a villain; they're both just imperfect. Naw, they're both villains. Too much hostility between brother-in-law and sister-in-law—it'll destroy the family, you'll see.

"Well, this is a surprise!" said a pleasant female voice. "The law takes a night off to go to the theater?"

Marian looked around to see Elizabeth Tanner beaming over her head at Page, looking more than ever like a movie star. With her was a balding, nice-looking man of about fifty with a half-smile on his face.

"Hello, Elizabeth," Page said with a sigh. "Enjoying the play?"

"Love it, simply *love* it. It's going to be a big hit, don't you think? Do you know my husband? Dr. Frank Tanner. Darling, this is Trevor Page, and, ah, Sergeant, ah."

"Marian Larch," Marian said, wondering if Elizabeth Tanner called her husband *Dr. Frank* at home.

"I wish you'd told me you were coming tonight," the other woman was saying to Page. "We could have made arrangements to come together."

"Ah, what a pity," Page said expressionlessly.

Dr. Frank smiled his half-smile.

"But now that we've run into each other," his wife went on, "we could meet later for a drink? Or a bite to eat, perhaps? How does that sound?"

"Lovely," Page said, "but Marian and I have already made plans for later. Maybe some other time."

Elizabeth Tanner looked at Marian for the first time. "I'm so sorry you were thrown out of the office this afternoon. But you have to understand, Edgar is getting a little paranoid. He's not used to having police all over the place."

She doesn't like my being here with Page, Marian thought. And: *No, I will not play this bitchy game.* "That's perfectly all right, Mrs. Tanner," Marian said in her cop-on-duty voice. "We pretty much got what we came for."

Tanner got the message; there was even a sparkle of amusement in her eyes. Just then the chimes sounded to summon them to the second half of the play. "Time to go in," she said brightly. "Trevor, you must come to our place soon, so we can all get better acquainted. Perhaps next week?"

Page made a noncommittal noise.

Elizabeth Tanner remembered to flash a smile at Marian and headed back into the theater. Dr. Frank trailed after her, the half-smile still on his face. He hadn't said a word the whole time.

The diplomatic thing would have been to keep silent, but Marian wasn't feeling very diplomatic at the moment. "Do you two have a history?" she asked.

"No," Page said emphatically, and then laughed. "It's just that Elizabeth is interviewing potential fourth husbands, and I seem to have made the list of candidates."

They went back inside. "For insurance, you mean?" Marian said as they took their seats. "Since her first two husbands died on her?"

"Something like that. Elizabeth works very hard at the 'total woman' game. Being a high-powered business executive isn't enough. She wouldn't dream of living her life without a husband somewhere in the background to give her respectability—one that doesn't make too many demands, of course. And she's had exactly one child, enough to authenticate her womanhood. When I first met Elizabeth, she talked a great deal about motherhood but very little about her son. And oh yes—she paints or sculpts or something, to give expression to her 'creative' side. What a cliché Elizabeth is.''

Marian didn't know whether to laugh or to feel sorry for the woman. She was glad when the lights went down and the curtains opened on Act II of *The Apostrophe Thief*.

The battles prepared for in the first act were now being fought, and the weapons the two antagonists used were the other characters in the play. Skirmish after skirmish was played out, with each one changing the lives of the participants in some way. About halfway through the act came the only scene in the play in which the two co-stars were alone together on the stage. It was a strange, edgy scene, in which it only gradually dawned on the audience that these two adversaries were attracted to each other, the way soldiers sometimes come to love their enemies. Sheila and Richard circled each other warily, dancing around this unexpected erotic element that had emerged to confuse what had been up to then a clear-cut hostility. But in the end each of them saw responding to their mutual attraction as a form of capitulation, and they both backed off.

"Whew," Trevor Page said.

A murmur ran through the audience, and there was much shifting of weight in the seats. Marian sat there with her mouth open. That scene was one of the most sensual things she'd ever seen, and the two actors had never once so much as touched each other. Whew indeed.

The play ended with the two generals of the internecine war figuratively killing each other off. Sheila was successful in her attempt to dislodge Richard from his position of authority in the family business and within the family itself, but she wasn't able to do so without discrediting herself as well. The result of all their manipulating had been to draw the other characters together in a new unified front against them both. The last thing the audience saw was the entire family gathered together around a buffet table, laughing quietly and talking, making plans, in a scene of subdued celebration from which Sheila and Richard were excluded. Those two sat on opposite sides of the stage, apart from the others, staring at each other, wondering what had gone wrong.

The curtains closed. Dead silence.

Then a roar exploded from the audience—cheering, clapping, even some yelling from the more vociferous of the playgoers. Marian didn't know much about playwriting or the craft of acting, but she did know she'd witnessed something extraordinary that evening. So did everyone else in the audience; during the curtain calls, they greeted each member of the cast as a new Olivier. And when Kelly and Ian Cavanaugh at last appeared, holding hands and smiling, the noise was deafening.

Then Cavanaugh did a gracious thing. With a little bow and a one-handed gesture toward Kelly, he made his final exit of the night, yielding the stage to his co-star. As one person, the audience rose to its feet, excitedly cheering the new star they'd seen created that night. Marian's hands hurt from pounding them together so hard. A man approached from the side of the stage, handed Kelly a huge bouquet of flowers, and disappeared.

Kelly Ingram stood there alone, with her triumph and her armful of flowers, openly basking in the waves of approval that flowed up to her from the audience. For the first time, Marian began to understand why her friend had been drawn to the acting profession in the first place. On impulse she turned to Trevor Page; they wrapped their arms around each other in a big hug, sharing the good feeling the evening had generated. On the stage, with a natural performer's instinct that had nothing to do with experience, Kelly knew the exact moment that the applause peaked and made a graceful, smiling exit.

Marian collapsed back into her seat. She was totally, utterly exhausted.

SEVENTEEN

BACKSTAGE, the Broadhurst was wall-to-wall people. With Trevor Page in tow, Marian tried to work her way through the amiable, jostling crowd toward Kelly Ingram's dressing room. A TV camera was recording the cheerful chaos for posterity, or at least until the next newscast. A shouted interview was being carried out with a television actor, a former co-star of Kelly's. He thought the play was real terrif, he said.

The door to Kelly's dressing room was open, and the well-wishers and congratulators crowded in there were showing no sign of leaving. Marian gave up on trying to work her way in and looked around to find she'd lost Page. She found a place against the wall out of the crush where she could wait for the crowd to thin.

After a while it did, although plenty of lingerers remained. Page *excuse-me*d his way over to Marian, laughing at the scene he found himself in. "This is almost as good a show back here. Have you seen Kelly yet?"

"Can't get in. I thought I'd just wait—you don't mind, do you?"

"Mind? I wouldn't miss it for the world."

Eventually Kelly shooed all her visitors out so she could take off her make-up and change. When she came out of the dressing room, she spotted Marian against the wall and started toward her; but four or five people closed around her and hurried her toward the stage door. Kelly looked back over her shoulder and called out to Marian, "Bradenton Towers, penthouse apartment A!" Then she was gone.

Marian and Page looked at each other. "Do you suppose that was a clue?" the latter asked.

"Could well be. Care to check it out?"

"By all means."

It took them a while to get a cab, but at last they found one that took them to the Bradenton Towers building in the East Eighties. The condominium had a doorman dressed the way all doormen used to be dressed, like a general in a Franz Lehar operetta. "Name?" the general barked. Marian told him her name, wondering if she should add her rank and serial number. The doorman checked a list he had, nodded, and marched away.

"I think we're supposed to follow," Page said.

The military doorman unlocked an elevator, commanded them inside, and punched a button marked A. He stood at parade rest as the door began to close, inspecting them. At the last second Page snapped him a salute.

The elevator door opened in a foyer of a luxurious apartment already crowded with people. When no one appeared to meet them or check their credentials or whatever, Marian and Page exchanged a look and a shrug and joined the party. Most of the people there were clustered in three little islands, the centers of which were Kelly Ingram, Ian Cavanaugh, and a small, dark woman. "That's Abigail James," Marian told Page.

A roving waiter came by and gave them each a glass of champagne. A buffet table had been set up along one wall, but the party guests were still riding their high from the play and weren't yet interested in food. "I wonder who our host is," Page said.

After a while the group around Abigail James was down to two people; Marian and Page joined them. When their turn came to talk, they introduced themselves and expressed their enthusiasm for the play, trying to avoid the usual clichés. The playwright answered with what was obviously a practiced public persona, polite but distant.

Then Marian asked *the* question. "Ms James, we were wondering if you would explain about the title. *The Apostrophe Thief* ... what does it mean?"

A pronounced change came over Abigail James. First she looked startled, then a smile appeared on her face—a genuine one, not one manufactured for public appearances. "Do you know," she said, "you are the *only* person to ask me that?" Marian shot a glance at Cavanaugh. "No, not even Ian," the playwright went on. "Theater people would die rather than admit they don't understand something about a play."

"*No* one has asked you?" Page said skeptically.

"No one. Not the producer, not the director, not any of the cast. But since you did ask, I'll tell you. It doesn't mean a blessed thing." She laughed at their blank looks. "I just liked the sound of those words together, 'apostrophe' and 'thief.' High-handed thing to do, I know, but I was fairly certain no one would question it—not that I wouldn't have told the truth, if anyone had bothered to ask. Now all that remains is to see whether any of the critics will point out that the newest play on Broadway has an utterly meaningless title."

Marian and Page were both laughing by the time she'd finished. "Abby?" Ian Cavanaugh appeared behind her, then spoke over her head to the other two. "You'll excuse me, I hope—I must steal her from you." He didn't remember Marian.

When they were gone, Page laughed again. "No meaning at all. I feel cheated."

"Do you?" Marian said. "I don't." She looked over to where Kelly was surrounded by her usual contingent of admiring men and decided to butt in. "We've waited long enough," she said, putting down her champagne glass. "Come on."

The minute Kelly saw her she walked away from her admirers to meet her. The two women smiled speechlessly for a moment and then hugged each other close, both of them happy and excited.

After waiting so long to speak to her friend, Marian suddenly found she had no words. "Kelly, I am in *awe* of you!" she finally got out.

Kelly's smile got even bigger. "Never thought I'd hear that from *you*. Awe, huh? I hope it lasts at least ten minutes. Tell me I did good."

"You don't need me to tell you that, but I'll tell you anyway. You were better than good. You were magnificent. Sounds melodramatic, but it's the only word that fits. You *were* magnificent."

Kelly pursed her lips in mock-judgmental style. "I don't think it sounds melodramatic at all. I can live with magnificent. So, this good-looking man here—is he with you?" If Kelly was surprised at seeing someone other than Brian, she didn't let on.

"This is Trevor Page," Marian said. "Trevor, meet Kelly Ingram."

"It's an honor to meet you," Page said. "Just as it was an honor to be in that audience tonight. This is a night I will never forget."

"I like him," Kelly said to Marian.

They sat down on a sofa, Kelly in the middle, and talked of the play, of scary moments (from the actors' point of view) when things almost went wrong, of Kelly's relief that her first opening night was now behind her. After a bit, Page slipped away and left the two friends alone. Marian apologized for sounding proprietary, but, she said, she was so proud of Kelly she felt she was going to burst.

Kelly said she didn't mind at all. "You know, Friday isn't the best day of the week for an opening. We'll probably be here all night, and we have two performances tomorrow. I'll have to get up at the crack of noon when I should be sleeping."

"Does that bother you?" Marian asked. "Would you rather sleep than perform?"

Kelly made a face. "Hell, no. I wish we had *three* performances tomorrow."

That would change, they both knew, as soon as the excitement of the debut wore off. Marian was happy for her friend for another reason. If anyone had earned the right to put on airs a little, it was Kelly Ingram. But she was the same good-humored, self-ironic woman she'd been the entire three years Marian had known her. Maybe that too would change, in time, as her prominence in the theater grew. But Marian didn't think so. For one thing, Kelly had already enjoyed a sizable amount of celebrity from her television career, and that hadn't spoiled her. Besides, Kelly was just too *Kelly* to let herself be swayed by the flatterers and the sycophants her newfound status was bound to attract.

Marian glanced up to see Page talking to Ian Cavanaugh on the other side of the room. Kelly followed her look and said, "Who is he, Marian?"

"FBI."

Kelly laughed. "I ask you to tell me about a man you show up with on my opening night and all you can say is 'FBI'?"

Marian grinned. "I'm just getting to know him, Kel. He seems nice—but then, so did Brian, once."

Kelly sighed theatrically. "Thank *god* you mentioned him first! I was being so careful not to say the word 'Brian' until you did. What happened?"

"I'm not really sure. He seems to have turned into a monster sometime when I wasn't looking. Or at least his behavior has been monstrous lately. Oh, I don't want to go over all that, Kelly. Brian is out of my life now. That's the way he wants it."

"What about you?"

"That's the way I want it too."

"Are you sure?"

"Absolutely. The whole thing was a mistake anyway."

"Well, I will say you don't look as if you're about to jump out a window, so I guess I'll have to take your word for it. How'd you happen to hook up with the FBI?"

Marian told her a little about the East River Park murders, but not much; tonight was Kelly's night and Marian's concerns could wait. The hour was growing late; Kelly and her friends were waiting for the reviews, but that was a ritual special to them and Marian didn't want to intrude. She mouthed *Let's go* to Trevor Page across the room.

When he came over to say goodbye, Kelly said, "Listen, there are still some kinks to be worked out in the performance, but in another week or so we ought to have it right. Marian, would you and Bri—, um, Trevor like to see the play again?"

"Yes!" they said together.

"Sure you don't want to talk it over?" Kelly asked, deadpan. "Okay, I'll leave tickets at the box office again. Marian, I'll call you when we're ready."

They thanked her enthusiastically, congratulated her again on her successful debut, and left the party. In the elevator on the way down, Page said, "You know, I didn't get to taste one thing from that sumptuous buffet table. Would you like to stop for something to eat? I promise not to ask you whose name Kelly almost called me by."

"Yes, I could do with a bite," Marian said, taking him at his word about Brian. Then it hit her: if Page didn't know about Brian, Curt Holland must have kept that degrading scene at the gallery to himself. That surprised her.

They went to a West Side deli that wasn't crowded at that hour. At first they relived moments of the play, enjoying it all over again. Then the talk turned more personal. Page was a widower and had been for almost ten years. He'd worked for various government agencies, the last eight for the FBI. Marian said she couldn't remember the day when she didn't want to be a cop, but now the job was beginning to get to her more than it used to. He asked if she'd ever considered working for the Bureau; she said she hadn't. They talked about that for a while.

"It's not a bed of roses," Page said, "but you'd find the working conditions rather better than with the NYPD."

Marian laughed shortly. "Anything would offer better working conditions than the Ninth Precinct. I'm not sure I'd fit into your organization, Trevor. But I'll think about it."

"Good." He bit into a sour pickle and changed the subject. "I do like kosher food. These pickles are good, aren't they? I can't stand sweet pickles."

"Me either. Sounds like a contradiction in terms, doesn't it? Sweet pickle."

"Pickle relish is even worse."

"And yellow mustard."

Page nodded. "And greasy popcorn."

Marian went on with the game. "Magazine inserts."

"Television commercials."

"Oh, everybody hates television commercials," Marian scoffed.

"All right." He thought a second. "Newscasters who say Massa*too*setts."

"Very good. Pay channels that cut their movies and then pretend they're showing them complete."

"Newspaper ink that rubs off on your hands."

"Paperback books that fall apart *in* your hands."

"Raisin bagels."

"Ballpark organists."

"Country music."

"Plaid shirts."

"Plaid shirts?"

Marian nodded. "Especially wool ones."

"Hm. Sunflower kernels."

"I *love* sunflower kernels!"

It was three A.M. when they finally decided to call it a night. In the taxi on the way home Page asked if he could

come up; Marian said no. When the driver stopped in front
of Marian's building, Page asked again. She said no again.
They thanked each other for a wonderful time. Good night.

Upstairs, Marian wondered if she'd done the right thing;
it would have been the perfect ending to the perfect evening. It was sheer stubborn pride that had made her turn
him away; Marian didn't want to be one of those women
who knew no way to bounce back from a disastrous love
affair other than to hop into bed with the first man who
looked at her. Besides, there would be time later. If Trevor
Page was the man she thought he was, there would always
be time.

MARIAN WOKE UP after four hours' sleep feeling marvel-
ous. She dressed quickly and started a pot of coffee. While
the coffee was perking she ran down to a newsstand and
bought copies of all the papers she thought might carry reviews of *The Apostrophe Thief*. She picked up a couple of
bagels (no raisins) and hurried back upstairs. The coffee was
ready; she poured herself a cup and toasted one of the bagels before sitting down to read.

One review was mixed, but the others were raves. The one
in *USA Today* was of the a-star-is-born variety, running a
colorful picture of Kelly glaring heatedly at Ian Cavanaugh. But McPaper was for people who found television
news too complex; what the *New York Times* said was more
important. And the *Times* loved it. The writing, the directing, the acting, even the stage set—all were greeted as the
long-awaited cure for the legendary fabulous invalid's myr-
iad ailments. When Marian had finished the last review, she
went back and read them all again, savoring the words. Not
one of the reviews attempted to explain the title of the play.

But Kelly had made it. From now on she would be accepted as a serious, legitimate actress. No more sexpot roles.
No more fluff TV series. As of last night, Kelly Ingram was
exactly where she belonged: in a hit Broadway play.

Inevitably Marian's thoughts turned to the man she'd gone to the Broadhurst Theatre with the night before. She and Trevor Page were on different wavelengths politically, but she had to admit she liked just about everything else about him. He was a comfortable man to be with, and that was important, probably the *most* important thing to Marian. Little scenes and snatches of their conversations flashed into her head. Trevor wiping brown mustard off his mouth as they sat on a bench eating hot dogs. Trevor quietly and without rancor explaining why Curt Holland hated him. Trevor bringing her breakfast in the stationhouse Friday morning. Trevor telling her he'd never been in Edgar Quinn's apartment.

Oh shit.

Oh shit.

Marian's buoyant mood burst like a pricked bubble. He'd lied to her. Trevor Page had lied to her. He said he'd never been there, but he'd been in that apartment more than once, if Quinn's manservant could be believed. But why would he lie about a thing like that? Or perhaps it was the manservant who was lying? What did it mean?

Before she could figure out an answer, her doorbell rang. She looked through the eyehole and made a sound of surprise; it was Curt Holland. Marian opened the door. "How'd you get in the building?"

The shadows under his eyes were blacker than ever and his face was pinched and gray; deep creases ran down his cheeks and he needed a shave. Holland lifted a corner of his mouth in the half-smile, half-sneer that seemed to be his most characteristic expression. "Your security system here isn't the world's greatest. I walked right through it."

With the help of a lockpick or two? "I'll speak to the super. Did you want something?"

He looked at her a moment before answering. Then he said, "Are you truly an honest cop?"

Irritated, Marian replied, "That's a dumb question. Would I tell you if I wasn't?"

He waited a beat and then repeated slowly, "*Are* you an honest cop?"

What the hell? "Yes, I am, dammit. What's this all about?"

Holland pushed past her into the apartment. "I hope to god you are, because I can't nail him alone. Tell me who you think is behind the East River Park murders."

She closed the door. "Edgar Quinn. And an accomplice."

He looked her straight in the eye. "Right. And I know who the accomplice is."

Marian got a sinking feeling. "Who?"

"Trevor Page."

EIGHTEEN

"YOU *HATE* TREVOR PAGE," Marian accused.

Holland folded his arms and looked down his nose at her. "Therefore anything I say about him will be suspect. Correct?"

"I didn't say that."

"Yes, you did. You're quite right, of course—I despise the man. The reason—well, you needn't concern yourself about that."

"I already know the reason. He forced you to stop being a criminal and become a criminal-catcher."

For the first time since she'd known him, Holland looked surprised. "He told you that? Amazing... I wonder what he thought he had to gain. Sergeant, I want you to repeat to me what he said."

Marian sat down on the arm of the sofa. "What's the point? What difference does it make now?"

"I think the point is which one of us you're going to believe." He was overarticulating his words. "What did he tell you?"

With some reluctance Marian repeated the story about Page's supervisor discovering that Holland was moving funds illegally in order to collect on legitimate debts, earning a big commission on each transaction. She said the supervisor had offered Holland a choice between prosecution or putting his skills to work for the FBI. The supervisor, now dead, had passed his information on to Page, who now stood as the foremost threat to Holland's freedom. "I suppose you're going to tell me all that is one big lie," she finished.

"No," Holland said pensively. "In fact, it's fairly accurate—except that part about the supervisor. There was no supervisor. It was all Page's doing."

Marian stared at him. "I don't believe you."

Both corners of his mouth lifted. "What a surprise. I think I'd better tell you what I found, from the beginning. Do I smell coffee? Could I have a cup?"

"Sure, come on." She led him into the kitchen.

"You certainly read a lot of newspapers," Holland said, clearing off the table while she poured them both some coffee. "What shall I do with these?"

"Don't throw those out! Put them, uh, just put them on the counter there."

After they'd sat down and Holland had had a long swallow of coffee, he dropped a bombshell. "I found the money connection between Evan Christopher and Jason O'Neill."

"What? The arms dealer? It's not Edgar Quinn? Well . . . that's it, then, isn't it?"

"Wait, hear me out. As far as arms dealers go, Evan Christopher was not exactly one of the big boys. He kept all his money in one account in Geneva, except for a getaway stash in a Cayman Islands bank. I got into his Geneva account and started tracing his payments. He knew enough to shift the funds around some before they finally ended up where they were going, so it took a lot of time to chase each one down. But one of the payment trails finally led to a bank in Vienna, to an account in Jason O'Neill's name. Two payments, in fact, the last one only a week before the murders."

"Then Jason O'Neill did sell Universal Laser secrets."

"I don't think so. The dates on the bank entries jibe with the theory that O'Neill was selling out, the second payment coming so close to the murders as it does. If you look at only the bank entries, it appears pretty cut-and-dried. Jason O'Neill was dealing with bad people and they killed him."

"But you looked at something else," Marian said, not seeing where this was going.

"I looked at the bank's computer directory—I always check the directories, it's automatic for me. One thing the directory tells you is the dates the last times the various files were used. And the last time Jason O'Neill's account file was open was last Monday—two days after he died."

"I don't see what you're getting at. O'Neill wouldn't have had access to his bank account file anyway. Someone else was looking at it, someone who works at the bank."

"Possibly," Holland said, "except that every other bank file the money traveled through on its deliberately meandering journey from Evan Christopher to Jason O'Neill was also used on Monday. A rather extraordinary coincidence, wouldn't you say?"

Marian began to see. "It's not just someone else trying to trace the payments, is it?"

"Ah, you've spotted it." He looked pleased. "All that the directories indicate is the date the last time a file was *used*— that could be either the last time someone looked at an already existing file, or it could be the time the file was originated. But the back-up systems the banks use can tell you the difference. Just by checking the earliest date a file appears on the system, you know when it originated. And here's the point. Every single file connected with the money transfer between Christopher and O'Neill was originated last Monday."

"A set-up," Marian said wonderingly. "It's an elaborate set-up. To incriminate Jason O'Neill. That entire money trail was planted for you to find?"

"Exactly right. Sergeant, are you going to eat that other bagel?"

"What? Oh—no, help yourself."

Holland took the bagel to Marian's cutting board, sliced it in two, and popped the two halves into the toaster oven. "I was meant to find the money connection—which is genuine, by the way. Funds really were transferred. But the Vienna account in Jason O'Neill's name didn't exist before last Monday. So unless O'Neill discovered a way to do his banking posthumously, we were meant to find the account and say, 'Oh, well, that proves it. Case closed.'" He brought his toasted bagel back to the table. "Don't you have any cream cheese?"

"No... you'll have to use butter. But look, the fact that a phony money trail exists doesn't prove Trevor Page planted it. How could he get into all those banks' computers to diddle the records?"

Holland chewed and swallowed before answering. "It's not generally known, but the FBI collects access codes the way small boys collect baseball cards. Part of my, ah, induction into that august organization required me to explain my techniques of money transfer and donate all my laboriously acquired access codes. Most of the codes have been changed by now, but that's not the point. The point is that large numbers of codes are available to Page for the asking—all he had to do was select four or five banks and move Evan Christopher's money through them. And Page knows how to do it, because *I* taught him."

Marian nodded reluctantly, thinking about it while Holland finished his bagel. She was trying not to show how shocked she was; Holland's news had hit her like a fist in the stomach. If only she didn't like Trevor Page so much—ye gods, she'd even thought about sleeping with him. It was hard to cast a man she'd responded to that strongly in the role of villain, just like that; she needed time to adjust. But if Holland was right, Page was lost for good. Marian sighed and decided she needed a refresher course in How To Pick Your Men. "Holland," she said, "why did you come to me?"

"Process of elimination," he answered. "If I took this to your Captain DiFalco, he'd turn it into a political weapon. Your boss is dying to establish his own personal hot line to the FBI, and he's been cultivating Page to that end. Did you know Page had dinner at DiFalco's house earlier this week?"

"No, I didn't! Neither one of them mentioned it."

"They wouldn't. So DiFalco was out. As for the others—Foley is mentally incontinent, Sanchez would fall asleep on me, Roberts is a baby—"

"All right, I get the picture. And I accept the possibility that Page set up the false money trail. Edgar Quinn wouldn't have the kind of information necessary to do the job—the access codes and the like. It had to be someone with inside knowledge. But that still doesn't prove it was Page. There is one other candidate."

"Who?"

"You."

He looked at her through slitted eyes, his mouth turned down. "What's my motive?"

"What's Page's motive? I still don't know what this is all about. Do you?"

He expelled air from his lungs. "No, I don't know the *why*. But would I tell you the money transfer was a set-up if I'd planted it myself?"

"It doesn't seem likely," she admitted, and thought a moment. "There may be a way of resolving this—something I remembered just before you got here. Trevor Page told me he'd never been in Quinn's apartment, and Quinn's manservant mentioned he'd been there several times."

"When was this?"

"Ah...Thursday. Lewis—the manservant—was trying to get a wine stain out of the carpet. He said Page had caused it, although *he'd never spilled anything before*. That means he'd been there more than once."

"You're sure of all this?"

"I can hear Page's voice in my head right now asking me what Quinn's apartment is like, there's no mistake about that. But the manservant could have been wrong, or I could

have misunderstood him. That's something I can check."
Marian found Quinn's home number in her notebook and
tapped it out.

"Do you have an extension?" Holland asked.

"In the bedroom," she replied, and pointed. When she
heard the manservant's voice on the line, she said, "Lewis?
This is Sergeant Larch, NYPD. You had the pleasure of
tossing me out of Mr. Quinn's apartment a couple of days
ago."

"Ah yes, I remember it well," Lewis said. "The most exciting thing that happened all week."

"Hm. Lewis, you told me Trevor Page made that wine
stain on the carpet. Are you positive it was Page?"

"Perfectly positive. Absolutely sure. And even dead
cert."

"Did you see him do it?"

"No, but he was the only one in the room other than Mr.
Quinn, and I told you Mr. Quinn doesn't drink wine. Are
you suggesting we bill him for cleaning expenses?"

"How often has Trevor Page been there?"

"May I ask why this all-consuming interest in Mr. Page's
activities?"

"Lewis, please—it's important."

A heavy sigh came over the wire. "Oh, very well. He's
been here on half a dozen occasions that I know of, possibly more. I'm not here all the time. They do let me out once
in a while, you know."

"When was the last time Page was there?"

"Wednesday night. Sergeant, I enjoy Twenty Questions
as much as anyone, but I am growing weary of this little
game. Is there anything more you're going to ask me?"

"One thing more. Did the stain come out?"

"Like a dream."

Marian thanked him and hung up.

"He sounds English," Holland said, coming out of the
bedroom. "Well? Are you convinced?"

"Yes," she said. "Page lied about being on personal terms with Edgar Quinn. It was Page who brought the conveniently dead Evan Christopher to my attention. And Page had the means for setting up the false money trail."

"Conveniently dead—yes. Page is the supreme opportunist. A man he's never met has an accident in his home, and Page finds a way to use it."

"One thing I don't get. If you taught him all about how to move money around, why did he leave the dates in the banks' back-up systems to give him away?"

Holland smiled, this time with his eyes. "I didn't say I taught him *everything* I know."

Marian shook her head. "It's hard to think of Page as Edgar Quinn's accomplice—I sort of had Elizabeth Tanner pegged for that role."

"Page isn't Quinn's accomplice—it's the other way around. They're in it together, but Page is the one with the initiative. Quinn can be led."

Elizabeth Tanner had once said the same thing. "So now what?" Marian asked. "Wait a minute—Page set up the phony money trail on Monday? But that's the day he went to Washington."

Holland thought back. "You're right, that's the day he *said* he was going to Washington. That's my next step—I'll check with the FBI there. I hope I don't have to go to Washington." He went toward the phone; but before he could pick it up, it rang.

It was the Ninth Precinct desk sergeant. Captain DiFalco wanted Sergeant Larch at the stationhouse toot sweet.

"READ THAT," DiFalco commanded.

It was the lab report on blood traces found on one of the platform trucks Universal Laser used for moving office equipment around. The hematologist had been able to identify the DNA code of one of them; it was Conrad Webb's blood. "Bingo," Marian said.

"So now we know where the murders were committed and how they got the bodies out of the building," DiFalco said. "None of the protective mats had blood on them, though—the killers must have tossed them. But why'd they bring the platform truck back?"

"The trucks I saw all had numbers stenciled on them," Marian told him. "Someone was keeping track."

"Yah, that must be it. Okay, reconstruction time. From the beginning. Talk it through for me."

Marian thought a moment. "The beginning is the project Universal Laser is developing independent of the Defense Department, not Project Soundbender but the hush-hush one only a handful of people know about. The Washington liaison group was in on it—Conrad Webb, Sherman Bigelow, Herb Vickers, and Jason O'Neill. That sounds to me as if Edgar Quinn was about ready to go to the government with it. But whatever the project is, it's been kept secret from most of Universal's employees as well as from the Defense Department.

"But one of the liaison group let the cat out of the bag—one of them either sold information or was careless or whatever, but the whole company knew something had gone terribly wrong even if they didn't know what it was. Now this part is sheer speculation. Even the three innocent members of the liaison party didn't know which of their group was responsible, so they got together Saturday afternoon at Jason O'Neill's apartment to try to protect themselves by ferreting out the guilty one. They didn't succeed in fingering the talker, but they thought of a way they might find out and it involved going into Universal's offices—probably to check some records or correspondence or the like."

"That's a hell of a lot of speculating," DiFalco said.

"I know, but it's the only way this mess makes any sense. They couldn't go into the offices right away—for reasons unknown—so they hung out at O'Neill's place until around six o'clock. O'Neill had called his girlfriend at three and told her he'd be late. That meant they had to wait three hours to go check whatever they had in mind. But at around six they did go in, signing in with the security guard. The guard was sick, and the killers were already in the building, having just walked in during one of the times the guard was in the men's room."

"They could have made an appointment with the killers," DiFalco said. "That would account for their hanging around for three hours until it was time for the meet."

"Entirely possible," Marian agreed. "But whether the group was surprised to find the killers there or only surprised to find they were *killers*, all four murders took place in the offices of Universal Laser Technologies. One of the killers held a thirty-eight on the four men while the other killer handcuffed them together. Then one by one each man was shot, through the right eye, because the killers themselves didn't know which of the four men had blabbed. The message was 'See what happens when you talk?' and it was aimed at the other Universal people who are working on the clandestine project. The bodies were loaded on a platform truck, and they must have been covered by a couple of mats. Let's see, now, how would that work?"

"Speed it up, will you?" DiFalco said. "I have to be downtown in ten minutes."

"All right, I think I've got it. The two killers took the platform with the bodies into the elevator and down to the second floor. One of the killers remained with the bodies while the other walked down to the first floor, staying in the stairwell and watching until the guard got up and went to the men's room. Then the killer left the stairwell and hit the button that brought the elevator down to the ground floor. That's about the only way they could have worked it. They pushed the platform outside, loaded the bodies into the van they'd already stolen—that's premeditation right there. One of them sneaked the platform truck back in, and they drove the van to East River Park and dumped the bodies where they were sure to be seen. The protective mats must have had blood on them so they ditched them somewhere, the river maybe, and abandoned the stolen van on South Street. How does that sound?"

"It sounds damned good," DiFalco said, getting up from behind his desk.

"Wait a minute, Captain, I have something else. Curt Holland told me—"

"I can't wait," he said. "Trevor Page and I are making a joint statement to the press. I've got to get downstairs."

"Trevor Page?"

"There've been some new developments. That's why I called you in—I've got a surprise for you."

"But it's Page who was Quinn's partner!" Marian said to his retreating back. He didn't hear, or didn't want to. On her way to the stationhouse, she'd decided she didn't have the right to remain silent about what Holland had told her, despite the FBI man's misgivings concerning Captain Di-Falco. But Page was here, now...downstairs? A hard knot burned in her chest.

What was this press announcement about? She hurried downstairs after DiFalco.

NINETEEN

DOWNSTAIRS at the Ninth Precinct stationhouse, the high-ceilinged main room was crowded with reporters and camera operators. Captain DiFalco and Trevor Page were standing with their backs against the battered, chest-high brass rail that separated the main desk from the sad stream of supplicants, complainers, nuts, and real victims that flowed through the stationhouse. The desk sergeant had left his seat and moved aside, safely out of the camera shots. No chance for a little stolen limelight with *two* Big Cheeses on the scene.

Marian found herself a place behind a file cabinet and watched. From where she stood, she had a three-quarters rear view of Page; he hadn't seen her yet. Again she felt that deep sense of loss. And she was uneasy for another reason; she should have thrown a hammerlock on DiFalco and *made* him listen before he appeared before the cameras shoulder-to-shoulder with Trevor Page. Since they were on Di-Falco's home turf, the captain spoke first.

"Thank you for coming," he said in a voice deeper than the one he normally used. "As you know, the Ninth Precinct and the FBI have been cooperating in the investigation of the East River Park murders." Not the *police* and the FBI, Marian noticed, but the Ninth Precinct; DiFalco was squeezing it for all he could get. "This joint effort has produced results that neither agency could have obtained alone. I'm pleased to announce that we expect to take one of the two perpetrators into custody shortly."

What's this?

DiFalco cleared his throat. "We have a warrant for the arrest of Edgar Quinn, president and major stockholder of Universal Laser Technologies."

"What?" Marian cried, her voice lost in the buzz of excitement from the news reporters.

DiFalco raised a hand to silence the reporters. "We're looking for Mr. Quinn now. He's not in his home, but we're sure he hasn't had time to leave the city."

Marian was thunderstruck. What was he doing, what in the *hell* was he doing? Getting a warrant, deciding the case was solved, making a public announcement before Quinn was in custody... all without so much as consulting her?

DiFalco went on, "Conrad Webb, Sherman T. Bigelow, Herbert Vickers, and Jason O'Neill were all killed in an attempt to keep secret a project Universal Laser has been working on. We have only recently learned that the project in question is a laser handgun."

Marian gasped, as did every other cop in the room. The reporters looked at them uncertainly, not grasping the significance.

"I'm sure I don't have to explain what this means," DiFalco said, and then proceeded to do just that. "A laser handgun would deprive law enforcement agencies all over the world of one of their most important defenses against crime. We've all seen make-believe laser pistols in the movies," he went on, milking it, "guns that shoot laser beams instead of bullets. You hear what I'm saying? No bullets. And no bullets means no ballistics. Without ballistics, a good ninety percent of firearms-related crimes would go unsolved. Without the deterrent of punishment, crime itself would skyrocket and become totally out of control. I want to take this opportunity to call upon the lawmakers of this country to pass immediate legislation to outlaw the manufacture, sale, and distribution of laser handguns."

An uproar broke out among the reporters. Marian was stunned. A laser handgun—no wonder Quinn wanted it kept secret. But what was Trevor Page doing taking part in this public announcement? And when did he and DiFalco work out the details? Why had DiFalco shut her out? She felt her face growing hot with anger; DiFalco had no *right* to make such an announcement.

It was Page's turn to speak. He signaled for quiet and when he got it, said, "The laser handgun has been no threat until now because no one had ever figured out how to make a power pack small enough to fit into the butt of a hand-held weapon. But Universal Laser has come quite close to solving the problem, and Edgar Quinn fully intended to capitalize on it. Quinn entered into partnership with an arms distributor named Evan Christopher, and the two of them together killed Webb, Bigelow, Vickers, and O'Neill when it looked as if one or more of them was leaking the secret."

"What's that name again?" one of the reporters yelled.

"Evan Christopher," Page repeated slowly. "Christopher died last Sunday in a freak accident at his home in Baltimore. We have no evidence that any third party was involved in the East River Park killings."

The reporters started shouting questions. Marian leaned against the wall behind the file cabinet and tried to think. The scenario had changed. Evan Christopher was no longer the big bad arms dealer who'd bribed Jason O'Neill to spill company secrets. Now he was the big bad arms dealer who'd helped Edgar Quinn kill four men. Page must be running scared to pull so drastic a switch. He had to have seen he wasn't going to be able to keep Quinn out of it; his original plan of putting the blame on Jason O'Neill and the near-anonymous Evan Christopher was scrapped and a new one fingering *Quinn* and Christopher substituted instead. Page couldn't have had much time to make up his mind, but what he'd decided was that Quinn would take the heat for both of them. All this time Page had evidently been cultivating Marian and DiFalco both; and sometime since she'd last seen him, he'd concluded he had a better chance with Di-

Falco. What if she'd let him stay last night? Would there have been any press announcement this morning?

The shouting had died down but the reporters' questions continued. Marian barely heard them; she had questions of her own. How had Page managed to convince DiFalco that Evan Christopher was Quinn's partner? And how was he going to explain away the money trail he'd left for Holland to find?

Holland.

If Page somehow knew that Holland had found what he was meant to find...that could become an embarrassment, now that Page was following a new script. Marian had left Holland in her apartment phoning the FBI in Washington. She moved to the nearest telephone and punched out her own number. Busy.

The press conference was over. Captain DiFalco was making his way out the front door, followed by a couple of reporters not quite ready to give up. She ran after them.

"Marian!" she heard Trevor Page call.

She pushed on. She caught up with DiFalco in the parking lot across the street and waited impatiently until he got rid of the reporters. He started to get into his car without acknowledging her.

"Captain! *Captain DiFalco.*" He turned, but before he could speak whatever excuse he had planned, she said, "Correct me if I'm wrong, but didn't you put *me* in charge of this investigation?"

"Of course you're in charge. There's no question—"

"Then what the hell are you doing deciding the case is closed without even telling me?"

His face turned dark. "Hold it. Who do you think you're talking to?"

"I think I'm talking to a police captain who knows better than to ride roughshod over his own investigators but who did it anyhow. I want to know *why.*"

"What's your problem, Larch? Did you change your mind about Quinn's being one of the murderers?"

"No, but—"

"Then what are you bitching about? We'll pick him up."

"I'm *bitching* about the way you've taken it on yourself to decide Evan Christopher was Quinn's partner. What's your evidence?"

He actually moved toward her as if he wanted to hit her. "You'd better get something straight. I don't account for myself to you, *you* account to *me*. You have to be reminded of that?" They stood glaring angrily at each other in the parking lot, the bright midmorning sun making them both squint. Then DiFalco forced himself to relax and went so far as to make a peace offering. "There wasn't time to bring you in on it—this all came up in a hurry. And there *is* evidence. The FBI found a money link between Evan Christopher and Quinn."

So that's how Page did it, the son of a gun. "It's evidence Trevor Page manufactured," Marian said. "He also made up a money link connecting Christopher to Jason O'Neill."

"What?"

"That's what I was trying to tell you when you left for the press conference. Evan Christopher didn't have any illicit connection with Edgar Quinn or Jason O'Neill or anybody else at Universal Laser. He was just a small-time arms dealer who died at the right moment and made a convenient patsy."

"You're telling me Page fabricated evidence just to close the case? You're wrong, Larch, dead wrong. Better forget it before you make yourself look foolish."

"But Captain—"

"I said forget it. This case is *closed*."

Then she understood. "You don't care if you got it right or not. All you want is the arrest. That business in your office before the press conference—what was that all about?"

Having me go over the murders step by step…to make sure there weren't any gaping holes to embarrass you? You don't give a damn who Quinn's partner really is."

He'd grown angry all over again. He moved in close, his face only inches from Marian's. "Larch, you're the best detective I got, but you ain't going *nowhere* until you get down off that goddamned high horse of yours. If you ever, *ever* speak to me like that again, I'll see to it you get every dirty, nasty little job that comes along. You'll spend your days in the Records Department, waiting for your pension. You'll work traffic detail. You'll sweep the floors and empty the wastebaskets and kiss Foley's ass before you ever get a decent case again. *Do I make myself clear?*"

Marian's breath was coming in shallow gasps. "Perfectly clear."

"Good." He got into his car, slammed the door, and drove away.

Marian lumbered over to her own car, still trying to catch her breath. She got in and rolled down the window; early September heat was no different from late August. She could request a transfer to a different precinct, but DiFalco would block it. Play ball, keep your mouth shut, be a good little detective. She started the car and pulled out of the lot.

As she drove she felt the familiar heavy weight of depression. What had happened to make Page change his mind? Last night he'd seemed so relaxed, as if he didn't have a thing to worry about. But then overnight he'd switched from his plan to incriminate Jason O'Neill and was now throwing Edgar Quinn to the wolves. For Page to pull such an about-face, something had to have happened.

Holland. Holland happened.

If there was a way for Page to know that Holland had found the money trail between Christopher and O'Neill but *had not reported it*…oh Jesus. He'd know that Holland had figured it out. Whatever Page and Quinn had once planned for the laser handgun was lost and all of Page's efforts would now be directed toward saving himself. Quinn was missing, maybe dead. And Holland? Holland's life wasn't worth the proverbial plugged nickel.

Praying that he hadn't left her apartment and gone where Page could find him—home, wherever home was, or the FBI building at Federal Plaza, Marian honked her horn anxiously at the car in front of her. When that didn't help, she reached the police light up to the roof of her car, getting her arm tangled in the connecting wire in her haste, and turned on the siren. The traffic ahead of her grudgingly edged over to the right.

No parking space in her block, of course; she pulled up next to a fire hydrant. The elevator took forever. Just as the doors opened at her floor, Marian looked down the hallway and saw Holland coming out of her apartment. "Stop!" she called. She ran down the hall, pushed Holland back inside, and shot all four bolts on the door.

He raised one eyebrow. "If you really want me to stay that badly—"

"Shut up and listen. When you went hunting for the money connection between Evan Christopher and Jason O'Neill, did you leave any kind of computer trail someone else could follow?"

"I left tracks, yes. It takes a lot of time to cover them up, and there was no need."

"Does Page know enough about computers to follow those tracks?"

Holland's eyes narrowed. "Yes, he does. It's not too difficult."

"He knows. He knows you found the trail he left, and you didn't say anything to him about finding it."

"Then he knows I'm on to him. Damnation! We've lost the advantage of surprise."

"It gets worse." She told him about Page and DiFalco's joint press conference, about how Page was sacrificing Quinn to save his own neck, and how the new scenario alled for Quinn and Evan Christopher to be partners in whatever scheme Quinn and Page had had going.

Holland listened carefully, absorbing it all quickly. "And DiFalco wouldn't listen when you told him? I'm not surprised. He's cast his lot with Page now—he'd lose face if he backed out. I've got to keep out of sight. It didn't look as if you were coming back so I was going home to get some sleep, but now I don't dare."

"No, you'll have to stay here. It should be safe—Page wouldn't think of looking for you at my place. There's something else. The hush-hush project that Universal's been working on?"

"The laser handgun, yes."

Marian clamped her lips together so her mouth wouldn't drop open. "How did you know?"

"It seems a number of people in Washington know about that. Let me tell you what I found out. Could we sit down? Not the sofa—I'd fall asleep."

They went back to the kitchen and sat at the table again; Marian tossed her raincoat over the chair back. Holland looked desperately tired, his face gray and bleak. One of the members of Universal Laser's liaison team, he said, had had a conscience. One of them, Webb or O'Neill or Vickers or Bigelow, was disturbed by this new weapon that could kill without leaving any trace except for a hole burned in some hapless victim's body—disturbed to the point where he was trying to do something about it. He'd informed three congressmen and two senators of what Universal Laser was working on and pointed out the need for legislation to suppress the futuristic weapon *before* it was ready for manufacture.

"But he informed them all anonymously," Holland said, "in statements written out on Universal Laser letterhead stationery. He'd managed to leave the letters where the lawmakers themselves were bound to find them, instead of some member of their staffs. And all five lawmakers were

on the liaison team's itinerary during their penultimate trip
to Washington. That's how Quinn knew the leak came from
one of the four men who made up the liaison group.''

"Uh, how?" Marian asked. "How'd we get from Sena
tor Whosit to Edgar Quinn?"

Holland rubbed his eyes. "Sorry, I'm not thinking in se
quence. Senators Wagner and Newbury as well as Con
gressmen Rock and Kincaid all had their staff check out the
story with Universal Laser. Congressman Torelli called Ed
gar Quinn direct. Denials all around, of course. But the in
formant had thoughtfully supplied each of the lawmakers
with the names of the other four he'd notified, so the five of
them got together and decided they were on to something.
They called in the FBI.''

"I was wondering how they got involved," Marian said.
"Page wouldn't have notified them."

But now too many people knew the secret for it to re
main a secret much longer; even the Universal Laser em
ployees who weren't working on the laser handgun had an
inkling of what was going on, thus propelling Quinn and
Page into a monstrous act in a desperate but doomed at
tempt to plug up the holes. Holland said he thought Quinn
must have called in the four members of the liaison team and
accused them as a group. That in turn led to their Saturday
afternoon meeting at Jason O'Neill's place.

Holland put his hands on his hips and stretched his back
without getting up. "It's entirely possible that they did fig
ure out which of them 'betrayed' the company. Then the
other three would have called Edgar Quinn and arranged a
meeting at Universal Laser. Quinn would have put them off
for a few hours, until he had time to contact Page and they
could decide what they wanted to do. So at six o'clock three
of the team forced the informant to accompany them to
meet Quinn...and found Trevor Page with him, armed with
handcuffs and a thirty-eight.''

"And the other three were shot gratuitously, as an object lesson?" Marian shook her head. "I don't think so. Edgar Quinn was genuinely fond of Conrad Webb. He wouldn't have taken part in Webb's murder unless he was convinced it was essential to his own survival. No, it's more likely the liaison team did *not* discover who'd leaked the secret, and they just wanted to meet again with Quinn in one last attempt to clear themselves. The informant would have no choice but to go along. Then when Page and Quinn couldn't identify him, they killed them all. I wonder..." she trailed off.

"What?"

"When the four men were handcuffed together and the first man had been shot through the eye—I wonder if the informant spoke up then and identified himself. He knew he was going to die, but he wouldn't want the others to die because of him."

"Unless the informant was the first one shot."

"Ah." Marian was silent a moment, feeling dejected. "Which one do you suppose it was?"

"Which one do you think?"

"Well, it wasn't Conrad Webb. Webb would cut out his tongue before he'd do anything to harm Universal Laser. Jason O'Neill was too dedicated to climbing the corporate ladder to knock it out from under himself. And I can't see Herb Vickers getting his act together enough to develop a social conscience overnight. That leaves Sherman Bigelow. He was a pretty standup type anyway—just the sort to be bothered by the development of an untraceable weapon."

"I would have said Webb."

"Webb? Why?"

"Primarily because he'd been with Universal Laser since the day it was born. For Webb it would be like watching a child growing up straight and strong and then inexplicably turning twisted. Going to Washington with the story would simply be a way of seeking help.'' Holland's words were becoming slurred.

It was a mystery doomed to stay a mystery. Marian and Holland both realized they'd never know which of the men had tried to stop the development of the laser handgun and whose good intentions had gotten all four members of the liaison team killed. ''What were Page and Quinn planning to do with the damned handgun anyway?'' Marian asked irritably.

Holland tried to stifle a yawn and failed. ''Oh, Page undoubtedly has little groups of people picked out all over the world that he wants to arm with superior weapons. Guerrilla groups, infiltrators. Good guys who'll fight against whatever force Page thinks is threatening the security of the land of the free and the home of the brave—said force subject to lightning-swift change, of course. Page is really a CIA man at heart.''

That made Marian feel more discouraged than ever. ''I can't think what to do next.''

''Nor I. Sergeant, I'm going to have to borrow your sofa for a few hours. I haven't had any sleep since Thursday night, and I'll not be of any help until I've done some catching up.'' He looked ready to collapse right there on the kitchen table.

''Use the bedroom,'' Marian said, putting her raincoat back on. ''I'm going out for a couple of hours anyway.''

''Now? Where are you going?''

''Personal matter,'' she said, and left.

TWENTY

KELLY INGRAM hadn't been up very long and her eyes were still sleepy. "Marian!" she cried. "Did you see the reviews? They *loved* us! Every single one of them loved us! Well, almost every single one. Come in, come in!"

Marian followed her friend into her kitchen, saying nothing but listening closely to Kelly's cheerful morning-after-the-debut chatter. Selfishly, that's what she'd come for; maybe she could absorb some of Kelly's upbeat energy and fight off the glooms. She accepted a cup of coffee but said no to a muffin.

"I was just starting to listen to my phone messages," Kelly was saying. "I had to turn the bell off, or I wouldn't have gotten any sleep at all! I must have a zillion messages—I didn't know I'd given my phone number to that many people. Oh, Marian, it's all worked out better than I ever hoped. Did you read any of the reviews?"

"I read every one I could get my hands on," Marian said. "In fact I read them twice. They all had such *respectful* things to say about you—"

"Yes! That's just it! They treated me with respect, even the one or two critics who were lukewarm about the play. Not one of them so much as mentioned all those tootsie roles I used to play on television. They treated me as if I have a right to be here!"

That brought a faint smile. "Is there any doubt? You do belong on the stage."

"Oh, *I* know that, but I just wasn't sure the rest of New York knew it. But now they do, snicker snicker, and ah ain't a-never gunna let 'em fergit it. Oh, *god,* Marian, I feel so good! Did you know David Lynch was there last night?''

Marian listened quietly as she tried to let herself be drawn into Kelly's world. She wanted to will away all thoughts of laser guns and treacherous FBI agents, of police captains blinded by personal ambition, of the man asleep in her apartment whom even now she had trouble trusting. She tried not to think of the manhunt then in progress, with Edgar Quinn running for his life. And in trying not to think of those things, of course she ended up thinking of nothing else. She brought herself up short and forced herself to listen to what Kelly was saying. Only Kelly wasn't saying anything.

Instead, her friend was looking at her worriedly. "Marian? What is it? What's the matter?"

Marian was feeling too sluggish to pretend to be cheerful but she did manage to say, "Just not enough sleep, Kel, that's all. Listen, I meant to ask you, who hosted the party we went to last night? I never did meet him, or her, or them."

But Kelly just shook her head. "Won't do, Marian. Don't try to change the subject. Something has got you down—I know the signs too well. Come on, tell me. What's eating at you?"

Marian was silent for a long moment, and then for the first time she put into words what had been on her mind for some time. "I'm thinking of resigning from the police force."

Kelly was shocked. She grabbed Marian's hand and started squeezing it, for Marian's comfort or her own neither one of them could say. When Kelly finally got her voice back, she said, "But, but you *love* police work!"

"I used to," Marian said. "It was the only career I ever considered. But the job has changed, or I've changed, or both. I don't like what I'm doing anymore. I don't like the place I work or the people I work with."

"Well, sure, criminals and murderers and—"

"I don't mean them," Marian said with a groan. "I mean the so-called good guys, the cops. The FBI. I don't like any of them, and most of all I don't like seeing them in *my* profession."

Kelly's eyes widened. "FBI? You mean Trevor?"

"Yeah, Trevor too. I've been building up to this for a couple of months, and Trevor Page is just the icing on the cake. Oh, it's all very involved, and all I want is to turn my back on it and walk away. There's another FBI agent, a man I don't completely trust—but I'm going to have to trust him, and I don't like that either. Oh, lord. When you're this miserable about your work, aren't you supposed to do something about it?"

"Like quit?" Kelly asked indignantly. "Is that the only solution you can come up with?"

"Frankly, yes." She thought a minute. "When you're a cop, you know you can never put an end to crime. But you do have a realistic hope of containing it, of limiting the harm it can do. Kelly, I no longer have that hope. Everything's out of control. I'm a cop, and I can't count on the cops anymore."

"You mean they're crooked? On the take?"

"No, not that. It's as if they've all been sucked into an attitude toward their work I can't live with... a way of doing things that pretty much neutralizes any good you might do. I have a captain who's more interested in promoting himself out of the Ninth Precinct than he is in catching the right perpetrator. I have a partner who's turned sour and who was never too bright to begin with. And the FBI...the FBI has been using the police for its own purposes. The end justifies the means, every time. No exceptions."

"Well, now, you know that isn't true," Kelly said pragmatically. "And I'm sorry, Marian, but I just don't believe there's nothing you can do about it. You're the most resourceful person I know, and I can see your situation must be pretty bad if *you* are thinking of giving up. I'd guess you're just kind of overwhelmed right now...but that's only right now. Don't make any decisions while you're feeling so down."

"Oh, I know better than that," Marian said with a faint smile.

"Good." Kelly looked at her watch. "Come talk to me while I get dressed—I'm supposed to be at the theater at one. I want to know what Trevor Page's part is in all this."

Marian was appalled. "The theater? Oh my god, you have a matinee today! I forgot, I completely forgot. Oh, Kelly, I'm sorry—I would never have dumped this on you if I'd—"

"Marian," Kelly said firmly. "Don't be a twitterhead. I would have been hurt if you *hadn't* come. But I don't know any of the details. How much can you tell me about your case? Is Trevor—"

But Marian was on her feet and gathering up her things to go. "Kelly, you should be thinking about your performance this afternoon, not about my problems. Put me out of your mind and concentrate on Sheila and *The Apostrophe Thief*. We'll talk later, I promise. I'll tell you all about the case." She took a deep breath. "I'll even tell you what Trevor Page did."

"*Mar*-ian!"

"'Bye, Kelly. Knock 'em dead." She gave her a quick hug and left.

It had rained while she was in Kelly's apartment, and the air was muggy and heavy. Marian stopped at a deli and loaded up on food, two bags full; there was no knowing how long Holland would have to stay at her place. And Marian needed to eat; she was getting a headache.

The rain started again as she ran from her car to the apartment building. Upstairs, she put the soggy bags down and unlocked all four locks. From the doorway, she could see straight into the bedroom. And what she saw was Curt

Holland, sitting up on the bed, his eyes glazed . . . aiming a gun directly at her.

"Holland," she said softly. "It's me."

When he'd focused on who she was, he lowered his gun and fell back on the bed, asleep again in an instant. Marian's hands were shaking as she turned the bolts in the door behind her.

In the kitchen she opened a carton of chicken salad and dipped in with one of the plastic spoons the deli had provided. But once she had the chicken salad in her mouth, her throat tightened up on her and she couldn't swallow. The day had finally gotten to her, the betrayals and the double-crosses and the sure-fire knowledge of trouble still to come. Noiselessly she slid to the kitchen floor and sat there, her back against a cabinet door and both legs straight out in front of her.

Seeing a loaded gun pointed at her when she came in was the last straw. Marian didn't blame Holland; he was only protecting himself. But getting shot as she entered her own home would have been a fitting climax to the day. The new alliance between DiFalco and Page was a dangerous one; DiFalco was willfully blind and Page was acting out of desperation. Of the two betrayals, Marian resented DiFalco's the most. Even worse than his threats was the dirty trick he'd played, springing his "solution" to the case on her the way he did—in public, so she couldn't stand up and say *Hey, there, Captain—you got it wrong.* She wondered about Edgar Quinn; it was hard to believe Page would let the one man who could incriminate him stay alive. Maybe Quinn was already dead.

If he wasn't, Page would be looking for him, the way he was sure to be looking for Holland. And if he found out Holland had confided in her, she would be next on his list. Trevor Page, the new "interesting" man in her life, would kill her without hesitation if he thought she posed a threat to him. In spite of DiFalco's self-congratulatory winding up of the case, it wasn't over yet. But how to blow the whole thing open before Page did any more killing? And how to keep from getting caught in the fallout? She had no idea; she was tired of the case and tired of thinking about it. How she wanted to walk away! It was as if the little Dutch boy had pulled his thumb out of the hole in the dike and said, ''To hell with this—I'm going home.'' With her eyes closed, Marian could see the cracks spreading across the dike.

What is the matter with me? she thought with a start. *Sitting on the kitchen floor thinking about dikes and deluges! Have I gone completely daft?*

She got to her feet, swallowed the chicken salad she'd been holding in her mouth all that time, and ate some more. She put the perishables away in the refrigerator, took a long drink of tonic water, stumbled in to the sofa, and collapsed.

THE PHONE ringing woke her up.

''Don't answer.'' Holland was standing in the kitchen doorway, holding a plate of deli meats and pasta salad. They listened to the message.

It was Page. ''Marian, this is Trevor—where are you? I've been trying to find you all day. Why did you run out this morning? I have much to tell you, starting with one Captain DiFalco and his grandstand play. That circus this morning wasn't my idea—I was under orders to go along with him.'' There was a pause. ''This thing isn't over yet, in spite of what the good captain may think. Marian, I do need to talk to you. Something's happened. Holland has dropped out of sight, and I think he may be the key to the whole mess. I need your help.'' Another pause, and Page's voice changed, softened. ''I want to see you, Marian. We can't let DiFalco's jumping the gun spoil last night for us. Call me.''

Holland put down his plate of food and turned on her in a movement that made her wince. His expression was glacial. ''Last . . . night.''

Marian flapped a hand at him. "Relax, you haven't delivered yourself into the enemy camp." When he continued to look icebergs at her, she said, "We went to a play, that's all. Don't create problems where there are none."

"You went to a play. I didn't know you were even that chummy."

Marian didn't like the implications of that. "And if you had known?"

"I wouldn't have come to you for help," he said bluntly. "How can I count on you to hunt down a man you've been he-ing and she-ing with?" Holland looked as if he wanted to strangle her. "I was a fool to come here," he muttered.

"No, you weren't," Marian said hotly, "but you're being a fool now. Goddammit, Holland, who the hell are you to tell me I won't do my job? *I'm* the professional here, not you. You're just a lawbreaker who got blackmailed into working for an organization you don't give a hoot about. I'm a hell of a lot more worthy of trust than you are. Now you get off my back—*do you understand?*"

He held his glacial look a few seconds longer and then eased into the sardonic, arrogant smile that Marian hated. "A very impassioned speech," he said with a faint sneer. "Almost convincing, in fact. Especially that part about trustworthiness. However, I'm sure you'll understand if I do not immediately fall to my knees in abject apology."

They glared at each other for a moment. Then Marian said, as calmly as she could, "Look, if I can adjust to the idea that *you* are the good guy, you can live with the fact that I went to a play with Trevor Page. It didn't contaminate me, you know."

For some reason, that got through to him. He even laughed, or came close to it. He shook his head and said, "We shouldn't be wasting our time fighting. Very well, I am the categorical good guy and you are unequivocally free of contamination. Pristine in your trustworthiness. Play back Page's message—there's one part I want to hear again."

She rewound the tape and pressed the START button. "...Something's happened. Holland has dropped out of sight, and I think he may be the key to the whole mess. I need your help..."

"That's the part," Holland said. "He's going to implicate me in his scheme to distribute illegal weapons, perhaps make me the mastermind. I would say that means Edgar Quinn is dead, and Page is setting the stage for killing me in a shoot-out. That must be what he wants from you. He needs a police witness to sanction the shooting."

"Then he must feel pretty confident he's going to find you."

"By now he has the entire FBI looking for me. That can do wonders for one's confidence."

Marian picked up the phone and tapped out the number of the Ninth Precinct. She spoke briefly to the desk sergeant and then hung up. "No sign of Quinn. Either he's evaded the dragnet or he *is* dead. Unless Page has some reason to keep him alive?"

"I can't think of any."

"Wait a minute, wait a minute," Marian said, frowning. "There's a time problem here. When did you figure out Page had laid a false money trail for you to find?"

Holland shrugged. "I finished up around ten last night. Why?"

"At ten o'clock last night Page was in the Broadhurst Theatre watching the premiere performance of *The Apostrophe Thief*. In fact, we didn't part company until three this morning. That means that since three A.M., he found out that *you* had found out, killed Quinn to cover his tracks, convinced DiFalco the case was closed, got the FBI to start looking for you, got the NYPD to start looking for Quinn— all before the ten A.M. press conference? No way he could have done all that in seven hours. Even if he'd run straight to Federal Plaza after dropping me off."

"That part's not out of character," Holland told her. "Page was in the habit of going in at all hours. But you're right about the time—he couldn't have done all that overnight. Maybe Quinn is still alive after all. You say you left Page at three?" His face tightened. "I must have just missed him. When I left the FBI Building at ten, I went out for something to eat and then just walked the streets for a while, thinking. At midnight I went back to the computer and retraced my steps to be sure I hadn't made a mistake. That took me about three hours."

"Then you did just miss him," Marian said. "If he went straight there. What's your procedure—would he have expected you to call him the minute you found the money trail?"

"No, I would have left him a message on the computer."

"And when you didn't..."

"And when I didn't, he knew he was in danger of being exposed. He must have spent the rest of the night making up a phony connection between Quinn and that hapless arms dealer who fell down and broke his neck. He put it all into the computer and printed out a copy to show DiFalco. I think it's safe to assume that I am also electronically linked to the arms dealer...or to Quinn."

Marian was thinking. "I want you to tell me something. Just exactly how much authority does Page have in the FBI?"

"As absurd as it sounds, I don't know. He reports to a man named Starbuck, but at times I've suspected Page has some inner-circle connection. Need-to-know is stringently observed within the Bureau, and as my immediate superior it was always Page who decided what *I* needed to know. He did have the clout to get himself assigned to the East River Park case."

"But Page might not be acting on his own?"

"It's possible, I suppose. He could just be carrying out orders."

Marian found that hard to swallow. "That would mean the FBI itself is behind this plan to distribute laser handguns! Come on, Holland! Do you know how paranoid that sounds?"

He sighed. "Yes, unfortunately. But whether Page is acting autonomously or not, he's still the one we have to get. All we have to do is find Edgar Quinn if he's still alive, convince DiFalco he and Page together killed the four men in East River Park, come up with some proof of what they were planning to do with Universal Laser's new handguns, and keep ourselves alive in the process."

"Oh, is that all?" Marian smiled wryly. "Then we'd better get started, hadn't we?"

TWENTY-ONE

TREVOR PAGE FOLDED his arms and leaned against his desk. "You still don't look as if you're feeling a hundred percent."

Marian smiled wanly. She'd claimed an upset stomach to explain her unavailability during the day, blaming the perfectly good deli food the two of them had shared...only the night before? "I'm all right. Just don't feel like climbing any mountains. So what's this hot new development you've got?"

"We found Edgar Quinn."

Marian's eyebrows rose; she'd been half sure the man was dead by now. "Where'd you pick him up?"

"JFK. With a ticket bought in a false name. He was heading for San Diego, then Mexico."

"When you say 'we' found him...?"

"The FBI. And no, we haven't notified Captain Di-Falco."

"Trevor, he's my superior! I can't—"

"Yes, you can. DiFalco left this afternoon for a little rest and rehabilitation in the health spas of Atlantic City and won't be back until tomorrow. He failed to notify you, didn't he? The man *wants* to be incommunicado. As far as he's concerned, this business is over. But with him gone, you're next in chain of command."

"Only because the lieutenant is on vacation. And he gets back Monday."

"That's enough time." Page stood up away from the desk he'd been leaning against. "Do you want another circus like the one DiFalco staged this morning? Your captain can't keep his mouth shut."

"You backed him up."

"I was ordered to back him up. You have to understand, Marian. Something happens in the FBI when one of our agents goes sour. The Bureau is totally unforgiving. Totally. Right now nailing Curt Holland is more important than all the laser weapons in the world. Going along with DiFalco this morning—well, that was a temporizing move. Buying time."

Ostensibly Page was talking about Holland, Marian thought, but every word he uttered could be applied to himself. The Bureau was unforgiving, he'd said. All of Page's great plans for illegally arming the friendlies of the world had come crashing down around his ears, and now his only concern was how to save his neck. Marian was uneasy; she had a role to play and she would play it, conning the conner. But some residue of the attraction she'd felt to the man still remained, a complication she'd never had to face before. She looked straight into his strong face, his intelligent eyes. And saw a murderer.

They were alone in Page's office at Federal Plaza; on an early Saturday evening most of the other offices were empty. It was possible that Page was indeed following orders from someone higher up the FBI ladder, but Marian didn't believe it. And whatever he was leading up to, it wouldn't do for her to give in too readily. "Look, I don't trust DiFalco's discretion any more than you do," she said, "but I have to get word to him that you have Quinn in custody. Where is Quinn, by the way?"

"In a safe house. We can use him to get to Holland. What would you say if I turned the collar over to you? Wouldn't that square you with DiFalco? You get Quinn, we get Holland."

Marian pretended to hesitate. She murmured some further demurral, making it as unconvincing as she could, and in another minute she'd let him talk her into it. From Page's point of view, she supposed, step one in his scheme was a success: he'd won a police accomplice to whatever bit of nastiness he had planned. For now she'd play a passive role, listening and nodding.

Page brought them each a cup of coffee. "Quinn is willing to testify against Holland in exchange for a reduced sentence. He claims the laser-smuggling plan was Holland's, and I'm inclined to believe him. I'll tell you why. We found a computer trail linking Holland to Evan Christopher, our dead arms dealer."

Marian forced a look of astonishment. Holland had guessed right. "That should seem to clinch it. How is Quinn going to draw him out of hiding?"

"We'll save Quinn as a back-up. But first we get a message to Holland, offering immunity from prosecution in exchange for information about his network of insurgents he wanted to arm."

Marian shook her head. "He'll never go for it."

"He went for a similar deal once before. And to sweeten the pot, we'll offer him his long-desired release from the FBI. If that sounds too generous, we'll make it a condition of the deal that he's to leave the country permanently."

"Get out of town by sundown?"

"Something like that. But if he doesn't go for it, then we'll let him find Quinn. And we'll be waiting for him when he does."

"The first way's less dangerous," Marian stated, and took a slow drink of coffee. "But how do we get in touch with Holland?"

Page smiled. "Easy. We leave a message on the FBI computer. He'll find it. If I know Holland, he's probably plugged in right now, trying to discover how much we know." Page pulled a legal pad and a pen out of one of the desk drawers. "Now, how should we word it?"

They worked together on the message, which they agreed should be kept brief. Marian made a couple of suggestions. Page listened with the same courteous attentiveness he always showed, seeming to approve of her recommendations but at the same time bringing the wording back to what he wanted in the first place while crediting Marian with having thought of it. *The master manipulator at work,* she mused wryly. She watched quietly as Page fed the message into the computer.

"There, that's done." He looked at his watch. "Nothing's going to happen right away—we'll have time for a bite to eat."

Marian shook her head. "Not for me, thanks. I'm still a bit queasy—I think I'll go home and lie down for a while. You'll call me the minute you hear something?"

He gave her his most charming smile. "Oh, yes. I will call you."

I'm sure you will, she thought dispiritedly.

She took her time driving home, not wanting to face Holland just yet. She felt sick about Trevor Page. Playing God, that's what he was doing, setting himself up to decide who lived and who died. Arming political groups to eradicate other political groups. Executing four employees of Universal Laser because one of them had had the effrontery to get in his way. Condemning Holland to death as casually as stepping on an insect. Page was hiding behind a badge to enforce his own personal law. And she'd thought Holland was the arrogant one.

Dominance, Holland had said that first day in Captain DiFalco's office. *Everything is always about dominance.* He'd been referring to Page's hold over him, Marian now understood, but she suspected he was right nonetheless. She thought back; it was true of the Downtown Queens when they imposed the death penalty on Mrs. Alvarez, promoting themselves to the status of godettes, perhaps. And Brian's deliberate humiliating of her at the art gallery...that was nothing more than a demonstration of which of them had the upper hand—*I dropped her, she didn't drop me*.

Once Marian had come across a bag lady who'd sold her "route" to another bag lady. Each old woman thought she'd put something over on the other; that's what the deal had really been about, outdoing the other. And Foley's ongoing refusal to accept Marian's authority—that wasn't about dominance? DiFalco's political game-playing wasn't much more sophisticated, one-upmanship hand-tailored to fit New York's police hierarchy. Who's on top, who's underneath. Every crime that had ever been committed was about mastery in some form—domestic violence, or robbery, or a kid defacing a building as a way of thumbing his nose at authority, or Son of Sam arbitrarily choosing total strangers to murder.

She stopped for a red light. Son of Sam. Sam's son. Samson. The strong man, with the power of life and death over others.

The light changed. If Page was telling the truth about Quinn's still being alive, his evidence would be enough to charge Page with at least one of the crimes he'd committed. Marian wished now she'd pushed him for the address of the safe house where he said Quinn was being held, but at the time it hadn't seemed like a smart thing to do.

Marian parked in the delivery zone of a printing company closed for the weekend. They had to find out first if Quinn was alive; then if he was, *where* he was. That was all. Piece of cake.

Upstairs she found Holland sitting at the small table that held her telephone, to which he'd hooked up a laptop computer. With part of her mind Marian noted his hair was wet and that he'd shaved and changed his clothing. "Where'd the computer come from?" she asked suspiciously.

"I went out and bought it."

"Out? You went *out*? Oh, Holland! Of all the hare-brained—"

"Before you burst a blood vessel, just listen a moment," he interrupted. "No one followed me—I made sure of that. You should be pleased to know this place is not being watched. And no sharp-eyed fed picked me out of the crowds. But I needed some things, not only the computer but clothing and a razor and the like. I'd been wearing the same clothes for two days."

He had on khaki pants and a black crew neck sweater— casual, off-the-rack garb that he managed to wear with a certain elegance. No slave to fashion, Marian nevertheless harbored ambivalent feelings toward men who wore clothes better than she did. "How'd you get back in? I didn't give you a key."

The sardonic smile. "I didn't need a key."

"Huh." *And so pleased with yourself because you didn't.* "I still think it was a dumb thing to do," she muttered. "You could have told *me* what you needed."

Holland disagreed. "You don't pick out a computer the way you buy a tube of toothpaste—I had to go myself. Now, are we going to go on arguing about whether I should have gone out or not, or are you going to tell me what Page had to say?"

Marian plopped down on the sofa and kicked off her shoes. She recounted in detail her talk with the other FBI man, repeating Page's words verbatim as often as she could. "So he has two plans to lure you out of hiding—the amnesty offer and Edgar Quinn. He figures if you don't go for the first, you'll go for the second."

"He figures right. You should have gotten the address of the safe house."

"What if he'd refused to say? That would have made it harder for me to pretend to go along."

"Possibly. It would have been better if we could've gotten a jump on Page—go for plan number two while he's still thinking plan number one. But he'll find a way to leak the address to us when he's ready. Right now I want to see that message you and he left for me."

"For which you just happen to have a computer handy. Page said you'd be plugged into the FBI system. What were you doing when I came in?"

"Take a look."

Marian got up to go look over his shoulder at the tiny screen. "What is it?"

"An account in a bank in Brussels—in my name. Opened at five-fifteen A.M. today. Crude, Page, crude."

"Is that the trail he laid connecting you to Evan Christopher?"

"Part of it. I knew he'd do something like this," Holland added, almost under his breath. "Page was rushed when he set this up—it's clumsy, full of holes. Easy to find." As Marian watched, he changed the name on the account from *Curt Holland* to *Trevor Page*.

She laughed shortly. "Will that help?"

"It can't hurt. Changing the name alone won't be enough—I'll have to come back later and try to figure out the identification codes. But if Page ever checks back, he'll just destroy the record. Once he knows I'm on to what he's doing, he'll stop. Page knows better than to play computer games with me."

"Modest, aren't you?"

"No." The bank's records disappeared from the screen and a new set of numbers and symbols appeared. The screen changed four or five times and Holland said, "Now we're in the FBI system. Since Page seems to be going for the obvious today, I'll just check my mail first. Ah. There it is."

EQ in custody. Can offer immunity and one-way ticket to country of choice in exchange for assistance in closing case. Respond immediately.

"Well, well—isn't that nicely put," Holland said ironically. "You read it and it says he wants information about the groups I'm supposed to be arming with laser weapons. I read it and it says he needs help counteracting Quinn's testimony. Damage control."

"How could you help?" Marian asked.

He shrugged. "By manufacturing evidence. By making sure Page left no computer trail incriminating himself." Holland made the screen change several more times, and then typed in his reply.

Require proof EQ alive.

"He'll see that as a test," Holland said. "It'll take him some time to set it up, if Quinn is still among the living as Page claims. But in the meantime . . ." He concentrated on the keyboard. "This will take a while. The file I'm going after is buried under several security layers."

Marian stifled a yawn and went into the kitchen. It had been a long and stressful day, and she was ready for it to end. But the kitchen clock said it was only 8:05, not quite over yet. Kelly's evening performance at the Broadhurst had just started. From the refrigerator Marian took one of the cartons of soup she'd brought from the deli earlier on. "Want some soup?" she called in to Holland.

"No." Still concentrating.

His failure to add a *thanks* irritated her. She heated the soup—kreplach, the pastries fat and bursting with meat—and was just pouring it into a mug when she heard a mild cry of triumph from the living room. She took a swallow of the broth and went back in, carrying the mug and a spoon with her. "What have you got?"

"FBI safe houses in all the five boroughs. If Quinn's alive, he's at one of these addresses." He scrolled down.

"So many," Marian murmured. "How can we check them all out? Wait—go back." Holland returned to the original screen. Marian quickly read through the addresses and said, "Okay." The screen changed and she looked at the rest of the list. She reached out and tapped the screen with a fingernail. "This one."

"Bleecker Street? Why?"

"It's the only address in my precinct."

Holland looked up at her in appreciation. "Of course! Page won't want to deal with police from other precincts—not when he has his own tame cop in the Ninth. The Bleecker Street safe house may not have been available when Page needed it, but it's still worth checking first." His eyes narrowed. "But neither you nor I can do the checking. I'm on the FBI wish list. And if Page saw you snooping around, that would blow our whole set-up."

"You think he's guarding Quinn himself?"

"Probably not, but it's not worth chancing. We need help. Do you suppose your partner Foley would lend a hand?"

Marian laughed raucously.

"Just thought I'd ask," Holland remarked dryly. "Isn't there anyone at the Ninth Precinct you can trust?"

She thought about it. "I think I trust Gloria Sanchez, but Gloria doesn't care to exert herself more than is absolutely necessary. Maybe we can get help from outside the Ninth, though. My former partner might pitch in, if I can get hold of him. Ivan plays hard on weekends. And there's a man in Intelligence who helped me out of a tight spot once—he might be willing to help again." She took a bite of kreplach and chewed.

"So?" Holland said, arching his eyebrows. "Why aren't you calling them?"

She pointed her spoon at the computer. "You seem to have the phone line tied up."

For once, Holland looked abashed. "Sorry." He shut the computer down. "It's free now."

Marian started calling.

TWENTY-TWO

AT ELEVEN O'CLOCK Saturday night the upper West Side coffee shop was crowded and noisy; the nearby Paramount had recently disgorged its movie audience, all of its members ravenous and all in the mood for talking after two hours of semi-silence. Marian had taken a seat by the window, barely beating the crowd. The city had finally realized summer was over; the cold drizzle outside had prompted someone in the coffee shop to turn on the heat. Whoever had done it, had overdone it; Marian was in danger of drowsing off. With her fist she made a clear place on the steamed-up window, not that there was much to see.

A waitress with raccoon eyes brought the coffee and peach pie Marian had asked for. The pie looked as if it had been around for a while, but the coffee was fresh and strong and she swallowed it down, welcoming the caffeine. She was waiting for Gloria Sanchez, who'd surprised her by saying yes to Marian's call for help. Jaime Romero from Intelligence had jumped at the chance; he'd been arguing with his wife when Marian phoned and was looking for an excuse to get out. Only Marian's former partner, Ivan Malecki, had dragged his feet; he had a date he didn't want to break, he said. But when Marian finished filling him in on what was going on, he'd immediately announced he was on his way.

Trevor Page had responded at once to Holland's demand for proof that Edgar Quinn was still alive. His computer-conveyed message said Quinn could be seen walking twice around the Lincoln Center Fountain sometime between 10:30 and 10:45 that evening. Holland himself couldn't check it out, as he'd surely be walking into a trap; and

Marian couldn't risk being spotted either. Ivan and Romero had never seen the men involved, so the job of determining whether Quinn was alive or not fell to Sanchez. She claimed no one would recognize her, because neither Page nor Quinn had ever seen her in her full-blown *latina* mode.

If Quinn didn't show at Lincoln Center, they'd know Page was bluffing and the place was probably staked out with a thousand feds. But if Quinn did show, that would tell them something too. If he was accompanied on his walk around the fountain by a man or men Sanchez couldn't recognize, then Page did indeed have the FBI behind him. But if Quinn's sole companion was Trevor Page, then Page was acting alone.

At that moment Ivan and Romero were watching the Bleecker Street address that was on the list of safe houses Holland had dug out of the FBI files. They were looking for a blond man with a triangular face to come out of the building, a man who might look as if he were being escorted against his will. If two or more men did emerge from the building in time to keep the Lincoln Center appointment, Ivan and Romero would try to discover how many people—if any—were still inside. It all depended on what the Bleecker Street safe house turned out to be; an apartment building or hotel would be easiest to check.

And Holland? Holland was still hiding out in Marian's apartment, busily using the new laptop to remove all traces of his existence from the FBI databanks.

Marian looked at her watch; five after eleven. It was one week ago exactly that she'd stood in East River Park and looked at four dead men handcuffed together. If everything fell into place and she did manage to nail Trevor Page, she'd have something to fling in DiFalco's face when she resigned. She was not above wanting a little payback; but even more than that, she wanted to go out with a bang.

The coffee shop opened to a gust of rain-laden air and Gloria Sanchez entered with a flourish, looking for all the world like Carmen Miranda wearing a raincoat. Startled, Marian waited until the other detective reached her table and asked, "Is that your idea of a disguise?"

"Hey, I fit right in." Sanchez pulled out a chair and sat down across the table. Then she looked at Marian with a slow smile. "He's alive."

Marian softly beat her fists against the table top. "Hallelujah! Who was with him?"

Sanchez's smile broadened. "The one and only Trevor Dead-Eye Page. Nobuddy else."

Marian let out the breath she'd been holding. "He *is* acting alone! I knew it, I knew it! Jesus, Gloria—the thought of bucking the entire FBI scared me shitless, but one renegade agent we can handle. Whoa...I'm jumping the gun. Did you spot any back-up?"

"Nope. I hung around after Page and Quinn left, and no trench coats stepped outta the shadows or nothin'. It's just Page, Marian. He's doin' a solo."

Marian felt like dancing on the table. She and Holland had talked about the feasibility of asking Sanchez to follow the two men, in case Marian was wrong about the Bleecker Street address. But they'd decided against it. For one thing, Holland insisted nobody could follow Page when Page didn't want to be followed. And for another, they might be putting Sanchez in danger. Marian hesitated a moment and then said, "Gloria, why are you helping?"

The other woman shrugged. "You're the only real cop I work with. You gonna eat that pie?"

Marian pushed the pie over to her. She felt flattered and guilty at the same time, but that was not the moment to tell her fellow detective she was quitting the force. Sanchez ate three bites of the pie and decided that was enough. They left the coffee shop and ran through the steady drizzle to catch a downtown bus.

On the way back to Marian's place, Sanchez asked, "What if they don' go back to Bleecker Street?"

"Then we'll just have to check out the rest of the FBI's safe houses in Manhattan. I don't think Page would keep Quinn too far away—he needs him to lure Holland out of hiding."

"Yeah, how's that supposed to work?"

"Well, we think Page is trying to set up a situation in which he shoots Holland—he'll claim self-defense or that Holland was trying to get away, and I'm supposed to be his witness. Don't know how he plans to work it. But what we're trying to do is make sure that situation never develops. We have to get Quinn away from Page, get him to talk. With Quinn's evidence, we'll just move in and make an arrest and nobody gets hurt."

"How you gonna get Quinn away from him?"

"Depends on what Romero and Malecki find on Bleecker Street."

The drizzle had turned into a steady downpour, so both women were dripping wet by the time they'd run from the bus stop to Marian's apartment building. Upstairs, they found Romero and Ivan hadn't arrived yet.

Marian handed Sanchez a towel and told Holland that Quinn was alive and Page was acting alone. Holland surprised both women by throwing back his head and laughing out loud. "Ah, your splendid news is of *evangelical* proportions! There have been times in the past two years when I despaired of ever finding a way out of the perplexing bureaucratic morass Trevor Page has thrust me into, but now—thanks to you—now a bloody beautiful exit sign begins to blink in the darkness. Sergeant Larch, Detective Sanchez—I am forever in your debt."

Sanchez stared at him. "Holy frijoles."

His uncharacteristic exuberance wasn't dampened. "What's more, I like your outfit."

"Hm. Tell you the truth, Holland, I'da suspected *you* before Page."

"I already told him that," Marian said. "Want some soup? I think there's some left."

It was another half hour before Ivan Malecki and Jaime Romero got there. They showed up wet and grinning; the Bleecker Street address had indeed been the right one. Marian handed out more towels and introduced Gloria Sanchez to Ivan, who said, "Aw shucks. I thought you were Rita Moreno."

Romero looked at Holland and said, "You must be..."

"The bait," Holland said dryly. "Curt Holland, formerly with the FBI, now a fugitive from injustice. I owe a debt of gratitude to both of you, putting yourselves out like this."

Romero didn't like his manner. "We're doing it to help Marian."

Holland smiled his sardonic smile. "She has good friends," he said with unexpected graciousness.

"I wan' some coffee," Sanchez announced and headed for the kitchen.

When they all had coffee and found seats in the living room, Ivan and Romero took turns telling what they'd learned. The two men had never met before that night but found they worked well together. The address on Bleecker Street turned out to be a church, a fact that made Marian groan. "No, that's good," Ivan said. "It's an old, narrow, three-story brick building, and the Souls on Parade use only the first two floors—"

"The what?"

"The church that owns the building, Souls on Parade. I think they're from California. Anyway, the Paraders use the first floor for holding services and meetings and the like, and the second floor is offices and living quarters. The third floor is divided into two apartments.''

"One of which is leased by the FBI."

"We think both of them are," Romero interjected. The entrance to the two apartments was at the back of the building; the church was separated from the structure to the left by a sidewalk only about three feet wide. Romero and Iván had almost missed the two men they were looking for, because they were watching the only entrance they could see from the street, the one to the church itself. "But when we spotted that guy with the triangular face," Romero went on, "we knew we had the right place."

Romero had brought listening equipment with him. When Page and Quinn were out of sight, the two cops followed the narrow sidewalk around to the back where they found a flight of outside stairs. Romero hauled out his equipment and listened: Paraders on the first and second floors. At the top of the stairs on the third floor they were faced with two doors. Romero checked both apartments; nobody home.

Ivan said, "I was surprised they had no electronic security system, but I guess they figured the rigmarole of installing one would call attention to the place." He grinned. "Deadbolts and Yale locks, all of which can be opened."

Romero grinned back. "An' you just happen' to have a set of picks."

Ivan pretended to be affronted. "You know carrying picks is against the law. I merely said 'Open, Sesame' and the problem disappeared. One of those apartments is sure as hell occupied. Rumpled bed, take-out food cartons in the trash. But the other apartment hasn't been used in a *long* time."

"That's why we think the FBI rented both places," Romero said. "A fully functional apartment in the Village standing empty? No way. The feds wanted to make sure they didn't have any neighbors. And that apartment has another use as well. It's part of an escape route.''

"Wait a minute,'' Marian interrupted, trying to visualize the layout. "Two entrances, you said. That sounds like no hallway separating the apartments. Do they have a wall in common, then?''

"Sure do,'' Romero said. "And right off the kitchen in both apartments there's a . . . a pantry, would you say?''

"I guess,'' Ivan answered.

"From the kitchen it looks like a broom closet when the door is closed. But—and here's the cute part—you can get from one pantry into the adjoining one in the other apartment. The feds knocked a hole in the wall, just enough for a crawl space. We found the pantry door in the occupied apartment locked, to keep your man Quinn from getting out. But that's the escape route.''

"One moment.'' Holland had a question. "I assume the two rear entrance doors are in close proximity? If someone were watching both doors, how would escaping from one apartment to the next be an advantage? There must be another way out of the building other than the rear entrance.''

"You got it,'' Ivan said. "The empty apartment is on the side of the building overlooking that three-foot sidewalk separating the church from the next building. And there are fire ladders down the side walls of both buildings. You wouldn't even have to go all the way to the ground. Through the pantry wall, out the window onto the fire ladder, step across three feet of open space to the fire ladder next door, up to the roof and away.''

"It's a good set-up,'' Romero added. "No alley in back, no place at all for a surveillance team to hide. If the feds suspect the building's being watched from out front, they can come and go by means of the fire ladders without ever being seen from the street. Neat.''

Marian pursed her lips. "But with one glaring flaw. What better place for a stake-out than that empty apartment? Page must check it every time he comes in, but still—"

"Hold it a minute," Ivan interrupted her. He looked at the former FBI man. "Sorry, Holland, but I got to say this." He turned to Marian. "Are you sure you wanna go on with this? You're going against your captain's orders. You're harboring a fugitive. You're planning a B and E. The rest of us, we can claim we didn't know you were acting against orders—we don't take the heat. But you got no loophole, Marian. If we don't pull this off, you're in deep shit—you know that, don't you?"

"I know it," she said quietly.

"So think again, willya? Drop it right now and we all go home clean. Holland turns himself in and fights the charges with legal counsel the way everybody else does. If he turns himself in to you and not the FBI, you're a hero instead of a shoo-in for early retirement. Otherwise, you could even do time on a harboring charge, for chrissake." He jerked his thumb toward Holland. "Is he really worth the risk?"

They were all listening for her answer, including Holland. "It's not just Holland," she said. "Getting Quinn out of there alive is worth the risk. Nailing Page is worth the risk. Wrapping this thing up ourselves—oh yes. That's worth the risk."

Sanchez laughed. "You wan' to rub DiFalco's nose in it."

"I want to rub DiFalco's nose in it," Marian admitted.

"A noble motive," Holland said ironically. "But I'll take it."

"So we just move in on them or what?" Romero asked. "What are we waiting around for?"

"Yeah," Sanchez agreed. "There's five of us and one of him. Let's go get 'im."

"Not...a good idea," Holland said, his speech even more clipped than usual. "Once Page sees he trapped, he'll put a bullet through Quinn's head and there goes our evidence. You could conceivably arrest him for Quinn's murder, but that would do nothing to clarify the circumstances leading to the East River Park murders, would it? And it most assuredly would not extricate *me* from the imbroglio Page has entangled me in. No, we need to get Page away from the safe house, long enough for us to go in and bring Quinn out unharmed.''

"A diversion," Romero said.

They talked about that. Ivan went into the kitchen to make a fresh pot of coffee; he'd been there enough times before to remember where things were kept. Marian tilted her head back against the sofa and closed her eyes, listening to the voices around her. Tired as she was, she was amused to hear Gloria Sanchez's latin cadence gradually slipping away; she was sounding more and more like the black members of the Downtown Queens.

Romero was saying, "We've not only got to get him away from there, but we gotta make sure he *stays* away long enough for us to get Quinn out."

"Thass easier said than done," Sanchez growled in her newly husky voice. "Hey, Malecki—where's that coffee?"

Holland's eyes slid toward her. "What happened to Chiquita Banana?"

"It's ready," Ivan said, coming back in with the coffee pot. "You pour your own."

"Page isn't going to leave Quinn alone any more than he has to," Marian said to Romero. She waited her turn and poured herself a cup of coffee. "How can we be sure he'd stay away even if we got him out?"

"It wouldn't have to be long," Romero answered. "The problem is finding a place he *couldn't* leave immediately."

"Like where, for instance?"

"How about jail?" Sanchez drawled.

The other four looked at her a moment—and then all started talking at the same time. Finally Ivan yelled for quiet and said, "We couldn't hold 'im. Even if we set something up, some humbug drug bust, say—all he'd have to do is flash his I.D. An FBI agent? We couldn't even taken 'im in."

Romero began to laugh. "Marian, remember Large Marge?"

Her face lit up. "I do indeed!"

"Large . . . Marge?" Holland asked.

"She's a member of a girls' street gang called the Downtown Queens," Romero explained. "The last member, as it turns out. But Marge has a special talent. Remember what it is?"

Marian nodded. "Marge can relieve unsuspecting strangers of cumbersome burdens they carry with them. Like billfolds. She could lift Page's I.D."

"Is she that good?" Ivan asked.

"She's that good," Romero assured him. "She has a *great* way of distracting the mark."

"Aha," Holland said. "And this pocket-picking girl gangster will help us if we just ask her nicely?"

"She won't have much choice," Romero replied. "The rest of her gang is in jail for killing a woman and chances are Large Marge knew they were going to do it. She could still be charged as an accessory before the fact. I tell her we'll ask the DA's office to lay off if she cooperates. She'll go for it—hell, she's only sixteen."

"Ye gods," Holland said. "We have to depend on the assistance of *children*?"

"Wait till you see her," Marian said wryly. She turned to Romero. "Do you know where she is?"

He waved a hand dismissively. "I can find her."

"Okay," Ivan said, "but we still won't be able to hold Page long. Once he makes his phone call, the FBI will confirm his identity. We'll have to say gee, we're sorry, we thought you were a street pusher—and then let him go. He's gonna be in and out faster than you can read the Miranda warning.''

"We'll need only that long," Sanchez said. "Since the locks ain't no problem, we just go in and get Quinn. It's not like he's armed or nothin'.''

"A point of curiosity," Holland said. "What is this Large Marge going to do with Page's I.D. once she's lifted it? The minute he finds it's missing, he'll insist that she be searched."

The others were silent a moment. Then Marian said, "She'll have to pass it on."

"To whom? Not to the arresting officers—who I presume will be Romero and Malecki. That's too risky. We need someone else there, someone who can take the I.D. and quickly disappear...somewhere."

"The ladies' room," Marian and Sanchez said together.

The three men exchanged glances and began to nod. "Yeah," Ivan said, "a public place like a bar where your Large Marge can approach him. She lifts the I.D., passes it to another woman who heads for the ladies' while me and Romero move in to make the bust. Now we need this woman."

"Not me," Sanchez said. "Page knows me and I don't have no reason to meet him in no bar."

"And not Marian," Holland said firmly. "Page is bound to be suspicious of every little thing that happens now. If she calls him instead of waiting to hear from him, there's no telling what he might do. It's too chancy."

Romero didn't think it was important. "Okay, so we get somebody else. But it'll work. And I get a piece of the bust."

Holland had his doubts. "I'm not convinced of the wisdom of this course of action," he said. "We bring in another outsider at the eleventh hour and expect her to play

Page along—a very wary and distrustful Page, I might point out. He's going to be *looking* for a set-up. Whoever this woman is, she'd have to be a good actor.

Marian smiled. "I know a good actor," she said.

TWENTY-THREE

ON SUNDAY Kelly Ingram had only one regularly scheduled performance, a matinee. Shortly before curtain she'd placed a call from her dressing room at the Broadhurst, tapping out the FBI number listed in the phone book. When the call was forwarded and Trevor Page's voice came over the line, Kelly launched into a second and wholly unofficial performance. She was worried about Marian Larch, she said. She'd been unable to reach her, and just now some guy named Curt Holland had showed up backstage looking for Marian and muttering what sounded like threats as well as saying a lot of other strange things and she was sure she'd heard Page's name mentioned and she didn't like being disturbed before a performance and she was afraid this Holland character might come back and what in the name of heaven was going on?

He'd bought it. When Page had pressed her for details of what Holland said, Kelly had replied she didn't have time to go into all that because the matinee performance of *The Apostrophe Thief* was about to begin. They'd made a date to meet at a bar called FiFi's after the performance.

The matinee had gone well. Her fellow actors had warned her that Sunday afternoon audiences were usually sluggish, but this one had been alert and responsive right from the opening line. With an effort Kelly shifted gears away from Abigail James's play to the one co-scripted by Marian Larch. Five people, including Marian, had coached her on this new role she was to play: four New York cops and an ex-FBI man—unusual directors, to say the least. She felt inexplicably calm, on her way to meet a murderer.

Trevor Page had killed four people, Marian had told her, ruthlessly slaughtering three people against whom he had no grudge just to make sure he got the one man who was causing him trouble. *You will never be alone with him,* Marian had promised. Kelly was still shocked to think a man with such a good, open face could be a killer. And he and Marian had seemed to hit it off so well together. But if Marian said Page was dangerous, then Page was dangerous.

FiFi's was a new bar in the theater district, one that was trying hard to establish itself as a place where celebrities liked to drop in. So Kelly made as grand an entrance as she could, at the same time trying to generate a *don't-approach-me* aura. The bar was busy, but the conversation faded to a whisper as the crowd realized who was standing there—and then quickly resumed on a lower key as the patrons all began asking one another if they knew that was Kelly Ingram who'd just come in.

Page was sitting at a small table; he rose quickly and came to meet her. But before he could say anything, Kelly asked, "Trevor, could we sit at the bar? Not quite so exposed."

"Of course," he murmured and followed her there, himself the object of candid looks of curiosity and envy.

Kelly let her eyes slide over Ivan Malecki and the man named Romero down at the end of the bar. In the ladies' room Gloria Sanchez was waiting to take Page's I.D. off her hands once she had it. And outside in a car, watching, were Marian and that dark-eyed, brooding man who seemed to be at the center of all the trouble. All Kelly had to do was keep Page here until this Large Marge made her appearance, whoever she was. *How will I recognize her?* Kelly had asked. Romero had laughed and said she'd know her the minute she laid eyes on her.

After they'd been served their drinks, Page said, "Kelly, this is important. I want you to tell me everything Curt

Holland said. Word-for-word, as well as you can remember.''

Kelly took a sip of her drink and looked deep into the eyes of the murderer. ''Who *is* he? I never heard Marian mention any Curt Holland.''

''He's on our wanted list.'' Page added no details. ''What did he say?''

Kelly made a show of thinking back, and then started on the story she was to tell, taking her time and stretching it out. She told him Holland had seemed distracted, demanding to know where ''Sergeant Larch'' was—very formal, he was—and accusing Marian and Page of plotting against him. He'd made a number of unspecified threats, Kelly said, of the *I'll-get-him-before-he-gets-me* variety. She even imitated Holland's manner of speech, clipping off her words and overarticulating.

Page was convinced. ''Did he say he was coming back? Did he drop any hint of where he was going?''

''Well-l-l,'' she drawled, ''he didn't exactly say he'd be back, but that was the impression I got. It's a little hard to be sure, you know—he didn't talk in complete sentences. He was always interrupting himself.''

Page frowned. ''That doesn't sound like Holland—he must be distracted indeed. Did he—whoa!'' He broke off as a brown-skinned arm the size of a leg of lamb suddenly draped itself across his chest from behind.

Large Marge had arrived.

Kelly had to tilt her head back to look at her face. Romero had been right; there was no mistaking Large Marge. The owner of the arm extending so nonchalantly across Page's chest was wearing a silver sequined top cut down to *there* and a Pepto-Bismol-pink skirt that was so mini it barely covered the essentials. And Marge had a lot of essentials. Well over six feet tall, big-boned, and not exactly skinny, instead of trying to conceal her size she flaunted it, much to Kelly's surprised delight. This girl was only six-teen? Incredible. Every eye in the place was on the young black woman; Large Marge was a *presence*.

"Hiya, sugah," she said to Page. "We know each other, don't we?" Her other hand began to caress the back of his neck.

Page appeared both annoyed at the interruption and im-pressed. "No, ma'am. I'd remember *you*."

"Well, mebbe I can help you remember." Her hands were all over him.

"Uh, I think you have me confused with someone else."

"Naw, I don't." Marge pressed a honeydew-sized breast against Page's upper arm; her hands never stopped mov-ing. "You *feel* familiar—y'know what I mean?"

He tried to put an end to it. "As you can see, I'm here with someone."

Marge threw Kelly a cursory glance. "Oh, hi." Then she oozed her way around Page's back and wedged herself be-tween the two of them. "That's all right, sugah," she said to Page. "I don't mind sharin'."

Kelly felt something plop into her lap. Quickly she cov-ered the I.D. folder with both hands.

"Sooner or later," said a new voice smugly. "Yep, I knew that sooner or later you'd lead us to your connection, Mar-gie-Pargie." Jaime Romero grinned ferally at Page. "We got you now, you sucker."

Page's jaw tightened in anger. "I'm not anyone's *con-nection*. I never saw her before a minute ago."

"Sure you didn't."

"You crazy, man," Large Marge said. "Nothin' goin' down here."

Ivan Malecki's long arm shot out and grabbed Page's wrist. "Keep your hands where we can see them."

"I was reaching for my identification!"

"Do it slowly," Ivan instructed. "One hand only."

All talk in the bar had stopped dead. A drug bust? In FiFi's? The two bartenders exchanged anxious looks, not knowing what to do.

Romero was searching through Marge's handbag. Triumphantly he held up two small white packets. "Nothing going down here, huh? All right, you two—assume the position."

"Excuse me," Kelly said, and fled to the ladies' room.

The last thing she heard as she pushed open the door was Trevor Page's voice: "My I.D.! She stole my I.D.!"

MARIAN AND HOLLAND sat quietly in her car across the street from FiFi's, waiting for the little farce in the bar to play itself out. Holland was miles away and Marian was struggling to find some kind of equilibrium for herself; the depression she felt was not the usual downer she went through when a case was nearing its climax. It was worse.

She'd been breaking the rules right and left; she'd even involved two civilians in the trap they'd set for Page. That was not her normal M.O.; most of the time she was able to observe the letter of the law as well as its spirit. But how easily she'd slid into subterfuge—disobeying Captain DiFalco's order to call the case closed, providing a hiding place for a man on the FBI's wanted list. That alone was a pretty strong indication it was time to start looking for a different profession. Providing she came out of this with her hide intact. The plan was for Gloria Sanchez to call Captain DiFalco and the FBI once they had Quinn in custody, but that might be too little too late.

It occurred to her that only nine days ago she'd been sitting behind the wheel of a different car with a different partner, when she and Foley had been waiting for the last of the Downtown Queens to show up. Things were different this time. Marian glanced at the man sitting tensely next to her. If it was bad for her, how much worse must it be for

Holland. How very alone he must feel—falsely incriminated, sought by a killer…and the only one he'd had to turn to was a policewoman he barely knew. But Holland had never whimpered, had never once said *Why me?* or complained of the unfairness of it. Right then Marian was aware of his physical presence in a way she'd never been before. Before, he'd been only a problem, a key piece of an overcomplicated puzzle she had to solve; she'd forgotten him as a person. And that was another mistake she never used to make.

"You've been quiet all day," she said. "What's bothering you?"

With an effort he came back from a great distance. "The locks. The way Malecki and Romero got into the Bleecker Street safe house using ordinary picks. Admittedly my experience of FBI safe houses is limited—I've seen only one, in Washington. But that one had a security system that would do a bank proud." He swiveled his head slowly to look at her. "It's too easy."

She nodded slowly, having wondered about the same thing herself. "A trap? Ivan got in safely, but the place was empty then. When Page has to leave Quinn alone, he's bound to take extra precautions. What's he likely to do?"

"Boobytrap the door, something, I don't know." Holland brooded over it. "But all my instincts are screaming 'Watch out!' The fire ladder down the outside wall…what do you say to going in that way?"

"I say it sounds like a good idea. That'll let us into the empty apartment and we can get into the other one through the hole in the pantry wall."

"Then that's what we'll do," he decided. He looked at the dashboard clock and then across the street to the entrance to FiFi's. "They ought to be coming out soon. I must say, Sergeant, I am impressed by your resources. Not only do three willing and able police detectives come running when you call, you are also able to pluck a Broadway star out of the air when we need one. When you said you knew a good actor, I had no idea you meant Kelly Ingram."

Marian smiled to herself. Kelly had been flattered and excited when Marian asked for her help; she'd gone to Marian's apartment that morning to be briefed on what they wanted her to do. Gloria Sanchez had shouted, "Well, aw*right*!" when she saw who the actor was that Marian that called. Ivan already knew Kelly; he'd met her the same time Marian had, three years earlier. But Romero just stood there with his mouth open, unable to speak. "Kelly and I have been friends almost from the day we met," Marian said. "It's so great when you find someone on the same wavelength as yours."

"Yes, it must be," Holland replied quietly. Marian shot him a look. "There they are," he announced in a different voice.

Across the street, Ivan and Romero were bringing out Page and Large Marge, both in handcuffs, both protesting vociferously. It was a toss-up as to which of the two was making the more noise; Marge wasn't a bad actor herself.

In spite of his tension, or perhaps because of it, Holland barked out a laugh. "That's Large Marge? Oh, magnificent." He laughed again. "And she picks locks, too!"

Marian started the car; they'd waited only to make sure nothing had gone wrong. She pulled away from the curb even before Ivan and Romero had gotten their prisoners into their car. She sped through a cross street just as the light was changing and headed toward the Village and Bleecker Street.

They were both silent during the drive downtown. When they reached Bleecker, Marian spotted a fire hydrant to park by; the safe house was on up a block or two. They left the car and started walking.

They could hear the church before they saw it; high-decibel rock pounded through the chill evening air, offering eternal deafness if not eternal salvation. Marian and Holland paused to get their bearings. A pink neon sign spelled out *Souls on Parade* in script over the door, which stood open in spite of the cold weather. Marian was warm, too warm, inside her down jacket. Three teenaged boys hurried inside without giving them a glance. The sidewalk separating the church from the building next door was so narrow Marian and Holland might have missed it if they hadn't known to look for it.

Holland led the way, playing a flashlight over the side of the building. The iron fire ladder was toward the back; it had a sliding bottom section that stopped a few feet over their heads. *I'll go first,* Holland mouthed over the music, putting his flashlight away. He jumped up and caught the bottom rung of the ladder and his weight slowly pulled the ladder down, the noise of its descent drowned out by the driving musical fervor pouring out of the Souls on Parade.

Marian waited on the ground, holding the ladder with one hand and shining her own flashlight up to the nearest third-floor window. When Holland reached the window, he motioned for her to turn her light off and took out his own. Carefully he examined the frame of the window, even peering inside the best he could. When he was satisfied the window wasn't wired, he placed his palms against the top frame of the bottom pane and pushed—and to Marian's surprise, the window lifted easily. Holland stepped through into the unused apartment. *There's another law broken,* Marian thought.

When he was inside, Marian climbed the ladder, which was on the shaky side. Her heart beating a little faster, she stepped over the windowsill and pulled out her flashlight again. Yes, the window had locks on the inside; why had Page left it unlocked? Behind her, the bottom section of the ladder pulled back up to its original position. Inside the building, the music took on a different quality; the melody dwindled to nearly inaudible while the bass line became more prominent. The wooden floor was vibrating in the empty apartment. Marian started hunting for the kitchen and the pantry.

She felt Holland's hand tugging her arm and followed in the direction he was leading. He opened a door and played his beam over a hole in the wall: the pantry. Marian crouched down and duck walked through to the adjoining pantry. The door between the pantry and the kitchen was locked, just as Romero had said it was. Marian held the light while Holland took out his picks; the first one he tried worked.

The apartment was dark. That was bad; could Page have moved his prisoner to a different hiding place? Or even worse, killed him? Still using her flashlight, Marian found the living room...and Edgar Quinn. He was alive, but there was a problem. He was tied to a chair, his mouth taped shut, and a bomb was strapped to his stomach.

Marian froze. Only when Holland found the switch and turned on the lights did her paralysis begin to dissipate. She caught a whiff of an unpleasant odor and it took her a moment to identify it as Quinn's sweat. Fear did have its own stench; nothing else smelled quite like it. Quinn's eyes were rolled up so only the whites showed, and he'd wet himself. The music pounded up through the floorboards.

Holland pointed. Marian followed his finger as he traced a trip wire connected to the outside door. That's why Page had left the window unlocked: so he could get back in. Holland pointed again; the bomb also had a timer, set for midnight—they had four hours. Page was protecting himself both ways; if someone found the safe house or if he himself was prevented from returning, the evidence against him would be blown to kingdom come—along with all the parading souls in the lower part of the building.

Holland ripped the tape off Quinn's mouth, none too gently. Quinn started screaming something, but they couldn't hear what he said over the uproar from downstairs. He seemed to realize that, because he took a deep breath and mouthed one word at them: *Page, Page, Page,* over and over again.

Marian wanted at least to untie him, but the ropes binding him to the chair were interwoven with the harness that held the bomb; too risky. The trip wire to the door was taut, running through a series of tiny pulleys positioned to keep Quinn from attempting to move at all. She couldn't see a telephone in the room, but they could never have made themselves heard anyway. Marian and Holland exchanged a look. They were going to have to leave him. She stood in front of Quinn's chair and pantomimed dialing and then speaking on a phone, but she wasn't sure he understood what she meant. He started screaming again when he saw them leaving.

Through the hole in the pantry wall, out the window. While climbing down the fire ladder, Marian decided it would be quicker to go back and use her car phone rather than look for a phone nearby. She hit the ground running, with Holland close behind. It took forever to run the block and a half to the car; and as they pulled away from the racket coming out of the church, Marian became aware of an unpleasant, high-pitched ringing in her ears.

Something else was ringing as well: the car phone. Marian scratched the paint in her haste to get the door unlocked. She snatched up the receiver and yelled, "What?"

"He's out," said Ivan Malecki's voice. "We couldn't hold him ten minutes."

"Oh, Jesus." She held the receiver out a little from her ear so Holland could bend in and listen.

"Did you get Quinn?" Ivan was asking. "Page ought to be arriving there any minute now. I've been calling—"

"We've got a crisis here," Marian interrupted.

"Quinn," Holland gasped and took off running back to the church and the third-floor apartment.

"I want you to call the bomb squad and give them the Bleecker Street address," Marian said to Ivan. She went on to describe what they'd found in the apartment.

"Shit! Are there people downstairs in the church?"

"Yes, they'll have to be evacuated. Ivan, make sure the bomb squad understands the bomb is hooked up to the door. They *must* go in by the fire ladder."

"Gotcha. God, Marian, if you'd used the door—"

"I know." She was trying not to think about that part of it. "Tell Gloria to make her calls to DiFalco and the FBI now—don't wait. Hurry, Ivan. Holland's gone back to guard Quinn since Page is on the loose, and he'll need back-up."

"You're not going back in there?"

"Have to." She broke the connection and ran as hard as she could back toward the cacophony and the danger.

TWENTY-FOUR

IT TOOK MARIAN three jumps before she was able to catch the bottom rung of the fire ladder. The climb wasn't any easier the second time; her sneakers kept slipping on the iron rungs. But at last she made it to the top and climbed through the window. The noise from downstairs—Marian could no longer think of it as music—was relentless. Her head was starting to throb in time with the bass rhythm.

But as she was crawling into the pantry, it suddenly stopped. Blessed, blessed silence! Through for the evening or only changing the tapes? She stepped into the kitchen and started toward the living room—and then stopped dead.

"—window was open," Trevor Page's voice was saying from the next room. "And the lights were on. I turned them off when I left."

Marian didn't dare breathe; a deep chill ran through her. Slowly and quietly she unzipped her jacket and slipped out of it. She reached around to the small of her back and drew her weapon from its holster.

Holland's voice sounded, cold and angry. "Do you plan on shooting me with my own gun? Don't you think that just might arouse *some* curiosity in official quarters?"

"Oh, I don't think that much matters now. But I didn't plan on your finding this place just yet. How did you find it?"

Holland evidently saw no reason not to tell him. "From the FBI's list of safe houses. This was the only one in the Ninth Precinct." He didn't mention Marian.

She edged up to the doorway and risked a look. Page was standing between Quinn and Holland; Quinn was crying.

Page had one gun pointed at Holland and another—his own, presumably—held loosely in the other hand. He'd been waiting for whoever had broken in. How pleased he must have been to see it was Holland.

Procedure called for her to erupt into the room shouting and going immediately into a crouch. But she didn't dare chance it, not with a gun pointed straight at Holland. So almost casually she stepped into the room, aimed her weapon at Page, and said, "Put the guns down, Trevor. It's over."

The look on his face made her stomach turn over. But unexpected as her appearance was, he still reacted quickly; he whipped up his other arm and pointed that gun at Edgar Quinn's head. Marian could see the beads of sweat on his forehead. "I'm bound to get one of them before you can drop me," he said in a tight voice.

"It wouldn't do any good if you got all three of us," Marian shot back, her own voice none too steady. "Do you think Holland and I are the only ones who know? Those two cops who arrested you in FiFi's—they know. And a third is notifying DiFalco and your bosses right this minute. Where do you think we were just now? Calling for help. The bomb squad is on its way. It's *over*. Put the guns down."

Page's face had changed expression half a dozen times while she was talking; his poise was deserting him and desperation taking its place. "I know it's over," he groaned. "But I'm not going to prison. I'll never go to prison. And if you pull that trigger, I swear to god, Marian, I'll take these two with me. You put *your* gun down."

She looked straight into his eyes and knew she didn't have a choice; he meant every word of it. Holland and Quinn were as disposable to him as were the four dead men he'd left in East River Park. Slowly she lowered her gun and placed it on the floor by her feet.

"Good. Now kick it over here."

She did as he instructed. "If we don't stop you," she said, "somebody else will. There are just too many people looking for you."

His laugh was artificial. "You think I didn't plan for this possibility?" he asked arrogantly. "I have a dozen contingency plans. Ah Marian, Marian! Why did you cast your lot with *him*?" He jerked his head toward Holland. "Marian, do you have any idea of what you've done, of the plans you've ruined?"

"You mean your plans for arming terrorists with laser guns?" She started inching toward him, trying to move without being seen and praying that Holland was doing the same thing.

"*Counter*terrorists!" Page said sharply. "Those guns were never meant to be used in the United States. They were for men and women all over the world who aren't afraid to fight the threats to democracy that Americans are too blind to see. The accelerating ambitions of the Islam 'nation,' for one. And the Russians are still pulling our strings in spite of all that's happened." He snorted. "You think that's going to stop by itself?"

Marian inched a little nearer. "And you appointed yourself to straighten it all out."

"Somebody has to. The CIA has turned gun-shy." But Page was too keyed up to be diverted for long. "Enough talk, now. Move over there with Holland."

She was about six feet from him. "And all the heady power that comes with the job, deciding who lives and who dies—that has nothing to do with it, I suppose."

"I said move over with Holland! Do it, Marian, or I'll have to—"

Baaaa-rooooom! The music exploded like a burst of dynamite, making Page start in surprise. In that split second of distraction Marian launched herself toward the gun pointing at Quinn, aware that Holland was going for the other arm. She pushed Page's arm up; the gun discharged, sending a bullet into the ceiling. She got her hands around Page's wrist and twisted them in opposite directions, hard. The gun fell to the floor. She glanced over; his other hand was empty as well.

Just then a great pain shot through the lower part of her left leg, causing her to cry out; Page's toe had caught her just below the kneecap. Her legs flew out from under her and all three of them went down in a struggling heap. Marian was having trouble breathing; she was caught between the two straining men, as she had been from the very first day. Holland was on the bottom; Page was trying to reach around her to get a grasp on Holland's throat. She could feel Page's hot breath on her face as they all three fought to get some sort of purchase on the wooden floor that was again vibrating from the taped rock band blaring away below. Marian kept pushing back against Page, trying to move him to the right, away from Quinn and the bomb. But Holland was working against her, trying to move them all in the other direction.

Then she saw why: one of the guns was on the floor not a foot beyond his outstretched fingers. Page now had one hand around Holland's throat while Marian held off the other. Trying to ignore the pain in her left leg, she squirmed and twisted and got herself turned around, facing Holland and away from Page. Then she put her right foot on the floor and pushed as hard as she could. They moved a little. She pushed again; Holland's fingers could just touch the butt of the gun. She pushed one more time, but then Page got his hand free. He grabbed her hair and yanked her head up, preparatory to smashing her face into the floor. Holland jerked up his arm, pressed the nozzle of the gun against Page's right eye, and fired.

Nothing moved. Time hesitated.

After an eon Marian felt Page roll away. The report of the gun so close to her ear had temporarily deafened her. She lay collapsed across Holland—sick, shocked, trying to catch her breath. After a minute or two she began to hear the *thud-thud-thud-thud* of the music again. She felt Holland's fist pressing against her back; slowly, gradually, it relaxed into a hand. She wondered if her hearing would ever be the same again. *If only the goddamn noise would stop—*

And no sooner had she thought that than it did stop, as abruptly as it had begun. She could make out sounds of shouting and movement from below; the Souls on Parade were being evacuated. The bomb squad had arrived.

Marian sat up and turned to look at Page—and wished she hadn't. The bullet fired at such close range had blown out the back of his skull. Blood was splattered as far as the wall. Small lumps of pink brain tissue was turning gray upon exposure to the air. Marian gagged once, then shut her eyes and clenched her teeth, fighting down the nausea.

"Marian—are you going to be all right?"

Marian opened her eyes to see Holland kneeling in front of her. "In a few years," she said.

He leaned forward and placed his cheek against hers. "Thank you," he whispered. Then he stood up and went to check on Quinn, whose head had fallen forward so that his chin was resting on his chest. "He's fainted."

Marian slowly got to her feet, favoring the leg Page had kicked. "Do you blame him?"

Holland looked at the gun he was still holding. "I think this one's yours." He handed it to her and picked up his own gun from the floor. He left Page's where it had fallen.

Just then three men wearing bomb squad coveralls came in from the kitchen. They stopped, taking in the scene, their eyes traveling from Quinn and the bomb to Page's body and the splattered blood and back to the bomb again. "Jesus, will you look at this?'' one of them kept saying. "Look at it! Jesus. Jesus."

Yeah, Jesus, Marian thought. *Look at this.*

IT TOOK THE BOMB SQUAD only forty-five minutes to dismantle the bomb and free Edgar Quinn. By that time it looked as if most of Manhattan had moved down to Bleecker Street. The block where the church building was located had been cordoned off, but outside the barriers the Souls on Parade congregated along with all the other occupants of the block. Their numbers were swelled by the hordes of onlookers that dropped out of the skies every time something unusual was going on. Six Radio Motor Patrol cars were there and over a dozen uniformed officers. A fire truck was there. An ambulance was there. Two men with a stretcher and a body bag were there, waiting to go in after Page. Ivan Malecki, Gloria Sanchez, and Jaime Romero were there—as was Captain DiFalco, who, as the ranking police officer present, was able to place himself in charge of the ''operation.'' The FBI was there. The TV news crews were there.

Marian asked the medic for some painkillers; her leg was going to have one beaut of a bruise the next day, but there was nothing she could do about that. The bomb squad had just brought Edgar Quinn down, trembling and unsteady on his feet. He didn't make it all the way to the nearest RMP; his legs gave out and he sank down on a curb, dropping his head between his knees. Marian got to him before DiFalco did.

"Quinn?" she said, hunkering down so her face would be on a level with his. "We'll get a statement from you later, but right now I want you to tell me something. Quinn, do you hear me?"

He raised his head just as DiFalco got there. "You saved my life, you and Holland," Quinn said in a choked voice. "I'll tell you whatever you want to know."

DiFalco had the sense to keep quiet; gratitude was an ephemeral thing at best, and this particular expression of it wasn't directed at him. "All I want to know is why," Marian said. "You didn't need the money. You're not a violent man—why cooperate in the murder of four of your own employees?"

"I didn't kill them!" Quinn cried, alarmed. "Page shot them. I didn't even know he was *going* to kill them! They just wanted to talk to me, to try to figure out a way to find which of them had been talking to Washington about the laser gun. I'd, I'd told them I was going to let them all go if we couldn't find the guilty one. That was Page's idea."

"But you did go along with the murders."

"Page killed them before I knew what was happening! Even when he pulled out a gun and had me handcuff them together, I didn't think he'd *shoot* them! Then Page told me I was an accessory, so I had to keep quiet."

Easily led, two people had said of Edgar Quinn. Marian went on, "You still haven't told me why. Universal Laser isn't losing money. Do you endorse Page's politics or what?"

He shook his head. "I don't care anything about that. It's true Universal Laser isn't losing money, but we aren't going anywhere either." Quinn sighed deeply. "When my father was running the company, every year there was some big leap forward. But ever since I took over, people like Conrad Webb and Elizabeth Tanner kept telling me we were standing still. I thought keeping the FBI supplied with laser guns year after year would put us right at the top of the field." He shook his head again, as if he still couldn't believe what had happened. "I didn't know Page wanted those weapons for his own purposes. I thought I was dealing with the FBI.''

Marian looked a question at DiFalco. He shook his head and motioned to the nearest uniformed officer. ''Take him in and book him.''

So that's what it all boils down to, Marian thought. *Everybody wants to be bigger than Dad.* She stood up and turned to see Malecki, Sanchez, and Romero standing behind her. ''Did you hear all that?''

They nodded. ''Page just used him, looks like,'' Ivan volunteered.

DiFalco planted himself in front of Ivan. ''Who the hell are you?''

Ivan raised an eyebrow, but identified himself. ''Sergeant Malecki, Thirty-second Precinct.''

''What are you doing on my turf?''

''I called him, Captain,'' Marian interposed. ''We needed help. Ivan's my former partner.''

''Why didn't you call your present partner?'' Marian just looked at him; he knew why. ''Um, yah.'' He pointed a finger at Romero. ''You called Intelligence too?''

''I called Romero, yes. And Sanchez. They were all in on the bust.''

DiFalco started to say something and then thought better of it. He turned to Ivan. ''What'd you say your name was?''

''Malecki. Ivan Malecki. Sergeant.''

DiFalco grunted and turned away.

''Nice work, people?'' Sanchez prompted.

He turned back only to say, ''That was a good kill, Larch. Probably won't even be an investigation.''

Marian nodded automatically, vaguely wondering why DiFalco thought the police might need to investigate an FBI shooting.

''Yeah, it was,'' Romero said approvingly. ''You got 'im right through the eye! Pow! Is that poetic justice or what?''

Marian looked at the three of them nodding at her and it finally hit her: they thought *she* had shot Page. She turned and ran after DiFalco. "Captain! Wait!"

"Later, Larch," he said over his shoulder. "I have to make a statement to the press."

"But I wasn't the one—"

"I said later." He was swallowed up by a mob of people. *He's going to do it again,* Marian thought. He was just too eager to get out in front of those cameras and microphones. She tried to work her way through the crowd of newspeople, but they weren't budging an inch. Finally she gave up and went looking for Holland.

She found him standing alone, arms folded, watching all the activity around him with a look of bemusement. "Di-Falco thinks I shot Page," Marian told him.

"What!"

"He's in such a hurry to see his face on TV that he wouldn't stop to listen."

Holland laughed his sarcastic laugh. "Leave it to Di-Falco. He ought to—uh-oh."

Marian followed his glance. A man in a brown overcoat was bearing down upon them, fire in his eye. He stopped before Holland.

"Curt Holland," the man in the brown coat said. "You know, we used to have an agent named Curt Holland, but our computer doesn't seem to know anything about him."

"Hello, Starbuck," Holland said with a weary sigh. "I rather thought you'd show up."

"When one of our agents goes down," Starbuck said, "we want to know why—even when it's an agent who's turned. I know there was bad blood between you and Page, Holland, *bad* blood, going way back. If I find any evidence that you set up this little scenario as an excuse to kill Page, I'll see to it you'll spend the rest of your days in Leavenworth."

Marian was appalled. This was wrong, all wrong.

"Trevor Page was a murderer," Holland said icily. "What's more, he was using the Bureau as a cover for moving arms illegally."

"We know that now. But that doesn't give you the right to execute him. We have laws for that, or have you forgotten?"

"Don't be a fool, Starbuck," Holland said sharply. "I did not 'execute' him. Nothing was further from my mind."

"Hand me your weapon."

Holland's eyebrows rose, but then he smiled sardonically and handed over his gun.

Starbuck sniffed the barrel. "It hasn't been fired. Well, maybe you are in the clear."

Holland took his gun and looked at Marian, amused. "It just gets better and better, doesn't it?"

Marian didn't think it was funny. They were going to have to get this cleared up... and send Holland off to Leavenworth? They'd saved each other's lives in there.

Starbuck spoke. "Where's this Sergeant Larch who's supposed to have shot him?"

"Right under your nose," Marian said.

He seemed to notice her for the first time. "Starbuck, FBI," he said unnecessarily. "Sergeant, I need to hear it from you. You and Quinn were the only other ones up there."

And Quinn fainted while the fight was going on. "Yes," she said cautiously.

"I want you to tell me straight out if Holland had anything to do with Page's death."

"Oh, this has gone far enough," Holland said tiredly. "I only said I didn't *execute* him. I didn't say I—"

"Quiet, Holland, I'm talking to the lady."

"Yeah, Holland, keep quiet," Marian said. "He's talking to me."

Holland's eyes narrowed as he began to suspect what she had in mind. She glared at him, willing him to keep his mouth shut.

Starbuck said, "Sergeant Larch, if Holland is in any way responsible for the death of Trevor Page, I want you to speak up right now."

Do I have the RIGHT to keep it to myself?

"Well?"

Marian remained silent.

Starbuck nodded. "So Holland didn't shoot him after all. I just couldn't believe he'd pass up the opportunity."

"Want to sniff my gun?" Marian asked.

He smiled. "No, I'm sure your ballistics people will do all the testing that's necessary. Holland, I'd like you to come back with me for a debriefing."

"I have resigned from the FBI," he said, looking stunned. He couldn't take his eyes off Marian.

"Um, we kind of figured that out. But we want you to fill us in just the same. Come along. Goodbye, Sergeant—thanks for your help."

Holland allowed himself to be led away, still looking as if he'd been hit by lightning. Marian watched them go, wondering if she'd done the right thing.

DiFalco's press announcement was about ready to begin; the cameras and microphones were all in place. Marian wandered over to where Malecki, Sanchez, and Romero were lounging against an RMP; she found an unused piece of fender and joined them. They had a good side view of DiFalco.

"Kelly Ingram is furious with you," Sanchez told her. "Because you wouldn't let her hang around and see how it came out? I put her in a cab and sent her home, like you said."

"Thanks, Gloria. I'll call her tomorrow."

"Here we go," Romero announced.

DiFalco gave the reporters only the essentials. Trevor Page was planning illegal shipments of a laser gun currently being developed by Universal Laser. His accomplice in these plans was the president of Universal, Edgar Quinn. Page had killed the four men found in East River Park eight days ago because one of them was threatening Page's plans. Page himself was dead, brought down by police fire during the successful rescue of Quinn, whom Page had kidnapped.

"We were able to bring this matter to a successful conclusion," DiFalco said smoothly, "because of a special task force headed by Sergeant Marian Larch of the Ninth Precinct. I want to give credit to everyone who participated. Sergeant Larch's task force was made up of Detective Gloria Sanchez, also of the Ninth Precinct. Detective Jaime Romero from Intelligence. Sergeant Ivan, uh, Maleski, of the Thirty-second Precinct. And Agent Curt Holland of the FBI. It's this kind of selfless cooperation among the various departments and agencies dedicated to law enforcement that makes effective police work possible."

The four lounging against the RMP groaned and laughed softly. "So now we're a task force!" Romero hooted, not too loud.

Sanchez rolled her eyes. "Appointed by guess who. We shoulda known."

"He got my name wrong," Ivan complained.

"Shh," Romero cautioned. "Listen."

One of the reporters was asking if this Trevor Page was the same Agent Page of the FBI with whom Captain DiFalco had held a joint press conference only yesterday morning. DiFalco admitted that it was. There was a buzz among the reporters. One of them said, "You stood up there with a murderer and fed us a line of bull?"

DiFalco fielded that one deftly. "It wasn't bull, except for the name of the man behind the laser gun plot. We had to count on your understanding when the whole story came out. Page insisted on the press announcement, and we didn't want to arouse his suspicions by refusing. We didn't yet know where he was hiding Edgar Quinn, you see."

"Then you knew all along Page was behind it?"

"Of course," said DiFalco.

"Why, that lying son of a bitch," Sanchez muttered. "*No shame, no shame at all.*"

Marian felt as if she'd been pushed off a cliff. She knew better than to expect DiFalco to admit he'd been wrong about the case, but she'd never anticipated his taking credit for solving it. Credit for *her* work.

Ivan looked at Marian with sympathy. "What are you going to do?"

"I don't know yet. The worst thing I can think of."

The press conference was over. The crowd had thinned considerably, once the police gave the all-clear and the Bleecker Street residents started returning to their various buildings. Romero stood up straight and stretched. "I'm going home. Thanks for calling me, Marian. It was a good gig. As for DiFalco—well, he's a captain and you're a sergeant. Think it over very carefully before you do anything."

Marian promised she would and said good night.

Ivan waited until Romero was gone and then asked, "Are you all right?"

She sighed deeply and said, "Right now I'm kind of numb. But I'll be all right."

Sanchez put her hand on Marian's arm. "It's not a good idea to be alone now. Maybe I'd better stay with you."

"That's a nice offer, Gloria, but I just want to go home and collapse. Thanks anyway."

"If you start having nightmares," Ivan said, "give me a call."

She said she would. She told them both good night and then turned and walked away from the scene at Bleecker Street.

FOUR A.M. Marian sat yoga-fashion on her sofa staring at the television, the sound turned off. She watched Greer Garson say something heartfelt to Walter Pidgeon and didn't even wonder what it was.

The painkillers the medic had given her had reduced the ache in her leg to a point where it was barely noticeable; but they hadn't made her drowsy at all, a side effect she'd earnestly been hoping for. She needed the escape of sleep. Her big plan for flinging the solution to the East River Park murders in DiFalco's face along with her resignation—what a laugh. It was bad enough that DiFalco should steal the credit, but she couldn't even get the man to listen to her. Maybe she should go to the *Times* or one of the TV stations and tell the full story there. Announce her resignation publicly.

Except that she could never tell the *full* story. Only she and Curt Holland would ever know who really shot Trevor Page. Marian didn't credit Starbuck's suggestion that Holland was deliberately executing his old enemy; but the thought nagged at her just the same. After what she and Holland had been through together, she ought to know by now whether he was deserving of trust or not. She ought to know, but she didn't. The man was less remote now than he'd once been, but Marian didn't kid herself for one moment that she truly knew him.

Sanchez and Romero had been a pleasant surprise. She'd always known she could count on Ivan, but finding two friends where she didn't know she had friends had given her a lift. But something Sanchez had said...Kelly. Call Kelly in the morning. Early, before she had a chance to see a paper or a newscast.

Walter Pidgeon was saying something heartfelt to Greer Garson.

Marian sat there, dully watching the screen, wishing for sleep, wishing for answers. Sitting and watching.

The doorbell rang. At four in the morning. Marian dragged herself off the sofa and went to the door. Now who do you suppose could get past downstairs security so easily? She knew who it was even before she checked through the peephole.

She opened the door. Holland stood there with his fatigue sitting on him like a lead weight, but he still held his head up. They looked at each other for a long moment without speaking.

Then he said, "I have one more thing to ask of you. May I . . . come in."

"Yes," said Marian.

A Sheila Travis Mystery

MURDER

PATRICIA
HOUCK
SPRINKLE

on Peachtree Street

First
Time In
Paperback

NO MORE MR. NICE GUY

Prominent television personality Dean Anderson was as popular
as he was respected, but he had incurred a good deal of
animosity among family, friends and co-workers. Though the
police are willing to rule his shooting death a suicide, his old
friend Sheila Travis is not.

**Because of meddling Aunt Mary, Sheila gets involved in finding
Dean's killer.** No easy task with a long list of suspects that
includes a resentful ex-wife, an enraged daughter, a jealous co-
worker, a spurned admirer, a mobster with a grudge. The truth
goes deeper than either Mary or Sheila suspects. And it may
prove equally fatal.

Available in November at your favorite retail stores.

WORLDWIDE LIBRARY ®
TM

Take 3 books and a surprise gift FREE

SPECIAL LIMITED-TIME OFFER

Mail to: The Mystery Library™
3010 Walden Ave.
P.O. Box 1867
Buffalo, N.Y. 14269-1867

YES! Please send me 3 free books from the Mystery Library™ and my free surprise gift. Then send me 3 mystery books, first time in paperback, every month. Bill me only $3.69 per book plus 25¢ delivery and applicable sales tax, if any*. There is no minimum number of books I must purchase. I can always return a shipment at your cost simply by dropping it in the mail, or cancel at any time. Even if I never buy another book from The Mystery Library™, the 3 free books and surprise gift are mine to keep forever.   415 BPY AJJU

Name   (PLEASE PRINT)

Address   Apt. No.

City   State   Zip

*Terms and prices subject to change without notice. N.Y. residents add applicable sales tax. This offer is limited to one order per household and not valid to present subscribers.
© 1990 Worldwide Library.   MYS-93R

LAST REMAINS

Had sweet, fragile, silver-haired Jane Engle, school librarian and churchgoer, murdered someone and put the victim's skull in her window seat? Did Aurora Teagarden, fellow librarian and astonished beneficiary of Jane's estate—including house, cat and half a million dollars—want to expose her friend as a murderess?

An intruder's careful search alerts Aurora to the unsettling fact that somebody else knows about the skull. Where is the rest of the body?

"Harris provides some genuinely funny scenes..."   —*Publishers Weekly*

**Available in January at
your favorite retail stores.**

A BONE TO PICK

AN AURORA TEAGARDEN MYSTERY

Charlaine Harris

To order your copy, please send your name, address, zip or postal code, along with a check or money order for $3.99 (please do not send cash), plus 75¢ postage and handling ($1.00 in Canada) for each book ordered, payable to Worldwide Mystery, to:

In the U.S.

Worldwide Mystery
3010 Walden Ave.
P. O. Box 1325
Buffalo, NY 14269-1325

In Canada

Worldwide Mystery
P. O. Box 609
Fort Erie, Ontario
L2A 5X3

First
Time in
Paperback

Please specify book title with your order.
Canadian residents add applicable federal and provincial taxes.

 WORLDWIDE LIBRARY®

BONE

COFFIN AND THE PAPER MAN

Gwendoline Butler

First Time in Paperback

A
JOHN
COFFIN
MYSTERY

A PROMISE OF DELIVERY

Sixteen-year-old Anna Mary Kinver is raped and stabbed in the dank Rope Alley section of Leathergate. A former psychiatric patient, covered with blood, is picked up for questioning and subsequently let go.

Soon thereafter, John Coffin, chief commander of the Docklands district, receives the first in a series of notes from an anonymous letter writer calling himself "the Paper Man," who promises more bodies if Anna Mary's killer is not caught.

As the case goes unsolved, more bodies turn up. Who is the Paper Man?

"Coffin...solves a complex puzzle in this richly textured police procedural."
—*Kirkus Reviews*

Available in December at your favorite retail stores.

WORLDWIDE LIBRARY®

COFFINP